Her fingers itched to grab his shoulders and shake him. "You need to loosen up, city boy."

Caden pressed his lips together. "Why do you keep calling me that?"

Finally, a reaction. "You're from Tucson, aren't you?"

He picked up his plate and placed it in the sink. "Should I start calling you 'country bumpkin'?"

"Touché." Stacy crossed her arms. "I'll just have to find something else to tease you about."

Caden's eyebrows rose. "Why?"

"You get flustered easy. It's kind of cute." She winked.

His face turned red and he looked away.

"See what I mean?" She laughed and headed for the door. Before leaving, she said, "Fair warning. I plan to get an entire month's work out of you in one week. You better rest up."

Caden nodded.

She closed the door behind her and started down the path. Living in a tourist town, she was used to people coming and going. It never bothered her before, so why was she disappointed that he wasn't going to stay?

Dear Reader,

Welcome to Coronado, Arizona!

When I moved to Arizona in 1992, I thought I would see nothing but cacti, rattlesnakes and sand. Then my husband, an Arizona native, took me on a trip through the Coronado Trail, a beautiful road over 120 miles through the White Mountains and the Apache-Sitgreaves National Forest. Instead of cacti, I was surrounded by aspen, pine and fir trees. Instead of rattlesnakes, I saw elk, turkey, deer and porcupines. Instead of sand, I saw lush mountain meadows. That was all it took to turn this Texas girl into an Arizona fan.

I love stories of redemption, forgiveness and broken characters. When Caden and Stacy first started telling me their story, I knew I had to put them in a place that was as special to me as they were and I couldn't think of a better place than Coronado.

I hope this story touches you as much as it did me. I love to hear from readers. My email is leanne@leannebristow.com.

LeAnne

HEARTWARMING

His Hometown Redemption

—

LeAnne Bristow

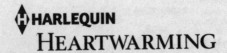

HARLEQUIN
HEARTWARMING

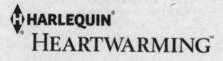

HARLEQUIN®
HEARTWARMING™

Recycling programs
for this product may
not exist in your area.

ISBN-13: 978-1-335-42677-2

His Hometown Redemption

Copyright © 2022 by LeAnne Bristow

For questions and comments about the quality of this book, please contact us at CustomerService@Harlequin.com.

Harlequin Enterprises ULC
22 Adelaide St. West, 41st Floor
Toronto, Ontario M5H 4E3, Canada
www.Harlequin.com

Printed in U.S.A.

LeAnne Bristow writes sweet and inspirational romance set in small towns. When she isn't arguing with characters in her head, she enjoys hunting, camping and fishing with her family. Her day job is a reading specialist, but her most important job is teaching her granddaughters how to catch lizards and love the Arizona desert as much as she does.

Books by LeAnne Bristow

Harlequin Heartwarming

Her Texas Rebel

Visit the Author Profile page
at Harlequin.com for more titles.

A special thank you to Dylann, Christy, Jackie, Misty and Janet. Thanks for never letting me give up on this story and for pushing me to tell it the way I wanted to, no matter how hard it was. Thank you for always encouraging me, cheering for me and kicking me in the butt when I needed it. I couldn't ask for a better writing family. And an extra loud shout-out to Trudi Harlan, who read and reread this story, making it better every time. You have no idea how much I appreciate you!

CHAPTER ONE

THE RINGING OF the telephone caused Stacy Tedford to quicken her pace. She made her way through the aisles balancing a cardboard box, a stack of notebooks and a metal cashbox. She stepped over a broken floor tile and around the candy bar display to reach the front counter.

She dropped the pile, sending notebooks sliding across the counter and onto the ground, and reached for the phone. "Hello?"

Silence.

Oh, well. If it were very important, they'd call back. She replaced the receiver on the old rotary dial phone and reached under the counter to turn on a small radio before moving around to pick up the mess.

Then she opened the cashbox to fill the register drawer for the day's sales. She marked the total in the logbook and flipped through the entries. This week had been slower than usual. Of course, the chaos of Memorial Day weekend had been a boost, but she was still behind her projected goal for this month.

An upbeat song started, and Stacy danced to the music, pausing only long enough to push the brew buttons on the coffee machines. While the smell of fresh-roasted coffee wafted through the air, she checked the ice cream machine in the deli section of the market. Except for the hum of the refrigerator units and the faint radio, silence settled around her. This was her favorite time of day. In an hour, the quiet would be disturbed by fishermen and families eager to get an early start on one of the nearby lakes.

She grabbed a cup of coffee and settled on a stool behind the counter. She flipped open one of the notebooks and ran her finger along the list of ideas she'd jotted down to increase revenue. Check marks were next to some of them. Updating the websites for the market and the campground had been easy. Her eye for design had earned her good grades in marketing classes during her short stint at the University of Arizona.

Her mother had been livid when Stacy'd quit college to come home and run the market, but what choice had she had? Her mom's Huntington's disease had progressed to the point that she could no longer live on her own. And now that her mother had checked herself into a nursing home, expenses had more than doubled.

If she didn't come up with twelve hundred dollars by the end of the summer tourist season, the nursing home would send her mother to a county facility. Much cheaper, but the quality of care was worse. And it was almost three hours away.

Her chest constricted. She couldn't let her mother be sent that far away. Coronado was their home, where Melissa Tedford had been born and where she wanted to die. Stacy would do everything in her power to honor her mother's wishes.

She glanced at her list again. One word was written bigger and underlined. *Bus*. She glanced at the calendar on the wall. Today's date was circled with bright red ink and her heart skipped a beat. Starting today, the empty lot next to her market would be the newest commercial bus stop. Passengers would be able to get out, stretch their legs, use the restroom and relax. Most importantly, they might spend money. Breakfast burritos at the deli, snacks for the road, drinks.

A tingle shot through her. She couldn't

wait to see if her persistence paid off. Would it be enough?

A loud thumping vibrated through the door. "Stacy? Stacy?"

Stacy ran around the counter and unlocked the front door. She stepped back to allow a set of elderly twins to enter. One woman sported bright pink hair, the other blue. "Good morning, Margaret. Edith."

The Reed sisters rushed past her with the energy of a whirlwind, despite being in their seventies. Edith stopped long enough to squeeze her arm. "You're late opening the store. That's not like you. Everything okay?"

Stacy looked at the clock on the wall. "It's only five after six."

Edith arched one painted eyebrow. "Better five minutes early than five minutes late."

"I told you not to say anything to the poor girl," her pink-haired sister scolded her. She gave Stacy a kind look. "Excuse her. You have a lot going on right now. Has Missy taken a turn?"

Stacy ignored the way her throat tightened and gave the woman a bright smile. "No. Actually, Mama had a good day yesterday."

The older woman pressed her lips together

for a moment. "You weren't at church, so naturally I assumed something was wrong."

Stacy ignored the comment and sat on the stool behind the counter. The women shuffled their way toward the coffeepots. Neither stopped talking long enough to hear what the other was saying.

Margaret approached the counter with her cup of coffee. "Are you still managing the campground for Frank? I heard the groundskeeper quit."

Stacy wasn't surprised that the ladies already knew about Luke. "Yes. He ran off to Nashville to become a country music star. Do you know anyone who needs a job?"

Edith let out a very unladylike snort. "I can sing better than that boy. Don't you let Frank saddle you with that job, too. It's enough he stuck you with the campground."

She shook her head. "I volunteered." Managing the campground for her uncle was easy. Customers checked in and paid at the store. When they checked out, she cleaned their cabin. Her uncle paid her a portion of the profits, and now that she'd updated the website and created a social media presence, profits were rising.

Besides, when her grandfather was alive,

her mom and dad had managed the market while she and her cousin, Coy, had helped Pap with the campground. She'd cleaned and decorated the cabins, Coy had handled care of the barn and horses, and Pap had taken care of all the maintenance and landscaping. It had been the perfect family business.

Then she'd left for college and Coy had decided to hit the rodeo circuit. Pap hadn't been able to manage everything by himself and had sold almost all the horses. Her mom's disease had become too much for her dad to handle and he'd started drinking. It was her uncle Frank who'd called her in Tucson and told her what was really going on.

Between the two of them, they'd managed to save the market and the campground from bankruptcy. Despite what the Reed sisters thought, helping with the campground was not an unwelcome chore.

"You work hard all day and spend all your free hours at the nursing home with your mother. You're never going to find a man if you don't make some time for yourself." Edith placed her cup next to her sister's on the counter.

"Oh, no. The last thing I need is a man.

Just coffee this morning?" Stacy rang it up on the register.

"You're out of the bear claws, Stacy." Edith shook her head. "I don't know how we can enjoy our coffee without one, but we'll try."

Stacy reached under the counter to produce two of the pastry treats. "I saw we were running low, so I saved some for you."

"You are a dear." Edith grinned. "Are you ready for the big day?"

"I think so." Excitement bubbled in her chest. "The bus doesn't stop until eight, so I'm going to start making burros now."

"Excellent," both women said in unison. "Do you want us to come by and help?"

"Oh, no. Millie will be in at nine." Stacy could only imagine the kind of help the sisters might offer. "I appreciate it, though."

When they left, Stacy opened a large box from behind the counter. She'd been rationing her inventory for the last month, holding back a portion of her bestsellers. Now she placed all the items back on shelves so that when the bus stopped, she would be fully stocked. Until she knew if the bus stopping at her market would be profitable, she couldn't afford to increase her inventory too much.

As soon as that was done, she moved to the

deli section and started making burritos on the hot-plate-style grill. Maybe someday the deli would be profitable enough to install a real grill, but for now, this one would have to do. She'd just wrapped the last burrito in foil and placed it under the heating lamp when she heard the rumble of the bus pulling into the dirt parking lot.

Her heart rate sped up and she pressed a hand to her stomach. This was it. Would this save her market and her mother?

THE SCREECH OF metal ripped through the air. Caden Murphy braced himself for impact. He waited for shattered glass to tear through his skin, warm liquid to seep into his clothes. Nothing. His chest tightened. Something was wrong.

Strong hands shook him and he struggled to open his eyes. "Mister. Wake up." Dark brown eyes stared into his own, worry etched on the older man's face. "Are you okay?"

Caden squinted at the brightness streaming through the windows. Where were the flashing lights? The wreckage trapping him?

"This is your stop." The man frowned at him.

The bus started to move and the man stood

to get the driver's attention. "Wait. This guy is supposed to get off here."

Another sound jolted Caden from the seat. He breathed in and out, willing his pulse to slow down.

Brakes. Just brakes. Get a grip.

The man stared at him from the aisle.

"Um...sorry." Caden rubbed his face. Stepping carefully past the man, he reached into the overhead compartment for his duffel bag. Everything he owned fit into the small brown bag. Still, he was the lucky one. At least, that was what everyone told him.

The bus driver eyed him. "We've been stopped here for twenty minutes. I was just pulling out when he told me you hadn't gotten off."

Had he slept that hard? It was probably the most sleep he'd had at one time in years.

"Sorry, didn't mean to put you behind schedule."

"No problem. See you next week when I come back through." The man grinned. "Unless you decide the mountain air suits you and decide to stay."

Caden pressed his lips together. No chance of that. Once he completed his mission, he doubted he'd be welcome. "I'll be ready."

A few moments later, Caden was alone in the middle of a dirt parking lot. The thick aroma of pine filled the chilly mountain air. *Good grief.* It was the middle of June.

For a moment, he closed his eyes and absorbed the sounds of the wind whispering through the tall trees edging the large dirt lot. He opened his eyes. His view was no longer obstructed by metal bars, but he wasn't free. Not yet. He had a promise to keep.

He threw the duffel over his shoulder and looked around. Coronado, Arizona. Population less than six hundred. How many times had he thought about coming here? And now that he was here, all he wanted to do was run away.

Except for the paved street, the town looked like a flashback to the Old West. Even the sidewalk was made from wood planks that echoed as he walked. A weathered wood building with Coronado Market painted on the side was the closest store.

Wooden shops lined the street in an array of bright colors. Chainsaw-cut bears and fish decorated the front of the log cabin hardware store on one side of the market. On the other side, a sign in the window of a bright pink candy shop boasted the best fudge in Arizona. Probably not as good as his grandmother's. A stab of pain twisted in his gut. He hadn't even been allowed to go to her funeral.

A lot of things had changed in seven years. Did phone booths still exist? Relief swelled his chest when he spotted a pay phone in front of the store.

He dug into his wallet, pulled out a business card and a calling card, punched in the numbers and held his breath.

"'Lo?" A muffled voice came across the line.

"Hi, Lieutenant Erikson. This is Caden Murphy." The tapping of his foot echoed against the sidewalk.

"Nice to hear from you so soon, Caden. You found a place to stay?"

"I just arrived, sir. I just wanted to thank you for letting me have this week to get things settled." Even though he'd served his entire sentence, he still had to be monitored for six months and had to get permission to leave Pima County.

"Happy to do it. You doing okay, son?"

"I'm fine." He swallowed. They both knew it was a lie.

"You served your time. Regardless of what happens this week, you need to forgive yourself."

Like that would ever happen. But there was no sense arguing. Erikson didn't understand. No one did. His best friend was dead because of him. No amount of punishment would be enough. "I know that, sir."

"I'll see you back in my office next week."

"Yes, sir." Caden placed the receiver back in its cradle.

He had one week. It wasn't long enough to fix all the pain he'd caused, but it was a start.

Smoke billowed from behind the restaurant across the street, carrying the aroma of slow-smoked barbecue with it. His stomach growled. Maybe breakfast was a good idea. He hadn't eaten since before he'd got on the bus, at least twelve hours ago. But first he needed to find a place to stay.

A community bulletin board hung on the wall next to the phone booth. Caden scanned the papers covering it. Lost and Found. For Sale. Even a few Missing Persons posters.

One advertisement caught his eye and he let out a sigh of relief.

Whispering Pines Cabins. Daily, weekly or monthly rentals. Inquire inside the market.

Bells jingled when he swung the market door open and stepped inside. Despite the building's worn appearance, the place was neat and tidy. Gouges marred the once beautiful wooden floor, and most of the shelves were probably older than he was. A deli hugged one side of the entrance, complete with a dining area. That was, if two tiny tables with chairs counted as a dining area. The other side of the entrance had a long counter with two cash registers. Behind the counter was another small table, a couple of chairs, and on the wall was a large wire rack of DVDs.

Overhead, the fluorescent lights flickered. He frowned.

The sound of someone clearing their throat interrupted his assessment of the lighting. He turned to his right to discover a pair of green eyes searching his. Dark green. Like the color of the pine trees that dotted the countryside.

Her eyes bored into him. "It's not much, but it's mine."

Caden lowered his gaze. "You have a nice place."

And he meant it. The building was old, but the homey atmosphere created by the colorful signs and trinkets hanging on the walls reminded him of his grandparents' house. He scanned the rest of the building. The market had everything. Bait. Groceries. Cleaning supplies. Even a little gift shop in the back corner.

"Thanks," she mumbled, and he was sure she thought he was patronizing her. "Coffee?"

"Please."

Walking around the deli counter, she pulled a Styrofoam cup from the dispenser and handed it to him. She shoved her hands in the back pockets of her jeans and studied him. "You got off the bus?"

He nodded.

"It pulled out a few minutes ago. Did you need me to see if I can catch the driver?"

He shook his head.

"Most people get back on before it leaves. Not many stay here on purpose." The apples of her cheeks puffed out slightly as a grin lit up her face. "Will you be here long?"

Caden stared at the smattering of freckles across her nose, reminding him of sunshine. Everything about her was warm and sunny. Right down to the golden highlights in her honey-colored hair. He blinked. "Um…no."

Impossibly, her grin got wider. She ran

her fingers through her long hair and pulled it into a ponytail at the back of her neck. With practiced ease, she slipped a rubber band from her wrist and wrapped it around the golden-brown locks before washing her hands in the sink.

"Hungry?" With a flick of her head, she indicated a small menu on the wall behind her.

He studied the menu. Not a big selection. Breakfast burritos or sub sandwiches.

"Sausage burro."

"Want chili on that?"

He nodded as the lights flickered again. "Do they do that a lot?"

She shrugged. "Depends on what you mean by 'a lot.' Have a seat. It'll just take a couple of minutes. The bus crowd wiped out the premade ones."

Caden dropped his duffel bag on the floor and sat at one of the tables. He retrieved his journal and reread the tattered pages. Each task was bigger than the one before it. He traced the notes with a finger and his chest constricted. Of all of them, this one would be the hardest.

"Your food's ready," Sunshine called from the counter.

He closed his book and walked over to the

counter. She handed a paper plate to him, and a jolt of awareness shot through him when his hand brushed hers. She winked. Heat crept up his neck. Turning away from her, he hurried to the tables and sank into the chair.

He unwrapped the stuffed tortilla and bit into it. Wow. Real eggs. Not the powdered kind they served in prison. Melting cheese dripped out of the end and he took another bite. The spicy green chilies made his eyes water. Heaven.

Out of the corner of his eye, Sunshine hummed while cleaning up the deli area. Her ponytail swung in rhythm with the music and he glanced at her left hand. Shame washed over him. He was here to serve out his parole, not flirt with the first pretty girl he found.

No matter. As soon as he completed his mission, he'd be gone.

CHAPTER TWO

STACY COULD SEE him from her vantage point in the deli. He was at a table, his back to her, and if he turned, he would catch her spying. But he didn't look around. He sat looking at a notebook for so long, she worried he had fallen asleep.

The bells over the door rang and a couple of local fishermen came in. She smiled at them. "Hey, Jake. Want the usual?"

Once she'd taken care of them and they'd headed out, she went back to chopping lettuce. But her eyes kept straying across the room. The handle of the knife pinched her thumb. "Ouch." She examined the spot. No blood, but if she didn't pay attention, she'd chop a finger off.

Until she put her curiosity to rest, she'd never get anything done. There was only one thing to do. She scooped up the lettuce and placed it in the bowl. The man had put his notebook away and started eating.

"Breakfast burro okay?"

He wiped his mouth with a napkin before answering. "It's good. Great, actually."

She untied her apron and stepped around the counter. The chair opposite him scraped loudly against the wooden floor as she pulled it out and sat. She interacted with strangers every day. One of her favorite games was figuring them out. Some loved to talk about themselves, their jobs, their families. Others wanted to escape from everything and gave off an I-don't-want-to-be-bothered vibe. This guy was different, though she couldn't say how.

She cupped her cheek with one hand and watched him devour the food. "Where in Arizona are you from?"

He wiped his mouth with a napkin again. "How do you know I'm from Arizona?"

Stacy chuckled. "You asked for a burro, not a burrito. So, where are you from?"

"Nowhere." Steel-gray eyes avoided her gaze.

"There's no need to be rude. Just tell me it's none of my business."

He raised his eyebrows. "Isn't that worse?"

Stacy shrugged one shoulder. "At least it's honest. Everyone is from somewhere."

"I grew up in Tucson. But I haven't lived there in a while, so I don't really consider it home anymore."

Ah. A city boy. "That wasn't so hard, was it? Where've you been?"

He stared at her for a moment, a hint of a smile beneath his scruffy beard. "None of your business."

She pressed her hand to her chest in an exaggerated gesture and used her best Southern accent. "Well, I never."

A low chuckle shook his chest. At least he had a sense of humor.

Leaning back in her chair, she studied him. His auburn hair hung in soft curls past his collar. A scruffy beard softened the rough angles of his face, but the telltale bump on his nose said he'd seen his share of scuffles. There was something familiar about him, although she couldn't place it.

He was from Tucson. Maybe she'd seen him at college. "Did you go to the University of Arizona?"

"No." He wiped his mouth. "Don't you have better things to do than watch me eat?"

She shrugged. "I'm trying to figure you out."

He leaned forward, his forearms resting on the table in front of him. "Why?"

Her breath hitched. It was the first time he'd looked her straight in the eye, and the intensity of it caused her heart to do funny things.

"Because you don't want to be." The answer slipped out before she had time to think.

He shifted in his chair. "Thanks for the company, Sunshine, but I should be going." Empty plate in hand, he walked to the trash can and tossed it in.

Stacy hurried to the front of the store while he pulled his wallet from the back pocket of his jeans and placed a ten-dollar bill by the register. She rang up his food and handed him his change.

He tucked the bills back in his wallet. "There's a sign outside about cabin rentals."

She reached under the counter and pulled a registration paper from the book. "Yes. The cabins are just around the corner. How long will you be staying?"

"Only a week." He took a pen from her and began filling out the form.

The bells chimed and the door opened. A middle-aged man in fishing gear came in and Stacy suppressed the urge to hide under the counter. The man had done nothing but complain ever since he'd arrived the week before. She regretted talking him into renting from her uncle's campground instead of staying at the fancy lodge down the road.

She gave the man her sweetest smile. "Good morning, Mr. Gordon. What can I do for you?"

"The sink in the kitchen is clogged again. I'm paying you good money for that cracker box you call a cabin—the least you can do is make sure the water drains."

She cast the visitor filling out paperwork a glance. "I'm sorry about that. I'll make sure it's taken care of right away."

"See that you do. If it's not taken care of by the time I get back this afternoon, I'll be checking out. And you can be assured I'll leave a proper review on your website."

Her stomach knotted as he exited the store. That was the last thing she needed. The extra income from the cabins was necessary to help pay her mother's bills. She glanced at the stranger again. Was he going to change his mind, too?

A few minutes later, he handed her the registration form.

She stared at the paper. Over half the form was blank. No address. No phone number.

"Um..." she started. At least he'd filled in his name. "Mr. Murphy, you missed some of the fields."

He held her gaze. "No, I didn't."

"Yes, you did." She turned the paper around and held the pen out to him.

He placed the pen on the counter. "I don't have a permanent address or a phone number. And I'm paying with cash."

He seemed to want to fade into the background and not be noticed. That was exactly what had piqued her curiosity about him, but now it aroused her suspicion. "Are you running from the law?"

One corner of his mouth lifted, hinting at a smile. "No."

She bit her lip. The man was hiding something, but it'd be easy enough to check on him. After all, her uncle was the sheriff. "In addition to the week's rent, I'll need a two-hundred-dollar damage deposit."

"There won't be damages." The words were clipped, but he placed money on the counter.

She stared at the bills. He was paying and she needed the money. Despite her apprehension, she pulled a receipt book from under the counter.

The front door bells chimed and her uncle Frank strolled in, dressed in his deputy sheriff's uniform. Caden rolled his shoulders back and stepped away from the counter. She grinned. Ex-military. Why hadn't she thought of that to begin with?

"Good morning, Uncle Frank."

"Morning." He went straight to the coffee.

"Cabin Eight's kitchen sink is backed up again. I thought you fixed it two days ago. Mr. Gordon is irritated."

"I'll get to it as soon as I can." Frank stepped between Caden and the counter and leaned closer to her. "Have you heard from Vince lately?"

Her eyes narrowed. "No. Why?"

"He's back in town," he said in a low voice.

Stacy tapped her pen on the counter. "So? What does that have to do with me?"

"I don't know exactly what happened before he left…" Frank brushed his thick mustache with the back of his hand. "But he wants to fix things."

Her entire adult life had been filled with people making excuses for Vince. First her mother. Then Frank. She couldn't be one of those people. Not anymore. "I'm done. I don't have time to worry about him anymore."

"Let me know if you hear from him." Frank's somber voice carried through the store.

"I won't. He knows how I feel."

"Stacy, he's your father. You can't…"

Anger swelled in her chest like a balloon. "He's. Not. My. Father."

Frank glanced back at Caden. "Fine. We'll talk about this later."

She fought the urge to roll her eyes. The last thing she wanted to discuss was her estranged father. She hadn't seen Vince in years and that was the way she wanted to keep it.

Her uncle waved some beef jerky at her before dropping a couple of bills on the counter and turning to leave.

She called out to him as he opened the door. "When can I tell Mr. Gordon to expect you?"

Frank ignored her and let the door slam behind him.

She gave Caden a bright smile. "Congratulations. You just put down a deposit for a cabin that may or may not have running water, pipes that drain and a roof that doesn't leak. Want to change your mind?"

A flicker of amusement danced in his gray eyes. "No. I'm staying."

"In that case, welcome to Coronado, Caden Murphy." She offered him her hand. "I'm Stacy Tedford."

Suddenly, the man's face paled. His eyes locked on the hand in front of him and a pained expression crossed his face. Stacy started to move around the counter. "Are you okay?"

CADEN SWALLOWED. SUNSHINE'S name was Stacy. Grayson's Stacy. For seven years, he had wanted to see her face-to-face, to tell her what he'd done and… What? Beg for forgiveness? No. His actions weren't forgivable. His stomach quivered like he'd just swallowed a beehive. That would hurt less than what he'd come here to do. And she was smiling. At him. Almost like she was glad he'd decided to stay. That feeling wouldn't last.

She rushed around the counter. "You look like you're going to pass out."

"I'm fine." He waved her away, his heart pounding.

He should speak his piece and get it over with. But the bus wouldn't be back for a week and he had nowhere else to go if she kicked him out of the cabin.

Lieutenant Erikson could arrange for him

to get a ride home. Caden caught himself. Home? He didn't have a home anymore. The accident had happened the first week he was home from the army. He'd been staying with his oldest sister until he could find a place of his own, and there was no way he was going back there.

His parents had offered to pick him up from prison. His mother would love to have him move back in, where she could hover over him and tell him things were okay, but he wasn't ready to face them yet.

No. He'd wait to tell Stacy why he was in Coronado. That would give him time to gather his wits and decide what to do next.

The bell over the door chimed and a family walked in. Another group followed and stopped to look at the deli menu.

Stacy went to the deli section. "I can drive you over to the cabin, but my help doesn't get here for another hour. Hope you don't mind waiting."

The thought of riding in a vehicle broke him out in a cold sweat. The thought of riding in a vehicle with her made him want to run. "I can find my way. Just give me the key."

She laughed. "It's easy to get to. You just

follow the signs. If you start walking now, you can be there by dark."

His auburn eyebrows furrowed. "How far is it?"

She shrugged. "By road, about ten miles, but I can show you a shortcut and you'll be there in less than ten minutes." She turned her attention to the family at the counter.

Caden took a deep breath and walked back to the table he'd eaten at. For more than a half hour, he watched her. She hummed along with the radio. She ran between the deli counter and the cash register as people came in, chatting with everyone, sharing jokes and smiling.

Stacy seemed happy. He swallowed. Was she really?

What did he expect? To find a twenty-six-year-old woman with a black veil draped over her face and still mourning the loss of a man she'd only known a few months?

His stomach roiled and he tried to swallow the sour taste in his mouth. His being here would only bring back bad memories. He shouldn't have come. The urge to pick up his duffel bag and run out the door almost overwhelmed him. This was going to be a long week.

Two little boys rushed by him, running

toward the candy aisle. "Slow down," their mother called after them, shifting the toddler on her hip.

A chorus of giggles erupted behind Caden. He glanced behind him just in time to see one of the boys jumping to reach the top of the metal candy rack. The shelving swayed. If the kid hit the shelf just right, the whole thing would topple since it wasn't anchored to anything. He glanced down the aisle where the mother was reading ingredients on the back of a food can.

One of the boys scaled the shelf to reach a candy bar at the top. He lost his footing as the shelf teetered. In two strides, Caden captured the falling boy with one arm and the candy rack with the other. Candy bars scattered across the floor.

Tiny arms clutched his neck. Caden wasn't sure who was more scared, him or the kid. His heart thumped. "You okay?"

Wide blue eyes stared up at Caden. "Uh-huh."

"Wesley Thomas Cooper, what did you do?" The mother rushed over. She stopped short when she saw the mess.

"I just wanted a candy bar." Wesley's bottom lip quivered.

Caden set the boy down.

A man walked up behind the mother and the little boy snapped to attention. Must be Dad. The man shook his head. "If you want to fish this morning, you best get this mess cleaned up now."

Immediately, the little boy bent down and started picking candy bars up off the floor. His brother, who'd disappeared when the crash happened, hurried over to help him.

"Thank you," the man said, reaching to shake Caden's hand.

Caden stared a moment and then grasped the man's hand. This felt alien to him…and oddly familiar, too. It'd been years since he'd done such a simple act. An act that, without words, conveyed respect and gratitude. Two things he hadn't had for a long time. Maybe he never would again.

He nodded and glanced around. No one else seemed to have noticed the commotion, thank goodness.

Stepping around the boys, he wandered down the aisle. Refrigerator units sat against the back wall, filled with sandwich meats and cheeses.

A low hum vibrated the air as one of the

units cycled on. Once again, the lights overhead flickered.

Dozens of books littered a long narrow table pressed against the side wall at the very back of the store. A handwritten sign read Free Book Exchange. Leave One. Take One. Caden found a Zane Grey novel he hadn't read and carried it back to the table.

He was in the middle of the second chapter when someone touched his shoulder. Startled, he dropped the book and turned. Stacy's eyes widened and she stepped back, holding her hands up in mock surrender.

It was then that he realized his arm was pulled back, his fist clenched. His breath escaped in a whoosh and he put his hands in his lap.

Concern pinched her face. "I didn't mean to scare you."

She probably thought he was a lunatic. He faked a smile and nodded at the book. "Guess I was a little too involved in what I was reading."

Her smile returned. "I thought I was the only one who did that."

How long before he quit jumping at every sound? He forced his gaze away from her and looked around. "Is the rush over?"

She laughed. "It hasn't even gotten started. But Millie's here, so I can run you over to your cabin now and be back before the lunch rush starts."

Caden followed Stacy's gaze to the girl sitting behind the counter. Long curly hair veiled her face but she didn't appear very old. "Are you sure she can handle things? I can wait."

His voice carried through the market and the girl looked up. Her eyes narrowed and she tucked a strand of hair behind her ear. "I grew up with four brothers. I think I can manage a few people wanting to buy bait."

Avoiding the girl's gaze, he bent to pick up his duffel bag.

Stacy headed for the door. "Coming?"

"Just a second." He opened his bag and pulled out a well-worn book to leave on the back table.

He could see Stacy approaching the entrance and hurried to hold the door open. The scent of coconut stirred in the air as she breezed past him.

He wiped his hands on his new denim jeans. How could his palms be sweating? Maybe it was the euphoria of being out of prison that had him on edge? No. His eyes strayed to the woman walking in front of him. It was knowing that as soon as she found out who he really was, he'd never see her smile again.

CHAPTER THREE

STACY'S SKIN TINGLED where Caden had brushed against her to open the door. Despite his gruff exterior, he'd obviously been raised with manners. The thought raised dozens more questions. Did he have family in Tucson? Why did he have enough cash on him to pay a two-hundred-dollar deposit without batting an eye? Why was he so secretive? And why was her skin still tingling where he'd touched her?

She motioned for him to follow her.

"How are we getting there?" He stopped at the edge of the dirt parking lot.

"We're taking a shortcut." Instead of heading to her truck, she followed a narrow trail that disappeared into the forest behind the store.

The crunch of leaves behind her was the only indication he was still there. Sunlight filtered through the thick canopy of trees, leaving the trail covered in shadows. She inhaled the mixture of fresh pine and dirt, letting it lift her spirits. She'd spent so much time inside lately that she'd almost forgotten how much she loved the area.

The path forked and she turned right, then climbed a slight ridge. She stopped at the top to wait for Caden. She took in the scene below. A lush green meadow spread out before them, with a tiny log cabin sitting at its edge. Several more cabins perched along the tree line. A large barn loomed on the far side of the meadow, with horses grazing nearby. It was a scene she would never tire of.

"Where'd the town go?" Caden asked.

"See that dirt road?" She pointed to her left. "Take that about five miles to the main road. Then you follow the main road for another five miles."

"Or just cut through the forest." Caden nodded. "Do the horses belong to the campground, too?"

"No. We rent the stables out for campers who want to bring their horses."

He nodded again. "Have you thought about offering trail rides?"

She shot him a look. "We used to. But it's hard to do without someone able to take care of the horses all the time."

Stacy jaunted down the hill a little too fast.

She shouldn't be irritated with him. It was a logical question, and he didn't know it was a sore subject with her. She stopped at the closest cabin and waited for him.

Tucked behind the rest of the cabins, this one offered more privacy. She had a feeling it was the one he'd have chosen for himself. "I put you in the caretaker's cabin. I hope that's all right."

The cabin was made of the same hewed logs as the others, but that was the only similarity. Where the other cabins had large porches and bright green shutters, this one was much smaller. The unpainted door and trim around the windows enhanced the weathered appearance of the structure.

Caden stared at the cabin and she wondered if she'd guessed wrong. "It's the smallest because it was designed for a full-time caretaker and the rest are for families or groups. I can move you to a larger one if you—"

"It's fine." Caden held up his hand. "I don't need much room and I won't be here long."

Stacy stood in front of the door. This had been her grandfather's cabin. All the caretakers Frank had hired since Pap's death had been local, so it was only rented out when the rest were full, which hadn't been often. And even then, it was to people she knew. So why this guy? Why now? She unlocked the door and went inside.

A counter, sink, stove and refrigerator marked the kitchen area. An oak table sat in the corner with two straight-backed chairs. On one side of the room, a rock fireplace took up most of one wall, and the stairs leading to the loft hugged the opposite wall.

Threadbare carpet squared up against the wood floor, dividing the kitchen area from the rest of the room with a sofa in the middle. Caden patted the back of it, sending a cloud of dust in the air. He coughed.

Stacy opened the refrigerator and was relieved to see the light come on. "We haven't rented this one out in a while. Let me know if something needs repaired."

He raised one eyebrow at her. "And you'll fix it?"

She let out a soft chuckle. "Don't say you weren't warned."

He walked over to inspect the fireplace. A thick layer of dust coated the mantel. "How long has this place been empty?"

"Six years." Stacy fought the lump building in her throat. It was hard to believe that Pap had been gone that long.

"And you don't have a caretaker?"

Stacy sighed. "The last one lived locally, so he didn't need the cabin. But he ran off to Nashville last month. He thinks he's going to be the next big country music star."

"You run the market and take care of the campground?" Caden's lips pressed together, his eyes locked on hers. "Seems like a lot of work."

She shrugged. "Normally, all I do is register guests and take care of paperwork. The caretaker does the maintenance and cleaning. It stays busy during the summer, but that's just a few weeks a year. Besides, I get twenty-five percent of the profits. No customers, no money."

He grimaced. "And you need the money."

"My mom's in a nursing home. This income helps me keep her in one close by."

Her cheeks flamed. Why had she told him that? She ducked down under the sink and pretended to browse the cleaning supplies. Once her face cooled off, she popped her head back up. "What brings a city boy like you to a little hole-in-the-wall like Coronado?"

"I have to take care of something for a friend," he said. This time, he was the one avoiding her gaze.

Her smile brightened. "You have friends here? Who? I probably know them."

He shook his head. "They've never been here."

"Okaaayy." Could he be any more vague? If she didn't have so much to do, she would ask more questions. Later, though. Definitely later.

She pointed to the stairs. "The bedroom is in the loft. Sheets, towels and blankets are in the bathroom closet. They probably need to be washed, though."

Her footsteps seemed loud in her ears as she climbed the steps to the loft above. "Why did you come to town on the bus? Don't you have a car?"

"No."

She leaned over the rail of the loft, long hair falling around her face as she stared at him. "Really? Why not?"

The corner of his mouth twitched. Then he gave her a slight smile. "None of your business."

She laughed. "You're learning, city boy."

She pulled back over the rail and finished inspecting the room. Satisfied with what she found, she clomped back down the stairs. "The good news is that the bed was covered with plastic wrap, so at least it's free of dust."

"And the bad news?"

"The pillows didn't fare so good. You're going to need new ones."

He frowned. "I can just roll up a blanket."

She ran a hand along the kitchen counter. "I hadn't realized how dirty the place was. I'll be back with more cleaning supplies and take care of it this evening." It would mean skipping her daily visit with her mom, but she had so much to do... Besides, her mother didn't recognize her most of the time.

"No, thanks. I can manage."

"Nonsense. You're a guest. I'll be back—"

"No."

She stiffened at the harshness in his voice.

He shook his head and added, "I'd rather do it myself."

"Suit yourself." Turning away from him, she hurried outside.

Apparently, his closed-off behavior wasn't just a ruse. He really didn't want to be around anyone. She walked over to the lean-to on the side of the cabin where all the tools were stored. It didn't take her long to find the tool-box and a bottle of drain cleaner.

Emerging from the dark shed, she blinked as the sun blinded her. And ran right into something hard.

Hands gripped her shoulders and steadied her. "Sorry." She stepped back to put some space between them.

"What are you doing?"

"As long as I'm here, I might as well unclog that pipe. Who knows how long it will take for Frank to get to it."

A fancy SUV rumbled by, kicking up dust as it passed the cabin. Stacy groaned. "Never mind—Mr. Gordon is back early. I better go."

"Do you know what you're doing?"

She waved the drain cleaner in the air. "I know how to use this. Hopefully, that'll unclog the kitchen sink. At least for the short term." After a few steps, she turned back to him. "By the way, city boy, don't leave any food out, and be sure to use the trash cans correctly."

Humor flickered across his face. "Is there a wrong way to use a trash can?"

"Yes. If you don't close them right, the bears get in them."

His eyes widened. "Bears? This close to houses?"

She grinned. "Have a nice afternoon."

CADEN RUBBED THE back of his neck as she walked away. Guilt twisted his stomach. He stepped into the lean-to and scanned the tools hanging on the wall. The shed was cleaner than the cabin. How often did Stacy have to act as the maintenance person? He dropped a large crescent wrench into a bucket, followed by a couple of rags folded neatly on the shelf.

There was no sign of her on the dirt road when he stepped back into the sunlight. He took off in the same direction she'd gone. Three cabins away, he recognized the SUV that had driven by earlier.

He knocked on the door and waited. Somehow, he didn't think Stacy would appreciate him offering to help. That was exactly why he was barging in instead of asking for permission.

The same man he'd seen in the market opened the door. Pressed slacks and a dress shirt replaced the more casual clothes he'd been wearing earlier. Caden nodded at the man. "I'm here to help with the plumbing."

"Fine, fine." The man stepped to the side. "I'm late for a meeting. I expect things will be working and cleaned up by the time I get back."

"Yes, sir." He waited for the screen door to slam shut before facing Stacy's glare. He flashed her a fake smile. "He seems like a nice guy."

He could almost hear her grinding her teeth. "What are you doing here?"

He held up the wrench and bucket. "I thought I would offer to help. In case the drain cleaner doesn't work."

Stacy reached into the toolbox on the counter and lifted a larger crescent wrench out. "This ain't my first rodeo."

"Oh. I guess you've done this before." He could tell by the scowl on her face that his offer had insulted her.

"Frank never seems to find the time. Luckily, my grandfather made sure I could take care of myself." Turning her back to him, she ran some water in the sink and watched for signs the drain cleaner was working. "'Never put yourself in a position to depend on a man or anyone else,' he always said."

"Sounds like a smart guy. You were close?" It was a rhetorical question. He could see from the look in her eyes that her grandfather was special to her.

"Yes," she said, her eyes holding a faraway look. "He was my rock."

Caden shifted back and forth on his feet. "Is there something I can—"

Her cell phone buzzed in her back pocket and she held up her finger to stop him.

"Hello?" Stacy's expression fell and worry lines marred her forehead. "I'll be there as soon as I can."

"What's wrong?" The shattered look on her face disturbed him more than he wanted to admit.

"Nothing." Her chest rose, betraying her lie.

"Is it your mom?"

She nodded. Holding the phone to her chest with one hand, she used the other one to turn on the faucet. Her voice was barely a whisper. "She's having a bad day."

Caden stiffened. How was he going to be able to tell her the truth when seeing her upset like this tore his insides out? How could he purposely put her through pain?

He reached around her and turned the running water off. "Your mom is more important than a clogged drain. Go to her. I'll take care of this."

Conflict raged in her eyes.

Caden understood her trepidation. After all, she knew nothing about him. She certainly didn't know he'd worked for his brother's construction company every summer since he was fourteen. Or that he'd just received his contractor's license before he'd gone to prison.

"I can't." The words sounded more like a question.

"I'm not going to steal your toolbox and run."

She flashed him a dark look. "I know that."

"And I know how to fix a pipe. I can take it apart and put the whole thing back together if I need to."

The phone was still clutched in her hand. She looked down at it, then lifted her chin. "Okay. I'll be back as fast as I can."

"It won't take long, so don't rush on my account."

He didn't see her leave. It was a conscious decision. Instead, he focused on the sink. It wasn't until he heard the screen door slam shut that the tension left his body.

As suspected, the clogged drain required more than drain cleaner. It took less than a half hour to remove and clean the P trap.

He was on his way back to his cabin when a woman waved at him from her porch.

"Are you the maintenance man?"

After rescuing a wedding ring the woman had dropped down the bathroom sink, he ended up at three other cabins. He fixed another drain, a broken cabinet and a door that wasn't shutting. It was late in the afternoon by the time he walked toward his temporary home. His body ached from the work, but it was a good ache. He'd forgotten how satisfying it felt to put in a hard day's work because you wanted to.

An SUV pulled up beside him. He tried not to panic when the sheriff stopped and rolled down his window.

"Where you going with that toolbox, son?"

He stopped and looked Frank straight in the eye. "I'm putting it back in the toolshed."

The sheriff glanced at the cabin. "Why do you have it?"

"Stacy had something to take care of, so I offered to finish for her." It was on the tip of his tongue to add that if this guy was doing his job, he wouldn't have had to step in.

The man appeared skeptical. "She just walked off and let you take over for her?"

"It took some convincing, but yes."

Frank's eyes narrowed. "She's stubborner than a mule, so you must be mighty persuasive."

He pressed his lips together. "I am."

"And you know how to use those tools?"

"Yes. Do you?"

Frank's jaw clenched and Caden stiffened.

So much for keeping his mouth shut. Was the sheriff going to kick him off the property?

Frank ran one knuckle over each side of his bushy mustache. "How long you planning on being here?"

"Just a week."

Frank nodded, rolled up the window and pulled away. He turned into the driveway and parked in front of the toolshed. He got out and waited beside his vehicle.

Caden cut across the road and trekked straight to the lean-to. Frank was still waiting when he came out. He waited for Frank to speak first.

"Where are you from?"

"Tucson, originally."

"What do you do for a living?"

"I'm between jobs right now." In this economy, lots of people were out of work. And he wasn't lying.

Frank let out a breath of frustration, recognizing Caden's evasive tactics. "What was the last full-time job you had?"

This would be tricky. How much was he obligated to tell the man? No sense in trying to hide the truth. It'd be easy enough for Frank to check up on him. Still, there was no reason to give him more information than was necessary. "I was in the army."

Frank's shoulders relaxed. "Nice. Did you serve overseas?"

"Afghanistan." Caden kept his body at attention. "You?"

"Marines. Desert Storm." Frank leaned against the side of his vehicle. "How long have you been out?"

"Seven years."

Frank's eyebrows lifted. "What'd you do after you got out? College?"

Caden took a deep breath. "I went to prison."

CHAPTER FOUR

STACY GLANCED AT the clock for the hundredth time. Ten more minutes until Donna arrived and she could take Caden clean sheets and towels.

He hadn't wanted her help cleaning the cabin, but he couldn't complain about fresh linens. When she'd left the nursing home, she'd stopped by his cabin to pick them up. He'd been nowhere to be seen, so she'd let herself in and gathered up everything that had needed washing. She'd managed to wash and dry everything in between waiting on customers.

The market was quiet except for a young family from the campground. She hung her apron up and closed the deli. The main cash register was across from the deli counter, which made it easy for her to see if anyone was ready to check out while she was making food for customers.

A young girl stood between the counter

and the deli, clutching a box of graham crackers. "S'cuse me. Do you have marshmallows?"

Stacy looked down at the freckled face. "I sure do. Are you making s'mores tonight?" She stopped in the first aisle and handed the child a large bag.

The small child grinned, revealing two missing teeth. "Yes. Mr. Murf made me a marshmallow stick."

"Mr. Murphy." Her mother stopped behind her. The woman stroked her daughter's head and shot Stacy a smile. "I can't tell you how helpful he's been today. I don't know how he keeps up his energy."

Was she talking about Caden? Stacy frowned. "I'm glad to hear that."

"He stopped by the cabin to introduce himself and see if we needed anything. I think he must have got it all done today."

Stacy's frown deepened. She hadn't been aware of any problems at the family's cabin. "What did he do?"

"He rescued my wedding ring from the sink, and after working in cabins all afternoon, came back and chopped wood for the firepit." The woman glanced around. Leaning forward, she placed one hand on the side of her mouth and whispered, "I could've watched him work all day." She winked.

Stacy gave her a small smile. "Enjoy your s'mores."

As the family was leaving, a plump woman with hair too dark to be natural held the door for them.

"Hi, Donna," Stacy greeted her.

She gave the woman a quick rundown of the day and then hurried to her apartment behind the store. Time to find out what Caden was up to.

She gathered the sheets, towels and blankets she'd washed for him and grabbed a couple of pillows. She set the items on top of the cardboard box she'd filled with cleaning supplies, toiletries and canned goods earlier. That should tide him over for now.

When she stepped outside, brilliant hues of purple, pink and orange streaked the sky. Even in the fading light, the trail was easy to find. Overhead, squirrels chattered, and the smell of pine trees engulfed her. Brisk mountain air was the best medicine for anything. It always soothed her soul.

As Stacy topped the ridge surrounding the cabins, she paused. Caden really had been busy. Stacks of firewood stood like soldiers next to the firepits. Already, families were gathered around the fire rings, some roasting marshmallows, others roasting hot dogs. The sound of laughter drifted in the air.

She made her way to Caden's cabin, balanced the box on her hip and knocked. Not a sound came from inside. She pushed the door open. "Caden?"

No answer. Maybe he wasn't there? She stepped inside. Setting the supplies on the counter, she walked through the cabin. The smell of soap hung thick in the air, but the bathroom door was open, the light off. She glanced inside. The mirror over the sink was still wet. He'd showered. So where had he gone? Stacy stepped out of the bathroom and headed for the loft.

At the top of the stairs, she paused midstep. The dim light streaming in from the window illuminated the bed in the center, Caden lying haphazardly across it. Thick arms supported his head, and dark red curls, still damp from the shower, left a wet circle on the mattress under him. He was wearing only a pair of jeans. She turned to leave, but something caught her eye and she stepped closer.

What in the world? Ugly scars marred

his muscular back. Dark red welts stretched out, almost as if something had been dragged across the skin. She fought the urge to reach out and touch him.

He stirred in his sleep and she jumped. The last thing she wanted was to be caught lurking over his bed. She fled down the stairs and began unpacking the box.

"When'd you get here?"

She glanced up. Caden leaned on the rail, his denim jeans hanging low on his narrow waist. She swallowed. "Um…just now."

"Hold on." He disappeared back into the loft. A few seconds later, he emerged, pulling a T-shirt over his head as he descended the stairs. Were there scars on his chest as well? It was hard not to stare at the thin material stretched across his broad torso.

Stacy chewed her bottom lip. She turned away before he could notice her interest. "You got a lot done today."

He held himself rigid, like a soldier at attention. "I like to keep busy."

"Why?" She lifted her chin. Ever since her mother had gone into the nursing home, people acted like she needed to be taken care of. She didn't want to be anyone's charity case, especially his.

Caden's eyes narrowed, just slightly, and he took a deep breath. "Your uncle hired me to do a few things around here."

Stacy frowned. "He hired you for the summer?"

He raised one eyebrow. "No. Just the week."

Leave it to Frank to take advantage of every opportunity. "How much did he offer to pay you?"

"Nothing." The muscles in his jaw tightened. "I get to use him as a reference when I leave."

"Are you looking for a job?"

He avoided her gaze. "Yes."

She crossed her arms over her chest. "You do know we're looking for a new groundskeeper."

"I heard." He peered into the box on the counter. "What's all this?"

"Clean towels and sheets."

"Thanks," he mumbled and carried the items toward the bathroom. "Beats drying off with an old shirt."

She waited for him to return to the kitchen. "Frank offered you the permanent job and you turned it down?"

"Yes."

"Why?"

His gray eyes pierced her. "I'm only here for a week."

"You have another job waiting for you?"

"No." He set the box on the counter and picked up the pillows she'd left there.

"Where are you going when you leave here?"

He avoided looking at her. "I don't know."

"Do you have a wife or girlfriend waiting for you?"

Caden held the pillows in front of his chest. "No."

Stacy let out a sigh. "You have no job, nowhere to go and no one waiting for you. What's your rush?"

He lifted his chin and sucked in a deep breath. "I just can't stay."

"Suit yourself, city boy." She picked up the now-empty box from the counter but paused, not yet ready to leave.

Caden opened the refrigerator and took out packages of ham and cheese.

"Do you cook?" she asked.

"Nope, but I was about to make a sandwich. You want one?"

Did that mean he didn't like to, or he didn't know how?

A streak of yellow mustard covered the bread slices on the plate in front of him. Stacks of ham and cheese followed.

"I never saw you come into the market today. Where did you get food?"

With his sandwich assembled, he sat at the table. "The family in Cabin Four picked it up for me."

She frowned. He let strangers bring him groceries but wouldn't let her clean the cabin for him.

While he ate, her gaze roamed the room. It was neat. Too neat. No books on the coffee table. Nothing haphazardly thrown on the counter. There was nothing to show that the cabin was occupied.

"You don't travel with much, do you?"

No response.

Caden's reserved demeanor was driving her crazy. Did he get excited about anything? "Are you always so quiet?"

"Yes, ma'am."

Her fingers itched to grab his shoulders and shake him. "You need to loosen up, city boy."

He pressed his lips together. "Why do you keep calling me that?"

Finally, a reaction. "You're from Tucson, aren't you?"

He picked up his plate and placed it in the sink. "Should I start calling you 'country bumpkin'?"

"Touché." She crossed her arms. "I'll just have to find something else to tease you about."

Caden's eyebrows rose. "Why?"

"You get flustered easily. It's kind of cute." She winked.

His face turned red and he looked away.

"See what I mean?" She laughed and headed for the door. Before leaving, she said, "Fair warning. I plan to get an entire month's work out of you in one week. You better rest up."

Caden nodded.

She closed the door behind her and started down the path. Living in a tourist town, she was used to people coming and going. It had never bothered her before, so why was she disappointed that he wasn't going to stay? He was just another drifter passing through, but something about him had piqued her interest. If she could figure out why he intrigued her, then she could let it go.

Still, if she could convince him to stay

through the summer, it would make her life so much easier. He didn't have a reason to go, and she could offer him a job with free room and board.

Free room and board. She groaned and turned back to the cabin.

THE MOMENT STACY closed the door, Caden let out the breath he'd been holding. It was hard to think when she was in his space. And harder to breathe. She smelled like a tropical island. The worst part was, she had actually looked disappointed that he'd turned down the job.

He scrubbed his face with his hands. Staying for a week was a bad idea. Not much he could do about that now. He'd made a deal with the sheriff, and he wouldn't break his word.

The door burst open and he jumped.

"Oh." Stacy grinned. "Sorry. I should have knocked."

"Did you forget something?"

"I wanted to tell you to stop by the market before you leave and get your refund."

He frowned. "For what?"

She snorted. "Your payment for the cabin.

I'm not going to charge you rent for working."

Her gaze held his and neither of them moved. A low growl broke the silence. Her eyebrow quirked. "Was that your stomach?"

Caden nodded. The sandwich he'd just wolfed down had only seemed to wake his stomach up.

Her face softened and she opened the refrigerator door. "You need more than a sandwich for dinner."

"I've lived off less."

She frowned. "You really helped me out with Mr. Gordon today. The least I can do is give you a decent meal. Come on."

The scent of coconut stirred in the air as she breezed past him. He shouldn't follow her. He should stay away from her. His stomach growled again and he glanced at the still-empty cabinets.

By the time he got outside, she was almost to the trees. His hair was still damp from the shower he'd taken earlier, and the cool breeze hitting him sent goose bumps down his arms. He hurried to the trail and followed her through the forest.

When he emerged from the trees, she was waiting for him. He hadn't noticed the wooden door hidden by empty crates and stacked boxes at the back of the market building before. She unlocked it and waved him in.

"After you." Reaching past her, he held the door open. He waited for a light to come on before he stepped inside.

He looked around the open room. This wasn't the store. It was an apartment.

A rock fireplace, similar to the one in his cabin, dominated the center of the far wall, and dark wood paneling covered the interior. The rest of the room, however, looked like a rainbow threw up. A bright orange sofa stood in the corner of the main room. Pillows of every size, shape and color were strewn everywhere, even on the floor.

A long counter separated the kitchen from the rest of the room.

"Have a seat. It won't take me long to whip up something."

The kitchen was a sharp contrast to the dark wood paneling. Everything was bright. White tile. White appliances. White countertop. Neon-colored coffee mugs hung on hooks on the wall.

She added color and brightness to everything she touched. His heart stuttered when she gave him another smile. Pure sunshine. No wonder Grayson had fallen in love with her.

A dining room table had been pushed up against the wall. Or, at least, he thought it was a dining table. Stacks of papers, notebooks, newspapers and magazines covered every square inch. A few of the titles were written in a language Caden didn't recognize.

"Don't touch anything." Stacy barely glanced at him as she filled a pan with water. "You'll mess up my system."

"Your system?" Was she serious?

"Believe it or not, I know where everything is on that table. If you move something, I won't be able to find it when I need it."

"And you need magazines from 1992?"

"Yes."

She didn't offer an explanation and he wasn't about to pry, so he stepped away from the table and slid onto a wooden bar stool with a bright pink cushion.

From his perch, he watched her zip around the kitchen. "Don't go to any trouble for me, please."

"Don't worry about it. You did the work of three people today. You need food." She broke spaghetti noodles in two and dropped them into the pan of boiling water. "Besides, it's no trouble to open a jar of sauce."

Nothing he said was likely to change her mind, so he scanned the pictures on the paneled walls. Dozens of photographs, mostly of the same dark-haired woman. Was that her mother? They didn't look anything alike.

One picture caught his eye and he slid off his stool to get a better look. "Who's riding a buffalo?"

Stacy grinned. "My mom. She's a little eccentric." A flash of sadness crossed her face. "At least, she was."

"What's wrong with her?" He immediately regretted his words. "Sorry. It's none of my business."

Her eyes focused on the tomatoes she was chopping. "She has Huntington's disease."

"What's that?"

"It's a genetic disease that affects both the body and the mind. Basically, she's losing control over her body and her mind a little at a time, and there's nothing I can do to stop it."

"Genetic. As in inheritable?" Was Stacy facing a terrible prognosis in her future? His stomach clenched at the thought.

Stacy tossed the tomatoes with lettuce and

placed the bowl on the counter. "Yes. She inherited it from her mother. All her siblings have already died from the disease." Her eyes clouded over with emotion. "She managed to fight it longer than any of them."

Caden swallowed. "Could you—"

"No." She tipped the pan over a colander to drain the noodles. Reaching into a cabinet, she plucked a jar of spaghetti sauce from the shelf and tried to open it. "I'm adopted."

After a minute of watching her straining with the lid, Caden walked around the counter. "Here. Let me." His hand brushed hers as he took the jar from her. He ignored the way her touch sent his heart into an unsteady rhythm.

"Thanks." She tipped the open jar into the pan. "That's why I have all those magazines."

He glanced at the table again, confused. "I'm not following."

"My mom found me at an orphanage in Georgia when I was eight years old. I had a baby sister that was adopted before me. I want to be able to talk to her if she ever finds me."

"Georgia, as in the country, not the state?" Now the foreign language magazines made more sense.

"Yes. My dad said it was important for me to remember my heritage and even learned the language, too." A hint of sadness filled her eyes. "I have no idea where my sister went."

Caden's heart seemed to freeze. This woman had already lost one family. She was about to lose her mother. She had more reasons to be angry at the world than anyone he knew. Yet she wasn't.

Stacy placed two plates of food on the counter, saving him from having to respond. He'd eat, then leave. No more small talk. He couldn't let himself get involved in her life any more than he had to.

She sat next to him but seemed more interested in watching him than in eating.

Caden kept his eyes focused on his plate and didn't look up until everything was gone. "Thank you. That was good. I should be going."

"Don't be silly." She took their plates and slipped them into the sink. "Have some coffee."

Caden stood and willed himself to run for the door. But he didn't. Instead, he found himself sitting back down. Stacy handed him a cup.

"I hope coffee doesn't keep you up." She

took a long sip from her own neon-green mug. "It relaxes me and helps me sleep. Maybe I'm weird."

He didn't need coffee to keep him awake. Nightmares managed to do that for him. He hadn't slept more than two or three hours a night in years. "Are you ADHD?"

She almost spit out her coffee. "What?"

"Attention deficit hyperactivity disorder."

"I know what it is. Why would you ask me that?"

Oops. He'd insulted her again. "Caffeine has the opposite reaction in kids with ADHD and calms them down."

"No, I don't have ADHD." She pressed her lips together. Then she smiled. "At least, I don't think I do. That could explain a lot, actually."

Caden couldn't help but return her smile. "I drank a lot of coffee when I was a kid."

"Did it work?"

"Not as much as a trip to the woodshed with my dad."

She laughed and the sound sent a thrill through him. It was nice to talk to someone who didn't hold his past against him or judge him. Which was exactly why he couldn't let himself get too close to her. As soon as his secret was out, she'd never look at him the same way. Was it too much to ask for a few days of feeling normal?

CHAPTER FIVE

CADEN'S STEEL-GRAY EYES took on a pensive look as he stared at her. Stacy stopped laughing and cleared her throat. The silence should have been awkward, but it wasn't. He seemed like he wanted to say something but was holding back. Why?

She took a long sip of her coffee, studying him over the top of her mug. What caused the flash of pain in his eyes? Her mother always told her curiosity killed the cat. Mostly she said it to get Stacy's nose out of a puzzle book. And Caden was the most interesting puzzle she'd seen in a long time. It had nothing to do with his looks or the way his chest stretched his T-shirt and everything to do with the way he carried himself.

Keep telling yourself that.

If curiosity killed the cat, she might as well do it right. She took a breath. "Why are you in Coronado?"

Caden stared at her for a moment. He set

his coffee mug on the counter and stood. "I told you. I have to do something for a friend. Some unfinished business he wasn't able to take care of himself. And since the bus doesn't come back until next week, I'm in no hurry."

His cryptic answer didn't stifle her curiosity. "What kind of business?" She'd known he'd ignore the question. It hadn't stopped her from asking.

The corner of his mouth twitched. She could tell he was fighting the urge to say it was none of her business. She beat him to the punch. "I don't need to know the details. I just wondered if it was business-business or pleasure."

His brows pinched and emotion clouded his eyes. "Neither," he said, his shoulders drooping a little more than they had before. "Thanks for dinner, Sunshine. Good night."

She followed him to the door and watched him until he disappeared into the trees. He didn't look back. Not once.

Stacy knew of only one thing that could cause the type of pain she'd seen in his eyes. He'd lost someone close to him. She was all too familiar with that type of pain. She'd only been eight years old when she'd officially become an orphan, but the truth was, her birth parents had given up long before that.

The sadness on Caden's face reminded her too much of the other children she'd been surrounded with at such a young age. Try as she may, she couldn't recall one memory of her birth father smiling. He'd crumbled under the burden of a sick wife, hungry kids and not enough money. Who had Caden lost?

Rinsing out her coffee mug, she left it with the dishes. She stepped around the kitchen counter and stopped at the dining room table. She scanned the room. Pillows strewn everywhere. Piles scattered on the coffee and end tables. Caden must think she was a slob.

He had spent a long time looking at the pictures on her wall. Stacy stepped closer, trying to see them as a stranger would. Colorful picture frames fought for space on shelves crammed with knickknacks. She ran her hand along the frames. Pictures of happier times, when her mother had been healthy. Vibrant. Before the crippling effects of Huntington's disease destroyed her body. Now it was trying to take her mind as well.

There weren't any pictures of the two of them together. Stacy had been too scared of strangers to allow one of them to hold her precious camera long enough to snap a picture of her with her new mother. It took a few minutes to locate a photograph with Stacy in it. A small, skinny child with stringy brown hair and a huge smile. The smile was fake.

After being engulfed in sadness for the first portion of her life, Stacy had been determined that her new life in America would be a happy one. So she'd faked it. She'd faked it until she hadn't needed to fake it anymore. It was a skill she'd honed well over the last twenty years.

A sharp rap at the door made her jump. Caden must have forgotten something. She hurried across the room and threw the door open.

The man standing there wasn't Caden. Her heart leaped into her throat.

"What do you want, Vince?" She stepped outside, closing the door behind her. Dark brown hair stuck up all over his head, but his dark eyes were clear—not what she'd expected at all. He was close enough that she should have been able to smell the alcohol on his breath, but cigarette smoke was the only odor clinging to him.

"Did you know they may kick your mom out at the end of the summer?"

How had he found out? She clenched her jaw. Someone at the nursing home was going to have a lot to answer for. "They aren't going to kick her out."

Vince waved a paper in front of her. "Then what's this?"

Stacy snatched it from him. Her hands shook as she saw the red Final Notice stamp across the bottom. "Where did you get this?"

"Please, Anastacia. Let me help." His voice cracked. "Let me come work in the market. The wages you would pay someone can go straight to the medical bills."

For a moment, she was tempted. After abandoning his family, paying her mother's medical bills was the least he could do. But asking him for help would be admitting she couldn't handle things on her own. "I've already taken care of it."

Vince's eyes narrowed. "You're a terrible liar. Always have been. Even when you were a little girl."

He was wrong. She'd been exceptionally good at lying when she was little. She'd had to be. He was the only one who could see through her. Part of her missed the man who used to hold her on his lap, tweak her nose and tell her to stop trying so hard to be strong. That it was okay to ask for help.

Too bad she hadn't seen that man for many years. She sucked in her breath. "It's not your problem."

"Of course it is. She's my wife."

"Ex-wife. You picked a bottle over us."

"I haven't had a drink in four years."

"You're a terrible liar, too."

"I'm not lying, *chemo sikharulo*." He lifted his chin. "I promised your mother when she went into the nursing home I would stop. And I did."

Stacy stiffened at the Georgian term of endearment. She folded the paper in two and slid the bill into her back pocket. "Go back to the bar, Vince."

Vince's dark hair fell across his forehead. "I went to the bank today. I'll have the bill taken care of by the end of the month."

She'd heard that before. When the initial expense of the nursing home had drained her mother's meager savings account, he'd promised to pay all the expenses. After the third missed payment, Stacy had taken over the responsibility for her mother's care.

Bringing the account up to date had meant selling off the rest of the horses, including her beloved Maze. And she'd been doing fine until recently. Her mother's quickly failing health was rapidly increasing the cost of her care. Stacy wasn't sure how much more it would go up, but she knew better than to count on Vince for anything.

Vince shook his head. "Talk to me."

Her stomach churned. Talking to him would dredge up memories she didn't want to deal with. "We don't have anything to talk about. Good night."

She turned to go back into the apartment, but the doorknob refused to turn. Crap. What a time to lock herself out.

"I'm not going to let Missy get sent away."

"Just go home."

Vince slowly moved toward his truck, and she tested the door again. Maybe the bedroom window was open. She couldn't remember.

Empty crates stacked against the wall cast eerie shadows in the already-dark area. With a sigh, she began clearing a pathway to her window.

Something ran across her foot. She screamed and jumped back. Whatever furry creature it was must have had a family, because another furry shadow darted toward her.

Her heart pounded and she turned to run.

The world tilted as her shin hit one of the crates and she tumbled over it. She threw her hands out to catch herself. Waves of pain traveled up her arms as the gravel bit into her palms. The air rushed from her lungs as the rest of her body slammed into the ground.

CADEN MENTALLY MADE a list of things he wanted to do the next day. The grass needed to be mowed, the hedges trimmed. He'd seen a Weed Eater, and Frank had told him there was a riding lawn mower in the large shed at the back of the campground. Caden had found the shed, but there'd been a padlock on the door.

Turning around, he jogged back toward Stacy's apartment. He doubted she would hand over the key without asking him a million questions, or teasing him again, but he could always hope.

A scream broke the silence of the forest. Stacy? He broke into a run. Emerging from the trees, he saw Stacy's porch light casting shadows in the empty lot. Stacy lay on the ground, a larger figure looming over her.

Dropping his shoulder, Caden slammed into the man with everything he had. They hit the ground and rolled. In seconds, Caden had regained his balance to stand between the man and Stacy, his fists clenched.

The man rose and staggered a moment. He was at least sixty pounds heavier than Caden, but Caden managed to hold his ground when the guy tried to push his way past him. *Stay calm*. He gritted his teeth.

If the last seven years had taught him anything, it was how to read body language. Which was why it was easy for him to dodge the blow that came flying at his head. Instinct took over and his own fist connected with the man's pudgy gut. While he was doubled over, Caden threw an uppercut to the man's jaw, sending him to the ground.

He turned around and offered his hand to Stacy. She was shaking. Caden longed to pull her close, but he didn't dare. Even in the diffuse lighting, the scrapes on her hands were easy to see. Taking one of her hands in his, he ran his fingers lightly over the injured area. No blood. That was a good sign.

"Did he hurt you?"

"No." She pulled her hand away. "I tripped over a box."

The air rushed from Caden's chest. A box? He'd punched a guy over a box. Great.

He pinched the bridge of his nose and squeezed his eyes shut. He didn't want to admit that prison had changed him, but this was proof that it had. He'd been in his fair share of scrapes inside, but he'd never been one to throw the first punch. Or, at least, he'd never used to be.

His sister had berated him for pleading guilty and begged him to take the deal offered by the state's attorneys, but he'd refused. She'd warned him that prison would change him. At the time, he hadn't cared. Anything was better than the pity he'd seen in every face that had looked at him. Even a jail cell.

What had happened to him?

Brushing her jeans off, Stacy nodded. "You knocked him out?"

He swallowed. "I thought he was trying to hurt you."

She raised one eyebrow and gave him a smug smile. "Where's your white horse?"

"Horse?"

"Your horse. Aren't all knights in shining armor supposed to ride up on a white horse?"

He was no knight. The furthest thing from it.

The man on the ground moaned.

Caden nodded toward her apartment door. "Get inside and call the sheriff. I'll watch this guy."

Stacy ran one hand through her long hair, pushing it away from her face. "I can't. I accidentally locked myself out. My phone's in there, too."

"Come on." He took her elbow and guided her to the apartment door. Pulling out his pocketknife, he opened it and, in a few short seconds, had the door open.

"How'd you do that so fast?"

"I got locked out of a lot of places when I was a kid." He folded the blade and slipped it into his pocket before stepping aside to let her enter.

She nodded. "I forget my keys a lot, too."

"I never forget keys," he said. When she gave him a puzzled look, he shrugged. "I have four older siblings. They locked me out of their rooms. I wanted in."

He waited outside as Stacy picked up her phone and called someone, presumably her uncle. Leaning against the wall, he kept an eye on the unwelcome visitor.

"Frank'll be here in a minute." Her gaze fell on the man and sympathy flickered across her face. "I hate what alcohol has turned him into."

"You know this guy?" A memory from that morning came back to him. She'd had a brief conversation with Frank about someone. Her father? His blood ran cold. Of course. The man was the same build as Frank. Same hair color.

"He used to be my dad." Stacy's voice was soft.

Caden's stomach dropped. He'd been in town one day and he'd done something stupid enough to send him back to prison. For one crazy second, he thought about running. But where would he go? Besides, he'd made a promise and he wasn't going to let Grayson down again.

Frank's SUV pulled up and Caden's heart went into overdrive.

The sheriff nodded at him. "What happened?"

He stood straight. "I was on my way home when I heard Stacy scream. By the time I got here, she was on the ground and he was standing over her."

Frank's eyes opened wide. He turned to Stacy. "Did he hurt you?"

She shook her head. "No. I tripped over a box. That's why I was on the ground."

Frank reached down and yanked Vince up by his collar.

"Aw," he protested. "Knock it off, Frank. I didn't do anything."

Frank shoved the sulking Vince toward his SUV. "Go get in the truck and wait for me." Then he turned his attention to Stacy. "What's going on? Why was he here?"

Stacy shook her head. "Who knows why drunks do what they do?"

"I'm not drunk." Vince's voice bellowed from the vehicle. "I have to take care of Missy."

She crossed her arms. "Just get him out of here."

Frank's bushy mustache twitched and he shook his head. "I thought he was doing better."

"I told you. I'm not drunk!"

Shaking his head, Frank turned his attention to Caden. "Thanks for watching out for Stacy."

He was thanking him? What kind of town was this? Frank knew he was on parole. Why wasn't the sheriff slapping handcuffs on him and throwing him in the back of the SUV?

She stood next to him, watching Frank drive away. "Well, Mr. Murphy, what am I going to do with you? You show up in town with nothing but a duffel bag, rescue me from the clutches of Snidely Whiplash, and you don't talk much. The strong, silent type. I find it interesting, even if it is a little cliché."

He stiffened. She shouldn't think of him as some kind of hero. "I'm not Dudley Do-Right."

She nudged him with her shoulder. "And I'm not Nell Fenwick, so relax. I'm not going to recommend you for a medal."

Some of the tension melted from his shoulders.

"I'm surprised you caught my reference. Most people don't know old cartoons," she said.

"Snidely Whiplash was my grandmother's favorite villain."

"Mine too. I learned to speak English watching cartoons. I still have the entire collection of *The Adventures of Rocky and Bullwinkle* on VHS tapes."

He crossed his arms over his chest. He didn't want to have anything in common with Stacy. He didn't want to like her. But he did. He squeezed his arms tighter, trying to push away the pain in his chest.

"You better get inside and put some ointment on your hands." Caden nodded at the open door to Stacy's apartment.

She frowned as she stared at her palms. "I already forgot about it."

Caden was struck with an almost irresistible urge to touch his fingers to her lips, just to see if they were as soft as they appeared. One day was all it'd taken for him to be wrapped around her finger.

He pushed his hands deeper into his pockets. He was just about to leave when he remembered why he'd wanted to see her to begin with. "Frank said there's a riding lawn mower in that big shed at the back of the campground, but it's locked."

"I haven't opened that shed in years. It may take me a while to find the key."

"As long as it doesn't take more than a week," he joked.

"That's right. You're leaving on the next bus." Her teeth caught her bottom lip. "You can still change your mind. I would really appreciate the help."

His heart skipped a beat. She was flirting with him. If Grayson were still alive, she wouldn't be pleading with him for help. But Grayson wasn't here. He was.

How long would it take to get the cabins

and the campground in good enough shape to make it through the summer tourist season?

He took a deep breath. "A month. I'll stay for one month."

CHAPTER SIX

STACY GROANED AND reached out from under the covers to hit the snooze button. Five more minutes. Then she'd be ready to tackle the day.

Today was her day off, but she still didn't have time to sleep in. Millie came in early to open the market so Stacy could spend the morning with her mother and the afternoon cleaning cabins and seeing to repairs. But with Caden here, she might get to relax for the first time since... Well, she couldn't remember.

Once she was up, she took her time getting dressed before peeking into the market to make sure things were going well. She rummaged through the papers on the dining room table until she found the most recent copy of the Georgian newspaper from her hometown. Then she settled on the sofa with a cup of coffee to skim through the headlines. Last, she flipped to the classified section.

What she'd told Caden last night was true. Vince had insisted she retain her home language even though her mother had feared it would make learning English harder. It was one of the few arguments she could remember her father winning. Reading the newspaper kept her native language fresh. Plus, if her baby sister ever reached out to her, she wanted to be able to communicate easily.

Remembering the kind of father Vince had once been made it easier to ignore the man he was now. Deep down, she knew he was good and caring. She'd been a daddy's girl from the moment the Tedfords adopted her. While she'd adored her new mother, it was her father who'd helped her learn English and adjust to the United States. He'd known what she'd needed before she had.

Unfortunately, you could love someone and not trust them. Vince had broken her trust too many times and she wasn't about to risk her mother's well-being by expecting him to live up to his word. Not this time.

The extension to the market phone rang, but Stacy ignored it. It was her day off. A few minutes later, the intercom buzzed. Tossing the paper aside, she answered.

"Yes?"

"The phone is for you."

"Thanks, Millie." She let go of the button and took the call. "This is Stacy Tedford."

"Hi, Miss Tedford. This is Bryce with White Mountain Electrical."

Stacy retrieved her planner from the dining room table. "I hope you're calling to schedule a visit." It had been almost three months since she'd requested an electrician come look at the store.

"Yes, ma'am. I'm heading your way next Friday. How does two o'clock sound?"

She wrote it in the book. "I'll see you then."

It was probably a waste of time to have him come out. As nice as it would be to operate all of the reach-in coolers without tripping a breaker, until she got the nursing home paid off, there was no way she could afford a huge repair bill. She would just have to make it through until winter using half the coolers.

She tapped her pencil on the open planner page. Her brow furrowed. She was supposed to do something this morning. What was it? She skimmed her never-ending list. Some of the chores she could check off because Caden could take care of them. Oh! Caden. He wanted the key to the old shed.

After digging through her junk drawer

with no luck, her eyes fell on a rolltop desk tucked in the corner of the living room. The desk had been her mother's, and Stacy hadn't once opened it. Despite the fact that her mother would never be well enough to return home, she couldn't bring herself to go through her mother's personal documents. She slid the top drawer open and found a handful of keys, with no idea if she had the right one.

Shoving the keys in her pocket, she opened the door to her apartment and stopped. Even the huge ponderosa pine trees couldn't block the mountains looming over the valley. The morning sun had yet to make an appearance over the rim of the mountains, but still managed to paint the sky with hues of pink and gold.

Leaning against her door, she breathed in the smell of the forest and listened to the birdsong. Rarely did she let herself think back to the place she'd lived before the Tedfords had adopted her. The memories of her birth family were vague, but she could remember the mountains behind her home with striking clarity. Maybe that was why this place had always felt like home.

Home. Her heart swelled. She couldn't imagine living anywhere else. Sure, she'd left for a little while. Eager to escape the growing tension between her parents, she'd gone to college in Tucson. What a mistake that'd been.

Cities made her miserable. She missed the crisp air, pine trees and open spaces. Even falling in love hadn't stopped her from rushing back when Vince had called her to say she was needed at home.

She wondered if Caden would be up. If he wasn't, she'd leave the keys outside the door where he'd find them. She wasn't about to walk in on him again. Her heart fluttered at the memory. This was silly. She was almost twenty-seven years old. Much too mature to feel giddy at the prospect of seeing a boy. And since when was she attracted to redheads? Even ones who looked like they'd just walked out of an action movie? Problem was, she was even more attracted to his quiet demeanor and the way he carried himself.

She topped the ridge behind the campground, looking over Caden's cabin for any sign of activity. Her stomach dropped. No lights on. He must still be asleep. She'd drop off the keys and come back after lunch.

Her feet didn't make a sound on the damp grass as she approached the cabin.

"What are you doing?"

Stacy jumped. She pressed her hand to her heart. "You scared me to death. I didn't think you were awake yet."

Caden sat on a tree stump, a cup of coffee in his hand. "I'm an early riser."

Something in his voice was off. She stepped closer. He was wearing the same clothes he'd had on the night before. "You look tired."

Caden shook his head. "I'm sorry about hitting your dad. I shouldn't have jumped to conclusions."

"I hope you didn't lose any sleep over that," she said. "I'm glad you came along when you did. How else was I going to get back in my house?"

His jaw twitched. "Still, I shouldn't have overreacted."

The breeze picked up and she rubbed her arms with her hands. "My relationship with my dad is complicated." Caden didn't need to hear about her personal problems.

"Yeah. Mine too." He stood from his make-shift chair. "Would you like some coffee?"

"No, thanks. I'm going to have breakfast with my mother this morning."

Caden nodded. In the dim light, Stacy could

see dark shadows under his eyes. He must have been really upset about last night.

She waited a few moments before breaking the silence. "I hope you didn't decide to stay because you feel guilty. I..." She searched for the right words. "I appreciate your help. But I don't want you to stay if you don't want to be here."

His brow furrowed. She held her breath, waiting for him to reassure her that she hadn't bullied him into agreeing to stay.

"The bus doesn't come until Monday, but if you want to leave before that, I will drive you to Springerville or Show Low. They have buses that come through twice a week."

"Do you want me to leave?"

Stacy shook her head. "No. But I don't want you to feel obligated."

"I don't." One corner of his mouth curved and her heart skipped a beat.

He cocked his head. "Is that why you came over so early?"

Oh! The keys. "You wanted to get the riding lawn mower from the storage shed. I'm not sure which one it is, so I brought them all." She pulled the handful of keys from her pocket.

He cupped his palm and she poured the

keys into his hand, the heat from it sending shivers up her arm. "Thank you."

"You're welcome." She looked up into his face and her breath caught. How could two little words make her heartbeat race? Maybe it wasn't the words but the gratitude in his clear gray eyes. She was in serious trouble.

CADEN CLUTCHED THE KEYS, still warm from Stacy's pocket, in his palm. He'd been too wired too sleep the night before. Even a three-mile jog hadn't helped, so he'd gone for a walk through the campground, making a mental list of a dozen other things he could do. The trick was figuring out how to get them all done in a month.

When he'd seen her top the ridge, he was sure she was coming to evict him. Now that that wasn't a concern, he could hardly wait to get started.

"I hope it doesn't take all day to find the right key," she said.

He set his coffee mug on the tree stump and walked to the large Conex box at the end of the yard. It was the only metal building in the entire campground and stood out like a sore thumb against the log cabins.

Even in the pale morning light, Caden had

no problem reading the letters on the padlock hanging from the door. He looked through the keys in his hand and then chose one. The key slid into the lock effortlessly.

"How'd you do that so fast?" Stacy said when the lock popped open.

"All skill, darlin'." Caden held the key up for her. "And it helps that this key is the only gold one and is the same brand as the lock."

She crossed her arms. "Why didn't I think of that?"

"You just have to notice what's around you." He yanked on the door. Nothing. He yanked again.

With a laugh, she stepped closer and placed her hands next to his. "One. Two. Three."

They both pulled and the door gave way with a groan.

She peered inside. "Everything you need for yard work should be in here."

Caden took a quick inventory. Ax. Chainsaw. Lawn mower. Toolbox. And fishing poles. Lots of them. "Do you rent poles to the campers?"

"No. Those were my grandfather's. Do you fish?" Something in her tone gave him pause.

"Why wouldn't I?"

She shrugged. "You're from Tucson."

"Maybe so, but I know how to fish." Or, at least, he did. It wouldn't be the same without Grayson. He stepped into the shed to take a closer look at the supplies. Stacy strolled around to the back of the shed. She never seemed to stay in the same place for more than a few seconds. He continued to riffle through the shelves.

The back wall of the metal shed shook as something crashed into it. Caden ran outside. "Are you okay?"

"Yes." Irritation laced her voice. She bent over a hunk of twisted metal and pulled at it. "Help me move this junk."

Caden stepped closer. It was an old motorcycle. Adrenaline shot through his system. A symbol of freedom without the responsibility of a passenger. He stepped between her and the beast and carefully stood it upright. "Whose is it?"

"It belonged to my daredevil cousin." She smiled. "He used to scare me to death on it. I was glad when he discovered a safer hobby."

The seat was still intact. He ran one hand over the leather. "What hobby was that?"

"Bull riding."

He raised one eyebrow. "That's safer?"

"If you ever saw him riding this thing on mountain trails, you'd agree."

Caden gripped the handlebars of the bike and gave it a test turn. "Did you ever ride it?"

Stacy cocked her head to one side and grinned. "I am going to plead the Fifth."

He tried to imagine her speeding around on the bike. From the way her dark green eyes sparkled when she looked at the motorcycle, his guess was that she was as much of a daredevil as her cousin.

"I wonder if the garbage truck will pick it up?" Stacy glared at it.

He couldn't resist teasing her. "Trying to get rid of the evidence?"

She made a face at him. "I'll have to get Frank to haul it to the dump."

The dump? He resisted the urge to stroke the rusted Kawasaki. "How much do you want for it? I'll buy it."

"That thing hasn't run in twenty years," she snorted. "If you want it, you can have it."

"Thanks." Caden rolled it away from the shed and dropped the kickstand. Grass brushed the undercarriage of the motor. Good thing mowing was the first thing on his to-do list. Well, the second thing.

First, he had to let the sheriff and his parole officer know he wanted to stay in town a little longer than planned. He doubted there would be a problem with it, but he didn't want to risk getting in trouble.

"I better go." Stacy jammed her hands into the back pockets of her jeans. "And thanks. I'm really glad you agreed to stay, even if it's only for a month. Funny to think we were complete strangers just yesterday. It feels like I've known you forever."

That sobered him. She wasn't a stranger to him. He'd thought of her almost nonstop for seven years. "Thanks."

Her eyes narrowed and she tilted her head. "I can't wait to hear about the mysterious business that's got you hanging out in Coronado. I'll bring some lunch over around one. You can tell me about it then."

Caden drew a sharp breath. What would she say when she found out she was his mysterious business? "I can fix my own lunch."

"Forget about it. The less time you have to spend on other things, like making lunch, the more time you have to work around here." She winked at him. "See, I actually have an ulterior motive."

He nodded. "True, but I wouldn't want to waste time talking during my lunch. I'll come to the deli and get it when I have time for a break."

Her eyes narrowed again and she put her hands on her hips. "Fine, but if you don't show up, I'll bring it to you."

He suppressed a smile as he watched her walk away. Stubborn woman. She would learn soon enough that he was just as stubborn as she was. For now, he could bide his time. When he left, she would hate him, but he would know that he'd done a little to ease some of her burden.

As soon as she'd disappeared down the trail, he retrieved his coffee mug from the stump and stared at the cabin. He'd never had a place all to himself before. With five kids in the family, Caden had always shared a bedroom. Four years in the army and seven years in prison had ensured that he was never alone. Funny, being alone didn't bother him as much as he'd thought it would.

And the size of the cabin was comforting. After living in a cell for seven years, large places made him nervous. It was too easy to get distracted and have someone approach from behind. He pinched the bridge of his nose. He had to quit thinking in those terms.

No one would sneak up on him here. No one cared what he did or where he went.

Once inside, he placed the keys on the counter and went upstairs to change clothes. Tomorrow, he would have to do laundry in the campground laundry room he'd noticed yesterday.

Sitting on the edge of the bed, he picked up a letter from the nightstand. His fingers traced the address of the home he'd lived in his entire life. How he missed his family! Especially his mother. By now, she knew he was out of prison, and was probably expecting him to come home. He'd written to let her know that he was okay but had to take care of some things before facing his family again.

While his mother would be upset that he hadn't come straight home, he knew his father would understand. When Caden had told him he didn't want to go to trial and wanted to plead guilty, his father hadn't tried to talk him out of it. As a district attorney for Pima County, his father had a lot of experience with cases like Caden's. While he supported Caden's desire to accept responsibility, he'd warned him what life would be like in prison and advised him to take a plea deal. Caden hadn't, but his father had supported him every step of the way.

Just before he'd left the courtroom, his older brother Patrick had shaken his hand. "When you're ready to come home, we'll be here, whether it's one year or seven. But don't come back until you can put this to rest. All of it. I don't want a shell of my brother. I want him whole."

Caden closed his eyes, remembering the tearful goodbyes from his family that day in the courthouse. A hollowness echoed in his insides. As much as he missed them, he didn't know if he'd ever be ready to go home.

CHAPTER SEVEN

CADEN'S SHOWER WAS QUICK. He didn't bother waiting for the water to heat up. He had a lot of things to do today and he didn't want to waste any time.

A slight chill hung in the morning air, especially under the canopy of evergreens that shaded the trail between the cabins and the store. He strolled past the market and to the main road in front of it.

To the left, houses and fields dotted the edge of the two-lane road that wove through the more residential part of town. To the right, signs beckoned summer visitors to come in and enjoy true Western hospitality. The road ended at a stop sign where the main highway cut through the little town.

He doubted the sheriff's station was to the left, so he turned right and headed toward the highway. With no pine trees to shield him from the sun, Caden was sweating by the time he got to the intersection. He paused at the stop sign. The main highway stretched ahead, curling its way through the distant mountains. In some places, the dark green of the pines mixed with the lighter aspens and blanketed the entire side of the mountain until he couldn't tell where one mountain ended and the next began. In other places, the blanket of green was interrupted by bright red boulders jutting into the skyline.

Coronado might be a small town, but it was spread out. To the right, he could see the American flag waving above some of the buildings on the main street. Large blue mailboxes were nearby. That had to be the post office.

Across the street was a gas station, a real-estate office and a tavern. Why did every town in Arizona, no matter how small, have at least one bar?

To the left was another cluster of buildings. A sign pointed them out as the library, fire station and sheriff's department. He headed that way. Hopefully, Frank was there and he wouldn't have to wait very long.

Caden paused in front of the glass doors and took a deep breath before entering. A forest of green plants sprouted from pots in every corner. This was a sheriff's office? It looked more like a nursery. Stepping past a large fern, he approached the counter. At least the glass partition between the lobby and the dispatcher was familiar. "I'm here to see Sheriff Tedford."

The gray-haired lady pulled a pencil from behind her ear and marked off something on the chart in front of her. "Frank," she hollered over her shoulder.

A moment later, the burly man opened the door and waved Caden inside. "I'm surprised to see you here. What can I do for you?"

Caden followed him to his office. At the campground, Frank had said he didn't have a problem with Caden sticking around. But that was before the altercation with Stacy's dad. "I'd like to talk to you about staying in Coronado until the end of the month."

Frank sat on the edge of his desk. "When I offered you the maintenance job, you told me you'd be leaving at the end of the week, no matter what. Why did you change your mind?"

"I agreed to stay until the end of the month to help Stacy out, since she's juggling the market and the campground."

The man's eyes narrowed. "You seem to

have a lot of interest in my niece. Is she the reason you're staying?"

"Yes, but not the way you think." Caden's throat was so dry, he could barely swallow. He couldn't explain why he wanted to stay without telling Frank who he was and what he'd done. He launched into his story before he lost his nerve. It was the first time he'd talked about the accident to anyone.

The memory of his best friend sent sharp pains through his chest. His throat constricted and he closed his eyes, sucking in a deep, pained breath. The slamming of a drawer jerked his head up.

Frank held a folder from the filing cabinet next to his desk. "Ben Erikson told me a lot about you."

"Oh?" He sat in a wooden chair as Frank sifted through the file.

"I gave him a call after our little heart-to-heart."

Caden tried to calm the erratic beat of his heart. The parole officer liked him. At least, he thought he did. "And what did he say?"

Frank gave Caden a somber look. "Ben says you could've gotten a much lighter sentence but you refused to plea-bargain. Not even when the judge told you to consider it. Why is that?"

He took a deep breath. "I was guilty."

"He also said you turned down all attempts at parole."

Caden wiped his hands on his jeans. "I just wanted to serve my time."

Frank crossed his arms. "You got some kind of death wish I should know about?"

"No, sir."

"Any reason I can't trust you in my town or around my family?"

"No." Caden's pulse pounded. "I told you before, I'm not here to cause any trouble."

Frank raised one eyebrow. "Stacy might not agree."

How was he supposed to respond? "I just want to set things right."

Frank leaned back in his chair. "He also said you wouldn't lie to me. I have to say I'm surprised. Most men in your situation would."

"I don't lie."

"But you don't want Stacy to know the truth yet, either."

He shrugged. "Would she let me help if she did?"

"No. She'd likely throw you out on your

ear." Frank grinned, leaning forward to rest his elbows on the table. "You seem like a stand-up guy. Stacy needs a few more of those in her life. She's been trying to do things on her own for far too long."

Caden's heart leaped. "So I can stay?"

"On one condition."

Caden nodded. "Anything."

Frank removed his hat, running a hand through his dark, wavy locks. "Her mama is dying. I doubt she'll make it through the summer. Stacy hasn't spoken to her daddy in years. I know you've heard bad things about Vince, but he was telling the truth. He was as sober as a preacher on Sunday morning."

Caden chewed on his bottom lip. What did this have to do with him?

The sheriff went on. "There are things Stacy doesn't know. It's not my place to tell her, but she won't give Vince a chance to explain."

"And you think I can get her to talk to her father? Why would she listen to me?"

Frank stroked one side of his mustache. "I don't know. You seem to be on a mission to find forgiveness. Vince wants that, too."

"I don't know what I can do, but if I have

an opportunity, I'll encourage her to listen to him." What else could he say?

"I'll give Ben a call and let him know what's going on."

"Thank you, sir. I appreciate that." Caden stood and shook hands with the sheriff.

Feeling as if a giant weight had been lifted from his shoulders, he left the sheriff's department and headed to the post office. The hours noted on the door said it didn't open until 9:00 a.m., but the sign hanging on the door had been turned to read Open.

He tested the glass door, which opened easily. He could see the mail attendant, an elderly lady with pink hair, sitting behind the counter. A cowbell hanging from a rope clanked when he let the door close behind him.

"Welcome, young man. What can I do for you?" The postmistress smiled, her lips the same shade of pink as her hair. Long gold earrings dangled to her shoulders.

"I need a stamp."

"A book of stamps or just a stamp?" She pulled a paper out from under the counter and placed it in front of him. "We have lots of different designs to choose from."

"Just a stamp, please." He pulled the letter

out of his pocket. It didn't matter if the postage showed a bird or a flower, as long as it got his letter to Tucson.

The woman pursed her lips, but she took the letter from him and placed a stamp on it, accepting his coins along with it.

"You don't have a return address on here, son," she said. "Don't you want to add it?"

"No."

"Wait right there. Edith," the woman yelled over her shoulder.

Another elderly woman, this one with blue hair, shuffled in from the back. "What is it, Margaret?" She saw Caden and smiled. "Well, hello, young man."

He nodded. What was going on? The women exchanged glances and smiled.

"This young man doesn't want to put a return address on his envelope."

The blue-haired Edith launched into a sermon on how easy it would be for his letter to get lost without a return address. Finally, she stopped talking and handed him a pen. "I don't want to be responsible for this missing mail."

"That's a chance I'm willing to take."

"Don't you have a return address, son?" Margaret gasped. "That's it. You're one of those mountain men living off the grid up in the mountains."

"Oh, Margaret." Edith slapped her arm. "Does he look like a mountain man? Besides, he smells much better. Are you new to town? Where do you live?"

"New to town! Oh, how nice." The pink-haired one clapped her hands. "Oh, Edie, we should introduce him to Anastacia. You're not married, are you?"

"We should! He'd be perfect for our Stacy."

"Yes, she's been alone for much too long."

Caden tried to stop the women, but their chatter continued as they carried on the conversation without him. Only the clanking of the cowbell stopped them.

"What's going on here?" A man wearing a postal uniform stood with his hands on his hips.

Edith opened the half door that connected the waiting area to the postal area and hurried past Caden. Margaret followed. "We must be going. See you soon, young man."

Confused, he looked back and forth between the man and the women waiting for him at the door. "Do they work here?"

The man laughed. "No. They retired fifteen years ago. We never changed the locks, so they like to come in and help out."

Caden's eyes widened. "You let them?"

"Why not? They do a good job. No harm, no foul." He shrugged. "Besides saving me a ton of work, it makes them happy."

After making sure the real postman had his letter, he walked outside, looking around to make sure he wasn't about to be ambushed by the two women. The coast was clear, so he headed back to the campground.

Caden's mind raced as he walked. Fixing the broken things in Stacy's life was easy. Unclog a drain. Mend a cabinet. Mow the grass. Run some electrical wire. But how was he supposed to fix a broken relationship when he couldn't even call his own mother?

CLEANING CABINS ALL afternoon kept Stacy busy. But not busy enough to keep her thoughts from Caden. Maybe she should invite him to dinner. That would give her a chance to get to know him better. Her heart fluttered at the thought. She knew it wasn't a good idea to take too much interest in him. He'd made it clear he wasn't going to stick around Coronado. Still, he was a puzzle to her and she had never been able to leave a puzzle unsolved.

She hadn't dated since college. Even then, it had only been one man. She'd liked Grayson a lot. Maybe even loved him. But it never would have lasted. He'd wanted to stay in the city and she hadn't. He'd also liked to drink and party, and even though he never overdid it, she'd already seen too much of it in her life. They'd argued about it a lot. Her chest ached. If only he'd listened to her, maybe he'd still be alive.

It was late in the afternoon when she finished the last cabin. Only a few families were still at the campground and they all seemed to be gathered in the common areas. The smell of hamburgers drifted in the air, making her mouth water. She hoped Caden was as hungry.

A few of the adults were playing horseshoes and children chased each other around the grass.

"Hello. Having a good time?" she greeted a group of ladies sitting at the picnic table closest to the path.

"Hi, Stacy." One of the women nodded. "Would you like a burger? We have plenty."

She shook her head. "It smells wonderful, but I already have dinner plans. Thank you."

At least, she hoped she would have dinner

plans. Caden was nowhere around, so she went to his cabin. After rapping on the door with her knuckles, she waited.

"Come in," his muffled voice called from inside.

He was sitting at the small table, a hamburger and a baked potato in front of him. She crossed her arms. "Where did you get that?"

Caden wiped his mouth with a paper towel. "Cabin Four. A thank-you for rescuing her wedding ring."

She frowned. It seemed she wasn't the only one who worried about him eating. "I was going to invite you to dinner."

"You already offered me lunch from the deli every day and fed me dinner last night."

"Friends help each other. You work hard all afternoon and I always cook more than I can eat. It's what friends do."

"We aren't friends." He took a bite of the hamburger.

"I see." Heat flushed through her body. She hadn't really thrown herself at him, but it felt like she had. She turned to leave.

"Wait," he said.

She faced him, gritting her teeth to keep from saying anything.

"I'm sorry." The chair scraped on the floor as he stood. "That came out wrong."

"No, it didn't," she said. "You don't want to be friends. Fine."

His face scrunched. "It's not that. We just met. Don't go out of your way for me. I'm not worth it."

The pained expression on his face softened her anger. "You really believe that?"

Caden didn't respond.

"How about we try this again? Would you please have dinner with me tomorrow night?"

He frowned. "I can't."

She narrowed her eyes. "Can't or won't?"

"Can't." He pulled a piece of paper out of the back pocket of his jeans and handed it to her. "I've got a date."

She took the paper and deciphered the crayon scrawl. "Those stick figures seem to be awfully happy about being stuck with a sword."

"That's not a sword," he said. Stepping closer to her, he pointed at the line. "It's a family sitting at a table. I fixed Jaylean's bike for her today, so she invited me to dinner. Hot dogs."

She smiled at the picture. In two days, he'd

developed a better relationship with the campers than the previous maintenance worker ever had. It reminded her of her grandfather. He'd loved getting to know the campers. She handed the picture back to him. "There's no way I can compete with that."

"Maybe another time."

"I'll hold you to that, city boy. Have a good night." She turned to leave, but stopped at the sight of the motorcycle in the middle of the room. She stared at it. "Isn't that the motorcycle we found behind the shed?"

"Yes."

"Why is it in the living room?" Parts from the engine lay on newspaper and more pieces were stacked in a bowl.

He walked to the refrigerator and poured himself a glass of milk. "Want some?"

"No, thank you." She waited for an explanation but didn't get one. Finally, she had to ask. "Why is it in here?"

"It's too dark to work outside."

Stacy chewed on her bottom lip. "Why don't you just work on it during the day?"

"I don't have time." He sat back down at the table to finish his food.

"Do you think you can make time for dinner on Friday night?"

His gray eyes turned dark and stormy. "I don't think that's a very good idea."

"Why? Because we're not friends? Too bad." She rejoined him in the kitchen, where she saw an open notebook on the counter. She couldn't help a glance at the to-do list she saw there. Cabin One: stuck cabinet, broken window, missing screens. Cabin Two: leaky faucet in bathroom, sink clogged. The list went on. How did she not know about all the things wrong with the rentals? As the manager, shouldn't she know about them?

"Are there this many problems with the cabins?" A heaviness settled in the pit of her stomach.

"Not anymore." Caden rinsed his glass out in the sink.

"I'm sorry. I had no idea."

He put the notebook in the drawer. If he'd come out and told her to stay out of his stuff, the announcement wouldn't have been as clear as his actions.

"No wonder you didn't have time to work on the motorcycle today."

As busy as he'd been, there had to be something she could do for him. Tomorrow she'd ask Millie to stay a little longer and she'd give the cabin a good cleaning while he was out working, whether he wanted her to or not.

She looked around the room. The downstairs area was neat and orderly. Even the mantel looked shiny. Unable to resist, she walked over to the fireplace and ran her finger over the wood. Not a trace of dust. "Don't you ever sleep?"

"Not much."

"Have you tried cherry juice?"

He put his plate in the sink and avoided her gaze. He didn't seem to avoid talking to the campground patrons, so why did he try so hard to avoid a conversation with her? Maybe he just needed a little push.

"People say you should drink warm milk to help you sleep, but cherry juice is actually better for you. It has tryptophan in it." When Caden didn't respond, she continued. "You know. Tryptophan is the chemical in turkey that's supposed to make you sleepy. There's a lot more in cherry juice."

"I know what tryptophan is."

She bit her bottom lip. "You don't talk much, do you, city boy?"

"No, ma'am."

"Stop calling me 'ma'am.'" She sat on the

arm of the sofa. "I had a hard time sleeping when I was little."

Caden wiped the table with a paper towel. "Why?"

"I don't know. I guess I was afraid something bad would happen."

He furrowed his eyebrows. "Like a monster under the bed?"

"No. Like someone else I loved would die." Stacy pulled her long hair over one shoulder and twisted the end around her index finger. "I told you I was adopted from an orphanage in Georgia. My birth mom had been sick for a long time when my little brother started to get sick. I went to sleep one night and the next morning my brother was dead. A few weeks later, my mother died and social services came and took me and my baby sister to an orphanage."

Caden let out a soft whistle. "What happened to your dad?"

She took a deep breath and clenched her hands in her lap. "One of the sisters at the orphanage told me he died a few months later."

"What about your sister?"

"She was adopted less than a month after we arrived. They didn't want me…just her."

"I'm sorry." His voice was barely more than a whisper. He walked over to the sofa.

"Don't be. I don't even know why I'm telling you all this." She hugged her arms around her stomach.

What was wrong with her? She never talked about her birth family. She rubbed the palm of her hand across the ache building in her chest. She'd ripped the scab off an old wound she hadn't even realized was still there.

"Sometimes talking about something is the only way to heal from it."

The way he looked at her shot right to Stacy's core. If he were to pull her into his arms and hug her, she wouldn't have been surprised. As much as she might like to feel his strong arms around her, she didn't want a hug of pity. She'd had enough of that in her life.

She forced a laugh to lighten the tension. "That's deep, city boy. I never would have pegged you for a counselor."

His brow creased and he stepped back as if suddenly aware of how close they were.

She stood. "There are always plenty of breakfast burros in the deli. You're welcome to come get one in the morning. And I will see you for dinner at seven on Friday."

She pushed past him and darted for the door before he could argue.

CHAPTER EIGHT

CADEN SAT CROSS-LEGGED on the living room floor, cleaning parts from the motorcycle. If he was able to get the bike running, he'd leave Coronado with a clear conscience and new vehicle. And what would Stacy have? The knowledge that Grayson hadn't abandoned her and fewer things to do at the campground. She still had a dying mother and a father she didn't speak to.

The wrench in his hand slipped from his fingers. He couldn't do anything about her mother, but what if he could help her repair her relationship with Vince? Did she even want that? He'd seen the sadness on her face when Frank drove away with Vince in his SUV. She missed her father, even if she wouldn't admit it to herself.

He had to try.

After washing his hands, he took off at a jog until he came to the small RV park where Frank had told him Vince was staying.

His lungs burned and he fought to catch his breath as he walked to the last RV lot on the road. He knocked at the door of the small travel trailer and a large man opened it, sending a cloud of cigarette smoke into the air.

"Excuse me. Vince?"

The man let out a long, slow puff of smoke, his face shadowed in the dark. "Who wants to know?"

"I'm Caden Murphy. I came to apologize for…" What should he say? "Punching you"? "Defending your daughter"?

Vince stepped outside and rubbed his jaw. "That was you, huh? Nice hook."

Caden nodded. "I'm sorry. I didn't know you were Stacy's father."

"Would it have made a difference?" His face was somber. "If I was doing what you thought I was doing, would it have mattered?"

"No," Caden said honestly. "Not if you were really trying to hurt her."

Vince gave an approving nod. "Good."

Vince took one last drag from his cigarette and dropped it on the ground, grinding it out with his boot. "Frank tells me you just got out of prison."

Caden lifted his chin. "Yes, sir."

Vince raised one eyebrow. "You another one of his pet projects?"

"No, sir." How often did Frank take in ex-cons? "I'm here trying to right a wrong."

"Righting wrongs is sticky business. Sometimes you make things worse trying to make things better." Vince unfolded two rickety lawn chairs that had been leaning against the RV. He sat in one. "Why don't you tell me what you're trying to fix and exactly how my daughter is involved?"

Vince's protectiveness over Stacy made Caden feel better. He was doing the right thing, whether Stacy would agree or not.

He hated talking about Grayson and the accident, but he started at the beginning and ended with his arriving in town. "Frank thinks that I can help you and Stacy mend your relationship, but I don't know how. I don't even know what happened."

Vince's face was hard. "Frank thinks he can fix everything. I guess that's why he became a cop, but there's more to it than you know. Years of lies that I don't think can ever be healed."

Caden understood the pain in his voice. "What happened?"

Vince lit another cigarette. "Missy—Stacy's

mom—knew from an early age that she could develop Huntington's disease. Her mother and siblings died from it. All her aunts and uncles on that side of the family had it, too. She was living under a death sentence, and she knew it.

"Well, from the moment we graduated high school, she was determined to see as much of the world as she could. She didn't want to miss out on anything. And I wanted her to have it all." Smoke curled in the air around his head. "I got offered a football scholarship to play for Arizona State, but Missy didn't have time to mess with college, so I went to work at the market with her dad until we saved enough money to go on one of her adventures.

"I put as much money away as I could." His gaze was distant. "I knew we would need it for medical expenses later on."

Caden didn't say anything. Vince needed to talk as much as he needed to hear it.

"It was hard to save much money with Missy traveling all over the country." Vince flicked his cigarette to the ground. "We went to high school with a girl from Georgia. The country, not the state. After high school, Missy and Nina remained friends. Nina was always raising funds and collecting things to send to an orphanage in her hometown. When Nina's mother got sick, Missy convinced me we should go with her to visit. So we packed up and went to Georgia."

"That's where you found Stacy?"

Vince laughed. "Oh, Missy had planned to adopt a child there all along. That's why she insisted I go with her. We took a bunch of donations to the local orphanage from our church and that's when we saw Stacy. Skinny. Scared. And so sad it just made your heart break to look at her."

He paused to clear his throat. "We both fell in love with her immediately and refused to come home without her. It took all the money I'd saved to get her here. But it was worth it."

Vince's love for Stacy was so obvious, it made Caden's heart ache for his own father. "What happened to cause a rift between you?"

"Missy's symptoms started showing up before Stacy was in high school. We knew we wouldn't be able to hide it for long, but Missy insisted on not telling her. We started fighting about when to tell Stacy. I was scared. I was losing my wife right in front of my eyes and there was nothing I could do about it. I started drinking more and more. Missy hoped Stacy would meet a nice young man at college, get married and move away. Then she wouldn't be here to see Missy's decline."

Guilt slammed into Caden like a wrecking ball. If it hadn't been for him, Stacy would've had that life. "And I messed it up."

"No, you didn't. Stacy liked that boy, but she didn't love him. If she did, she wouldn't have been able to walk away so easily."

Caden rubbed the back of his neck. "Why did she walk away? Why did she leave school and come back here?"

Vince's face turned dark. "Missy had accepted her fate, but I couldn't. I applied for every experimental treatment program I could find. I was determined to find a way to hold on to my wife. But they were expensive.

"Then one day, the money ran out and the bank wouldn't give me another loan. I started drinking even more."

The pain on Vince's face mirrored the pain Caden felt.

"I didn't realize how bad my drinking was until, one day, Missy threw an empty bottle at my head and told me to get out." He shook his head. "I did, but only to try to get sober. The next thing I knew, Stacy had quit school and come home to run the store.

"Then Missy called me and told me she was checking herself into a nursing home. She couldn't stand the thought of Stacy going through what she had gone through with her mother. I begged her not to. I told her I'd take care of her, but she claimed I was too drunk to take care of myself."

He let out a long sigh. "And she was right."

Silence filled the air for a moment. Caden waited for Vince to continue.

"I promised her I would go to rehab, and when I got sober, I would bring her home and take care of her."

"Why didn't you?"

Vince's chest heaved. "She signed some paperwork that prevented anyone from removing her. But that was after she'd spent the last of our savings account on enrolling me in a rehabilitation program that I didn't know about until Frank was driving me to it."

"And Stacy got stuck paying for the nursing home."

"Only for the first year. As soon as I got out of rehab, I got a job driving a truck. I've been paying half of it ever since," Vince said. "Six months ago, I got laid off, so the bill has fallen behind again."

"Does Stacy know any of this?"

He shrugged. "Does it matter? The damage is already done."

How many times had Caden said the same thing when referring to the shame he'd inflicted on the family with his prison sentence? He found himself repeating the words his sister Sarah had said every time. "It's never too late."

And for the first time since his incarceration, he hoped it was true.

STACY HADN'T GONE to the campground the next day. She'd had enough to do around the market. Too bad it hadn't kept her mind off Caden. When he hadn't shown up by one o'clock for lunch, she'd packed a couple of sandwiches, a bag of chips and some water bottles into a small ice chest and sent it to the campground with Donna.

She'd felt much better when Donna had reported that she'd barely got more than a few words out of Caden, either. Maybe he was just a really quiet person. Still, Stacy couldn't shake the feeling that he was always on guard around her. But why?

Today, Caden hadn't visited the market, either. Was he busy, or did he just not want her to provide him with lunch? Part of her wanted to take lunch to him and remind him about her dinner invitation that night. The other part wanted to wait and see if he would show up.

Donna was busy at the cash register, so she went behind the deli counter to make Caden a sandwich. She couldn't let the man go hungry, even if he did want to avoid her. As she packed his lunch, she debated taking it to him herself or having Donna do it again.

The bells chimed and a loud voice called out, "Now, that's where I like to see women, standing in the kitchen, making her man some food."

Stacy dropped the knife she was using. A stocky man in a cowboy hat grinned at her, his dark blue eyes twinkling.

"Coy!" She raced around the counter and he caught her up in a giant bear hug. "What are you doing here?"

He tilted his hat back. "I decided to take some time off before the Luna Rodeo next month."

A dark-haired woman with long braids rolled her eyes. "What he means is he needs a few weeks to recover so that he *can* compete in the Luna Rodeo."

"Hi, Becky." Stacy gave her cousin's girlfriend a quick hug. "I wish I could say that surprises me, but it doesn't. What did he do this time?"

"Hey," Coy said. "I'm right here. You can ask me."

She arched one eyebrow at him. "Okay. What happened?"

"I got stepped on, that's all."

Again, Stacy looked at Becky. "What's he *not* telling me?"

"The bull stepped on his head and he's got a concussion."

"Are you just dropping him off or are you taking some time off, too?"

Becky shrugged. "I need to study for summer finals, so I'm staying."

Stacy had always admired Becky. The tiny cowgirl was as tough as she was smart. Somehow, she managed to remain one of the best barrel racers in the country and keep near-perfect grades in college. She was on track to graduate in record time and planned to go to veterinary school to specialize in livestock. Stacy suspected Becky would spend more time patching up Coy than cows.

Coy draped one arm across Becky's shoulders. "Do you mind if we put our horses in the corrals out at the campground?"

"You know you don't have to ask," Stacy said. "I was just about to run out there. If you wait a few minutes, I'll go help you. Donna, do you mind?"

Donna glanced at her from the cash register and gave her a knowing smile. "Not at all."

"Do you want a sandwich or something while you're waiting?" she asked her visitors.

"How 'bout an ice cream cone?" Coy asked.

She laughed and pulled a sugar cone from the dispenser.

It only took a couple of minutes for Stacy to finish packing the food. She walked outside with Coy and Becky. A large gooseneck horse trailer covered one whole side of the parking lot. She had never seen anything so fancy.

"Wow. Is that yours?"

"Yes." Coy answered at the same time that Becky said, "No."

Becky shook her head. "It's mine."

"Darlin', what's mine is yours and vice versa."

"Not until you put a ring on it." Becky held up her empty left hand and wriggled her fingers. "Until then, you can keep sleeping on the couch."

Stacy didn't wait for Coy to respond to Becky's jab about marriage. They'd been having the same conversation since they were sixteen years old. Becky wanted to get married. Coy didn't. It was usually best to ignore their arguments. "There's a couch in there?"

Coy laughed. "A couch. A kitchen. Flat-screen TV. Bathroom. Everything you need on the road."

"If y'all can manage to get this rig out of my parking lot without running over anyone, I'll meet you at the corrals."

Becky pointed at the diesel truck hooked up to the trailer. "We've got room if you want to ride with us. No sense taking two vehicles."

Stacy held up the small ice chest she was holding. "I've got to deliver lunch to the new groundskeeper, so I'm taking the shortcut. I'll probably beat you there."

"Dad finally hired someone to replace Luke?" Coy's voice carried a hint of hardness.

"Temporarily. He only agreed to stay until the end of the month, but he's done more work in the last five days than Luke ever did." She probably shouldn't have said that. Coy was already irritated with Luke.

They had once been good friends and Coy had taken it personally when Luke bailed just before the busy season. Stacy wasn't sure if their friendship would ever recover.

Coy waved at her as he climbed into the driver's seat. She didn't wait to see if he had any trouble getting the giant trailer out of the parking area. He'd been pulling trailers since he was tall enough to reach the gas pedal of Frank's truck and handled them better than anyone she knew.

The closer she got to the campground, the faster her heart rate increased. As she headed down the trail toward his cabin, she told herself it was because of the walk and not the thought of seeing Caden again.

It was silly to let him get to her like this. She would drop lunch off, then go meet Coy and Becky. If he was there, fine. If he wasn't, that was fine, too. She wouldn't stop and chat. She wouldn't even remind him about dinner.

Her heart went into a gallop when she saw him in the backyard, bent over a hunk of metal. *Well,* she thought, *here goes nothing.*

CADEN KNELT ON the grass, working on the lawn mower's engine. His hands were so covered in grease, he doubted they'd ever come clean. So much for making life easier.

Something touched the back of his arm.

He jerked his arm, banging his knuckle on the top of the engine. Pain radiated all the way to his shoulder. He turned, prepared to fight off whatever wild creature had decided to disturb his afternoon.

"It's just me." Stacy, carrying her ice chest, held up her free hand in surrender. "What are you doing back here?"

Rising, Caden picked up the rag lying on the grass and wiped his hands. "There's more shade back here."

Stacy took a deep breath, then wrinkled her nose. "You smell like gasoline. What were you doing, taking a bath in it?"

He nodded to the metal containers spread across the yard. "I'm not, but the carburetor is."

"I'm guessing it doesn't run?"

"My mom always said that with a little patience and TLC, most things can be fixed." Caden's chest ached. He missed her. He missed his family. But he couldn't go home yet. Maybe not ever.

Stacy held up the ice chest. "I brought

lunch. Want me to set it up on the picnic table or leave it in the cabin?"

"The picnic table is fine. I'll go wash my hands."

He tucked the dirty rag into his pocket and headed for the cabin. His chest expanded with an emotion he hadn't felt in a long time. It was silly to be happy about Stacy bringing his lunch. He'd missed her yesterday.

He washed his hands. Then he washed them again. That smell wasn't going to come off easily. Before heading back out, Caden grabbed two water bottles from the fridge.

Picnic tables were scattered in the campground's common area. Stacy was waiting at the one closest to his cabin. He handed her a water bottle and sat. "Thanks for bringing lunch. I didn't realize how hungry I was."

"No problem." She took a sip. "I had to come over here anyway."

He frowned. "You aren't doing more cleaning today, are you?"

"No, thank goodness. My cousin wants to drop some horses off at the corrals, so I was going to make sure the stables are still okay."

Horses? Caden perked up. "Can I come?"

Stacy shrugged. "Sure. Just don't get in the way."

"I'll try not to." He unwrapped the sandwich and stood. "It's a ways across the campground. I'll eat as we go."

They walked in silence, but Caden knew it wouldn't last long. Stacy was too inquisitive.

Sure enough, she asked, "Have you worked on the motorcycle?"

"A little."

"The common area looks great. Did you chop all that wood?"

He took a drink of water before answering. "Yes."

"The whole place looks better. How long are you willing to stay?" she teased.

Caden shrugged. "It depends."

Her face lit up. "On what?"

On you. He willed his heart to stop pounding. "If the motorcycle can be fixed."

"Then you'll stay for the rest of the summer?"

"No." If it could be fixed, he'd have some measure of freedom, but he still couldn't stay.

She turned to face him and rested her hand on his arm. "I really hope that you change your mind. Coronado isn't as exciting as the city, but it's not a bad place."

The touch of her hand sent shock waves

up his arm. To break the contact, he pointed at the dirt road. "That must be your cousin."

"Yes." Her pace quickened. "You'll like him. Everyone does. His girlfriend is super-sweet, too. She's a little shy, though. Sometimes people think she doesn't like them, but that's just because she doesn't talk until she gets to know someone."

"So she's a lot like you." He could listen to her rattle on all day.

Her eyebrows rose as she gave him a sly smile. "Did you just make a joke?"

"It happens." He'd do it more often if it meant seeing her smile.

Caden hadn't ventured this far from the main campground. A weathered barn sat just off the dirt road. Behind the barn, a large pasture was fenced off to allow horses access to both the field and the shelter of the barn.

The driver of the dually truck had already whipped around and was backing the horse trailer up.

"I'll open the barn doors," Caden said.

The smell of old hay, dust and manure greeted him as he did. Inside were rows of stalls on either side of the barn. An office, a large tack room and a washing area at the front of the building told him that this had once been a thriving operation. Sunshine filtered in from skylights through the dust hanging in the air. In the background, he heard the metal doors of the trailer swing open and movement from inside the horse trailer.

"Which stable do you want to use?" Caden called, ignoring the wave of homesickness the barn induced.

"The first one on the left will be fine, city boy." Stacy's voice was muffled.

He heard the clomping of hooves as someone led a horse off the trailer. He unlatched the gate to the stable and held it open.

"Caden Murphy?" A tall cowboy stared at him, holding the reins to a beautiful chestnut mare.

Stacy's eyes darted back and forth between them. "You know him?"

It wasn't until the cowboy grinned that Caden realized who he was. "Coy?"

Why hadn't it dawned on him that Coy Tedford might be related to Stacy Tedford? He looked at her and pointed at Coy. "This is your daredevil cousin?"

The cowboy dropped the reins and was next to him in just a few strides. He reached out to shake Caden's hand. "How are you? I haven't seen you since the high school rodeo finals."

"You know him?" Stacy repeated, her eyes wide.

"We competed together when we were kids," Caden told her.

Coy nodded. "Caden was top dog when I first started competing in the Arizona High School Rodeo Association."

It didn't surprise him to see that Coy was still rodeoing. He'd been one of the most natural bull riders he'd ever seen. "I was just glad you never took up roping. Competing against you in steer wrestling was bad enough."

Caden heard his name again and looked up to see Becky Maxwell at the corner of the trailer. He grinned as she rushed over to hug him.

"How's your hand?" Becky grabbed his right hand. "I see it healed okay."

Stacy looked at her. "What's wrong with his hand?"

Caden held up his right hand. The very tip of his middle finger was missing. "It got caught in the dally."

"I was the first one to him when it happened," Becky said. "He's the whole reason

I decided to go to veterinary school and not medical school. I figured dealing with a two-ton bull had to be easier than dealing with ornery cowboys."

Stacy rubbed her temples. "What's a 'dally' and how did it cut your finger off?"

"You've seen team roping before, haven't you?" Caden asked.

"Yes. One person ropes the head of the steer and one person gets the back feet," she said.

"Right," he said, glad she knew the basics. "When the cowboy ropes the steer, he—"

"Or she," Becky interrupted.

Caden nodded at her. "Or she, wraps the rope around the saddle horn to help hold the steer in place. That's called 'dallying.' You have to be fast and wrap it before the steer pulls too much or your finger or thumb can get caught in the rope."

Stacy's mouth dropped open. "Your finger got caught in the rope?"

He shrugged. "Just the tip. It wasn't too bad, considering. Most of the team ropers I know are missing a lot more than that."

"You still roped after that?"

Becky leaned on the horse trailer, her thumb hooked in the belt loop of her jeans. "Caden won the state championship for team roping that year."

Coy punched Caden in the arm. "I kept looking for you on the circuit after high school. Where'd you go?"

He braced himself for all the questions he knew were coming. "I joined the army." He hoped Coy would let it go at that, but he knew it wouldn't happen.

"I thought you wanted to go into the construction business with your brother."

Caden couldn't believe Coy remembered that. "I wanted to, but the deal was I could only do it after I served in the military."

"Why?" Becky asked.

He glanced at Stacy but continued. "Apparently, Patrick thought I needed time to grow up and learn responsibility first."

Suddenly, Coy burst out laughing. "Wait. Are you the city boy she was talking to when we first got here?"

Stacy crossed her arms and glared at him. "He told me he was from Tucson. What else was I supposed to think?"

She turned to Caden. "You don't live in Tucson, do you? I mean, in the city limits."

Caden shook his head. "No, ma'am. I grew

up on a ranch outside of Tucson. I've never lived in the city."

Her body stiffened and her chin tilted up. "I guess y'all can manage the rest of this without me. I need to get back to the store."

Caden watched her walk away. He looked at Coy. "What did I do?"

Coy scratched his head. "Beats me."

"You men can be so obtuse," Becky groaned. "You lied to her."

He shook his head. "No, I didn't."

"Did you let her believe you were from Tucson?"

"I am from Tucson."

She let out a sigh. "Did you correct her when she called you a 'city boy'?"

"No."

"Why?"

How could Caden explain that he enjoyed Stacy's teasing? He shrugged. "I don't know. I'm only here for a few weeks, so I didn't think it mattered."

Becky gave him a serious look. "Things like that matter to her. Everyone in her life gave her half-truths for years. It's one thing she hates more than anything."

Caden's throat tightened and he tried to swallow the sour taste in his mouth. If she got angry because he hadn't told her where he lived, what was she going to do when she found out who he really was and why he was there?

CHAPTER NINE

CADEN BOLTED UP in bed. Darkness pressed in on him and he gulped for air. Scrubbing his hands over his face, he tried to slow his heart rate. Would he ever get through a night without nightmares? Pictures of Grayson rolled through his mind and he shut his eyes, forcing the memories away. The therapist he'd seen twice a week in prison had assured him he'd get better in time. As soon as he learned to forgive himself. Looked like he'd be working on no sleep for the rest of his life.

The red numbers of the digital clock next to his bed glowed. Three thirty. He threw the blanket to the side. Might as well get up. There was no way he'd get any more sleep tonight. At least he'd made it thirty minutes longer than last night.

His muscles protested when his feet hit the cold wood floor and he stood and stretched. Physically, he thought he'd been in good shape. There hadn't been much to do in prison except work out. But after almost two weeks of working twelve-hour days at the campground, he'd discovered that lifting weights had nothing on manual labor. Not that he minded. Anything was better than sitting around with his thoughts.

He'd never worked this much in one day, not even in the military. Between pounding nails and chopping wood, Caden should have been too exhausted for nightmares.

But it didn't matter. He was used to surviving on four hours of sleep a night or less.

Caden stumbled down the stairs to turn the coffee machine on. He might as well work on the motorcycle since sleep wasn't an option. After coffee.

A few minutes later, he was sitting on a stump in what was now his backyard. He'd found the large piece of wood while dragging debris away from the drainage ditches circling the campground. It was too large for firewood but perfect for a makeshift chair. Steam rose from his mug and he waited for the coffee to chase away the grogginess.

Crickets sang a lullaby, and farther into the mountains, the howl of a lone wolf echoed. For the first time in years, Caden felt at peace. He gazed up at the stars. Had he ever paid attention to stars before? He was always too busy to notice trivial things like stars. Or trees. Or fresh air.

A noise disturbed the relative silence around him and Caden froze. Something was poking around by the woodpile at the side of the cabin. Bears were frequent visitors. Summer guests weren't always diligent about locking their food away, and an easy meal was too much temptation. Not wanting to attract attention to himself, Caden continued to sip his coffee and watch for the perpetrator.

Relief washed through him when he made out the silhouette of an animal much too small to be a bear. But something about the way it moved alarmed him. Short, choppy steps. It limped closer. The light from his open door was just enough for him to see the dog sniffing the ground in front of him.

At least, he thought it was a dog. Deep gashes ran along his hind legs. More cuts covered his face and one eye was sealed shut with matted blood. The dog's ribs could be seen, even through the shaggy coat.

Caden spoke softly. "Hey, boy, come here."

The dog jumped, but was either in too much pain or too hungry to run from him.

Keeping his movements smooth and slow,

he eased over to the animal. Carefully, he herded the dog toward the door of his cabin. The poor thing was hesitant to go inside, but Caden gently nudged him through the door and shut it after him. He didn't think the dog would get far if he tried to escape, but there was no sense making it difficult for both of them.

After he filled a bowl with water, Caden pinched up some sandwich meat and cheese and offered them to him. Instead of wolfing it down, the dog took them from his hand slowly, almost as if he were afraid Caden would take them away. Caden sat cross-legged on the floor and continued to feed the starving animal.

The dog looked to be a shepherd mix. His brown coat was splotched with black in places. Maybe. It was hard to tell with all the blood that matted his hair.

"What happened to you?" Caden stroked his head. The dog lay beside him and rested his head in Caden's lap. A deep sigh escaped the creature, and Caden continued to pet him. "We need to get you cleaned up and your cuts taken care of. You're going to have some nasty scars." Just like him. They were a good match.

The sun had barely started to rise when Caden cut through the forest trail to Stacy's store. The market wouldn't be open yet, but Stacy would be up. He hadn't seen her in almost a week and he wasn't sure if she would even talk to him.

He knocked on the door of her apartment. He waited. Using his fist, he pounded again.

"What?" Stacy threw the door open, a toothbrush in her mouth. Her eyes widened and her irritation melted into concern. "What's wrong?"

"I need some alcohol."

She recoiled as if she'd been slapped. "I don't sell alcohol. Try the bar down the street."

Caden caught the door with his foot when she tried to slam it shut. "Rubbing alcohol."

The fire in her eyes dimmed. "Oh."

"And bandages."

"What happened?" She dropped the toothbrush as her hands flew to his shoulders. She slid her palms down his arms, inspecting his limbs.

He sucked in a breath when she turned his hands over in hers. How could she smell like vanilla and coconut so early in the morning? She was like a tropical island.

"Where are you hurt?"

Shivers danced up his arm as her hand stroked his palm. He jerked away from her touch. "Not for me. For Max."

"Max?"

"My dog."

"When did you get a dog?"

"About two hours ago. Can I buy some alcohol and bandages? He's hurt pretty bad."

Leaving the door open, she hurried through the apartment to the market entrance. Caden stepped inside. The aroma of coffee filled the tiny room. He hadn't been there since that first day. Was it possible that the room was more colorful? A large canvas hung above the mantel. The abstract was a mishmash without any form or pattern he could detect. It looked like someone had stood back and thrown paint at it.

"Here you go." Stacy held out a paper sack.

"What do I owe you?"

"Later. I have to open the store." She twirled her key ring around her finger.

"Um, okay. Thanks." He hurried out the door and heard the click of the lock before he broke into a run.

A soft thump, thump, thump of a tail greeted him as he opened the door. The dog could barely lift his head, but he still managed to lick Caden's hand when he reached down to stroke the matted fur. He set the bag on the floor next to the dog and knelt beside him.

A few whimpers erupted from Max when Caden poured alcohol over the wounds. "I know, boy." Soothing words and gentle movements kept the dog calm as he continued to clean the wounds. It soon became obvious that Max's cuts were going to require stitches as well as medication to get rid of the infection that had begun to set in.

The dog whimpered and Caden set his jaw. Max needed him. And something deep down told him that he needed Max just as much.

A flip phone lay on the counter. Frank had dropped it off a few days ago, claiming that Lieutenant Erikson needed a way to get in touch with him when necessary. Quickly, Caden dialed the number to the store.

Stacy answered after only two rings. Even the sound of her voice sent his pulse racing. He took a deep breath. "Hi. It's Caden. I think Max needs stitches. Is there a veterinarian in town?"

"No," she said. "The closest vet is in Springerville. That's about a half hour away. You're welcome to borrow my truck, if you want."

His heart was heavy. "I don't have a driver's license."

Would Stacy be willing to drive him to the neighboring town? He hadn't ridden in a vehicle, other than a bus, in years. What if he freaked out in the car?

"Let me see if I can get Donna or Millie to cover the store. I'll call you back."

He sat next to the dog and cradled his head in his lap. "She's talking to me. That's a good sign, right?"

Leaning against the wall, he stroked the dog's ears and talked to him. He didn't realize he had drifted off until a knock at the door woke him up.

"It's open," he called out as he eased himself up.

The door swung wide and Becky entered. "Hi. Stacy asked me to come by and take a look at Max for you."

Disappointment flooded him as he led her over to the patient. Maybe Stacy wasn't speaking to him after all. But at least she'd called someone and hadn't ignored him completely. "How did you get roped into this?"

"I've been doctoring animals on the ranch my whole life. Wow." Becky crouched next to the dog. "This guy's been through some stuff, hasn't he?"

Max barely moved while Becky examined him. An occasional whimper was the only sound he made.

Becky got up and walked into the bathroom, returning with a towel. "Let's get him wrapped up so you can move him without hurting him too much."

The dog barely reacted. Only the slight rise and fall of his chest indicated he was still with them. Caden nodded. "Are you going to take us to the vet?"

"I volunteered," Becky said, "but Stacy said she'd do it. She should be here any minute."

"I'm here." Stacy came through the door. "How's the patient?"

"Stable for now."

Caden helped Becky tuck the towel gently around the dog. "He seems so much worse than when I found him."

Becky squeezed his arm. "He was on pure survival mode when you found him. That was the only thing that kept him going. Now he knows he's safe, so he's relaxed. Sleep is often the best medicine."

It took almost fifteen minutes for Becky and Caden to have the dog wrapped enough before Caden could carry him to the truck.

Stacy held the vehicle door for him as Caden cradled the dog to his chest and climbed in. A whimper escaped as he laid the dog on the front seat. "Easy, Max." Caden's low voice was almost a whisper.

She slid into the driver's seat and started the engine, glancing down at the dog on the seat between them. "He sure tangled with something, didn't he?"

"He's nothing but skin and bones. I fed him, but he threw it all up a little later." Worry laced his voice and he smoothed the fur between the dog's eyes.

Her chest tightened. How could this man care so much about an animal he just met? Swallowing the lump in her throat, she reached for the gearshift.

Caden's hand stopped her. "Put your seat belt on."

His touch sent tingles up her arm. She always buckled her seat belt before pulling onto the highway, but she didn't argue. Waves of tension rolled off him.

As soon as he heard the click of the belt,

the lines around his eyes relaxed and he put his own on.

She didn't glance at him again until they were on the highway.

Caden's face was ghost white, his lips pressed together into a tight line. His entire body was rigid, except for the rise and fall of his chest. "Are you carsick?" She let her foot off the gas.

He closed his eyes. "No. I'm fine. Just keep going."

Fine? He looked like he was about to jump out of the truck. Of course, dropping off the side of the mountain might not appeal to him. She pressed the brake as she approached a curvy stretch.

Caden sucked in a breath as she took the corner. Was it her driving that made him so nervous? Or the roads? She was used to curvy mountain roads, but he wasn't. She slowed to almost a crawl.

"No." Caden's voice cracked. "Don't slow down."

"If you keep your eyes focused ahead, it'll help. Let me know if we need to stop."

"I'm not carsick." His knuckles were white where they gripped the door handle. "I haven't been in a car in a long time. Just keep going."

She remembered the scars she'd seen on his back and it dawned on her that he could be suffering post-traumatic stress as the result of a car accident. She needed to get his mind off whatever painful memories he was dwelling on. "Take slow, deep breaths. Why did you name him Max?"

"I don't know. It just fit." He closed his eyes and breathed in through his mouth.

The dog nudged his hand and whimpered, immediately drawing his attention. Caden's gaze dropped to the animal and he began to stroke his fur. The tension in his shoulders eased as he started to talk to the dog. Stacy couldn't make out what he was saying, but the soothing voice seemed to comfort the animal. And focusing on something besides the road calmed Caden.

She sped up again. By the time she pulled into the outskirts of Springerville, his breathing was almost back to normal. She glanced at the man in the passenger seat. He gave a whole new meaning to the strong silent type. Yet the hurt animal in the vehicle wasn't the only one who was suffering.

She turned into the parking lot of the animal hospital and Caden let out a sigh of relief.

She stopped as close to the front entrance as she could. "Go on in. I'll park."

"Thank you." He got out and scooped the bundled dog up gently.

She found a parking spot and went inside. For his sake, she hoped the dog would pull through. She wasn't sure Caden could make the trip back up the mountain, especially if he lost the dog.

Caden was nowhere to be seen, so she approached the counter. "I just dropped off a man with a hurt dog. Has he been taken back already?"

The young man behind the computer nodded. "Yes. Becky Maxwell called to let Dr. Evans know the situation, so we were ready for him."

He didn't offer to take her to the exam room, so she sat and waited, her knee bouncing.

For over a week, she'd kept her distance from Caden. She still didn't like the fact that he hadn't been up-front with her, but maybe he had a good reason for not correcting her when she'd teased him for being a "city boy." Was it somehow tied to his accident? So many questions raced through her mind, but this was not the time to ask.

Every day this week, she'd taken his lunch to the cabin, but he was never there. She'd left the ice chest by the back door. In the mornings, the ice chest would be next to her back door. Always empty and always with a thank-you note.

Her phone chimed and she pulled it out of her purse, smiling at the notification. Someone had posted a five-star review for the campground.

Our stay at Whispering Pines Cabins was marvelous. The cabins are clean and the staff was very helpful and friendly. Caden really went the extra mile to make sure we had everything we needed.

This was what the campground had been missing. For the last few years, she, and whoever'd been helping out at the time, had kept a low profile. There'd been very little interaction between the campers and staff beyond check-ins and complaints.

She scrolled over past reviews, none of them five stars. Words like *quiet*, *rustic* and *quaint* were common. Nothing that would grab someone's attention and make them want to pick their campground over another.

The personal touch was what it had needed. Caden's touch.

Much later, the door to the exam room opened and Caden appeared, carrying Max carefully in his arms. He paused in front of Stacy's chair. "Ready?"

"How is he?" She stood and peeked at the sleeping dog.

"Better. I'd like to get him home before he comes out of it."

"Of course."

A man in scrubs handed her a brown paper bag. "This is his medication. Antibiotics for the infection, painkillers, as well as something for nausea."

"Thank you, Dr. Evans," Caden said, waiting for Stacy to hold the door open.

Once they were settled in the vehicle, she started the engine and Caden's body tensed. She reached for her purse, took out a notepad and a pen, and handed them to him. "Here, can you take some notes for me?"

His expression was puzzled, but he took the pen and paper.

"Today is the day I usually do inventory, so I need to make notes about things to check. You'll be saving me a lot of time when we get back."

All the way back to Coronado, she rambled about any item that came to her mind. And a few things the market didn't carry. It didn't matter. Her records were impeccable, but he needed something to keep his mind busy.

"Now, for your to-do list," she said as they got to the curviest part of the road. "I need you to check and double-check the barn, stalls and fences. I'm pretty sure the hay-loft has a bunch of moldy hay that didn't get cleaned out, so we need to get rid of it."

He made notes as quickly as he could. "Are you thinking of getting horses again?"

"If we did, what would we need for trail rides?"

Caden seemed to be bursting with ideas, jotting notes as he talked.

It was the most she'd ever heard him say at one time and she could've listened to him all day, but they were almost at the camp-ground. "You have really great ideas, but for it to work, I have to find someone that can not only manage the upkeep on the campground and cabins but understands horses. Do you know anyone like that?"

Caden's face was solemn. "No."

"That's too bad." She brought the truck to a stop. "Get out, then."

His eyes widened. "What?"

She laughed. "We're here."

He glanced around. Relief filled his expression. "I didn't even realize we were so close to home."

Her plan had worked. Happiness swelled in her chest. "Hand me that to-do list."

She held her hand back out. "No, both of them." She folded his list of notes about the campground and placed it in her purse. Then she crumpled the rest of the papers up and dropped them in the console. "There. Those jobs are done."

His stormy gray eyes went from the crumpled ball of paper to her and then back again. Finally, he looked at her. "Thank you."

"No problem, cowboy." She opened the driver's-side door. "You get Max and I'll make him a bed."

Inside the cabin, she pulled the blanket off Caden's bed and met him as he came in.

"Where do you want to put him?" she asked.

He nodded to an empty corner. "On the other side of the fireplace is fine."

She folded and arranged the blanket on the floor and he gently laid the dog down. Max's tail thumped and he opened his eyes. Caden squatted next to him and stroked the dog's head.

"I'm going to go. If I hurry, I'll have time to see my mom before Millie needs to leave the store," she said.

When she got to her truck, she noticed a small paper bag on the seat. With a groan, she took it back into the cabin.

"Hey, it's just me," she said, opening the door without bothering to knock. "I put his medicine on the counter. I'll bring you another blanket this afternoon."

Caden didn't answer. He'd lain on the floor and curled his body around the dog. Stacy walked over to him. Both he and the dog were asleep. She couldn't help but wonder which of them needed the other more.

CHAPTER TEN

WHEN STACY ARRIVED at the nursing home, the staff told her that her mother had refused to eat her breakfast.

Missy sat in her bed, staring out the window. "Hi, Mom." Stacy pulled the chair up next to the bed.

Silence. Although Missy's body could no longer respond, Stacy knew her mother recognized her. She could tell by the way her mom would squeeze her hand, or how her eyes would brighten when they looked at each other. But that was happening less and less. How much longer before her mind shut down, too? Already the jerky movements of her body, called chorea, had subsided, indicating her progress into late-stage Huntington's.

Stacy leaned on the edge of the bed, her arms folded on the railing. "I hate this. I hate seeing you like this and knowing there's nothing I can do."

The silence settled around her as she sat with her mom. She often spent hours talking to her, but today she just wanted to sit with her. Missy continued to stare out the window.

Stacy read a chapter from a book she'd borrowed from the home's library. Then she read a chapter from her mother's Bible. Rising, she walked around the bed to stand in front of the window. Missy continued to stare toward the window as if her daughter wasn't there. Stacy's heart cracked a little and she hurried out of the room.

She stopped at the nurses' station. "I need to speak to the director. Is Mrs. Hernandez in her office?"

"Yes. Is everything all right? Can I help you with something?"

Stacy didn't want to go into the details of her father's impromptu visit a couple of weeks ago. "I just need to speak with her about something."

She rapped lightly on the frame of the open door.

Mrs. Hernandez glanced up from her computer. "Hi, Stacy. Come on in."

Stacy entered and shut the door behind her. "I'm sorry to disturb you, but can you explain why my father showed up at my house a couple of weeks ago with this?" She slid the bill across the desk.

The director picked up the paper and frowned. "It is addressed to him, so he must be on the account."

"Since when?"

"I really couldn't say. You'll have to talk to the Phoenix office. All the accounts go through there." Mrs. Hernandez pushed herself up from her chair. "Is his being on the account a problem?"

"Yes."

Mrs. Hernandez walked over to a filing cabinet and placed a file in it. "I don't mean to be obtuse, Ms. Tedford, but you are behind on the account. If Mr. Tedford can contribute, isn't that a good thing?"

Stacy took a shaky breath. "Don't count on it. He hasn't followed through with one promise in years."

Mrs. Hernandez gave her a sad look. "You never know. He has yet to miss a Saturday, so there may still be hope."

"What are you talking about?"

"His Saturday visits," she said. "He has come to see her every Saturday since she was admitted."

Stacy shook her head. "That's impossible.

My mom has been in the nursing home for almost four years. This is the first time I've seen my father in five years."

Mrs. Hernandez raised her hands. "I don't know what to tell you other than he has been here every week for the last four years."

Stacy's hands were shaking and her stomach quivered. She didn't even know where her father lived. The bill was addressed to a PO box in Coronado. If he was here every Saturday, that meant he must live close by. "Thank you. I appreciate you letting me know."

By the time she got back to the store, she was emotionally drained. Frank hadn't returned her phone calls and she had no idea how to get in touch with Vince.

She needed something to keep her mind occupied, so she got her inventory sheet and started going through everything in the store.

"Where are you today?"

Stacy jerked her head around. "Hi, Millie. I didn't hear you."

The girl gave her a funny look. "You've counted those cans three times. Are you okay?"

"I'm fine. I just have a lot on my mind."

"How's the dog?" Millie had a soft spot

for animals. "I've been asking around and I posted it on Facebook, but so far, no one has reported him missing."

"Thanks. From the looks of him, he's been on his own awhile. Someone probably dumped him."

A scowl crossed Millie's face. "I'd like to get my hands on the people that think it's okay to leave a dog in the middle of the forest."

"Me too." She picked up her clipboard and went over her order sheet again.

When the last can was counted, Stacy rubbed her neck with one hand. Then she waved to get Millie's attention. "I'm going to email this order in. Buzz me if you need me."

No sooner had she finished sending her supply order in than a buzz sounded through the apartment. She hurried back into the store.

"I'm sorry, but I'm not letting you in the storeroom without permission from Stacy." Millie's voice was sharp.

"Look, little girl, Stacy is the one who called me. Now let me by."

Stacy covered her mouth with her hand to stifle a laugh. Despite Millie's tiny stature, she had a quick temper. Whenever her brothers wanted to get a rise out of her, all they had to do was call her a little girl. It was like waving a red flag in front of a bull.

She rounded the corner just as Millie straightened up to her full five-foot-one-inch frame, her mouth pressed into a hard line. Poor man. He was about to be subjected to Millie's fiery redheaded temper.

"It's okay, Millie. I'll take care of this." She saved the man in the nick of time. "You must be Bryce. I appreciate you fitting me into your schedule."

He reached out to shake her hand. "No problem. I need to find the fuse box, and if you could show me where I can unload my equipment, we'll see what's going on."

"You can park around back and I'll open the door for you." She hoped. The door was infamously stubborn about when it wanted to open.

She waited until Bryce left the storeroom before throwing her shoulder into the door. Nothing. Grunting, she hit it harder. Three more tries and it hadn't budged. "Stupid, stupid door," she said under her breath and kicked the metal with all her might.

"Need some help?"

She took a deep breath and turned to see

Caden. "What are you doing here? How's Max?"

"He's still asleep. I need to pick up some groceries and dog food. Then I'll get back to work."

"At the cabins? You're kidding, right?" Of course he wasn't kidding. "Take the day off and take care of Max."

She tried again to push the door open.

His gray eyes were laced with amusement as he strode across the concrete floor. She stepped back and let him try. When he couldn't budge it either, she didn't keep the smug smile off her face. Then she said, "On three. One. Two. Three."

The door gave way with a loud groan. She grinned. "That's us, two, doors, zero."

"We make a good team." Caden nodded.

The smile that crinkled his eyes was gone so fast Stacy wasn't sure she'd seen it at all. And she really wanted to see it.

A ladder appeared through the doorway, followed by Bryce with a tool belt hanging from his waist. "Thanks." He pushed his way past them and turned the corner. The end of the long ladder knocked Stacy into Caden.

Her pulse thundered in her ears, but she couldn't move. The ladder had them pinned against the wall. Caden's arms wrapped around her, shielding her from being bruised by the metal.

"Careful." His low growl was right in her ear and she breathed in the clean scent of soap and shampoo.

"Oh! Sorry." Bryce stepped back, giving them some space. "I'm trying to get around these boxes."

"I'll get them for you." Stacy pushed away from Caden's hard chest. Her hands shook while she shoved the boxes against the wall. When she looked up, Caden was gone.

THE IMPRINT OF Stacy's body against Caden's burned his skin. He escaped the storeroom as quickly as he could. The only thing that stopped him from heading back to the cabin was the fact that he was almost out of food for himself and he had none for the dog.

He shopped quickly. With any luck, he could pay and be gone before she came back to the front. Was it too much to hope he could avoid her for the next two weeks?

He placed the items on the counter.

"You're the one taking care of the cabins, aren't you?" Millie asked as she rang him through.

"Yes."

Her face lit up. "How's the dog you found?"

"He's going to be okay. It'll just take a while."

"I think it's really nice of you to take care of him like that," she said. "Are you going to keep him?"

Caden had initially thought he'd leave town on the motorcycle if he could repair it. There was no room for a dog on a bike. And he was pretty sure the bus didn't allow nonservice animals.

"Yes." The thought of giving Max to a stranger bothered him more than it should. He'd only had the animal a few hours.

Millie smiled. "I'm glad." She slid the grocery bag across the counter with a funny look on her face.

"What?" He glanced down at himself. Did he have something on his shirt?

"Nothing," she said. "Just…now I know why Stacy kept watching for you all week."

Stacy watched for him? He liked that idea. Too much. "Why does she have an electrician here?" he asked as he took out some cash.

"Fuses blow all the time. We can only run one cooler at a time, and if too many things are plugged in, we lose power. And you don't pay for your groceries. It comes with the job."

The lights overhead flickered. She looked up. "That happens a lot."

Caden thought through possible scenarios. Given the age of the building, he had a pretty good idea of what was wrong. If he was working for his brother's construction company, he could do the work for a quarter of what a big-city company would charge her. In half the time, too.

What was he thinking? He wasn't a licensed electrician, and it wasn't his business how Stacy spent her money. She wouldn't have called the guy in if she couldn't afford it. Still, he would offer to look if she needed a second opinion.

"Have a good day, Millie. I'd better get back." He reached for the door but had to step away as a large group of people filed through.

"Oh, no. Can you do me a favor?" Millie sent him a pleading look. "Get Stacy for me."

He nodded and headed to the storeroom. Stacy's voice was almost frantic. "Every wire?"

Caden took another step to peek around the corner. He knew the electrical business.

If the electrician was pulling a fast one on her, he'd be able to tell.

"Everything." Bryce had a notepad in his hand. "There's such a mess up there, I don't know how the market hasn't burned to the ground before now."

Stacy buried her face in her hands. "What will it cost?"

He pulled a calculator out of his front pocket and tapped some numbers with the end of his pencil. He looked at the notepad again and punched in more numbers. "With labor, travel fees and equipment costs, you're looking at ten to twelve thousand dollars, minimum."

Caden cringed. As much as he'd like to argue that the electrician was overcharging, the cost was average for the work he claimed needed to be done. He'd helped out with his brother's construction business long enough to know that the man was probably giving her a discount.

"It'll have to wait until the end of summer. I'll cut back on the equipment I'm running until then."

"I wish I could tell you that would work, but it won't. The wires needed to be replaced yesterday." The electrician gave her a sorrowful look. "Get a second opinion if you want, but I promise, I'm not trying to hustle you."

She sighed. "I know, but I can't afford it right now. What can I do to get by until then?"

He shook his head. "You can call my boss and see if there's some kind of payment plan he'll work out with you."

"Thank you."

The chances of a company waiting until the end of the summer for payment was next to nothing. From the worried look on Stacy's face, she knew it, too.

Bryce gathered his tools and handed her the estimate. "One more thing…" he said.

Caden didn't like the tone of the man's voice. He stepped into the room, making himself known for the first time.

Stacy didn't acknowledge him.

"I have to report this to the fire marshal."

"Why?" Caden and Stacy asked together.

"Those wires are that bad. It'll be up to him to determine how long you can stay open without making the repairs."

A few moments later, the electrician and his tools were out the door. Stacy shut the door and leaned her head against the wall. "What am I going to do?"

Caden didn't listen to the voice that told him it was none of his business. "I'll do it."

"Do what?" Her voice was muffled against the wall.

"Replace the wiring," he said. "To pay for the motorcycle." That should keep her from arguing.

He watched the rise and fall of her back as she took in deep breaths.

He couldn't handle it if she cried. He put a hand on her shoulder. "Please."

She turned to face him. "Even if you could do the work, I can't afford the wires and equipment you'd need."

"I already have everything I need. I just have to get it sent up here. Look, you'd be doing me a favor if you let me do this."

Her eyes narrowed. "How am I doing you a favor by letting you fix my market for free?"

After her reaction at the barn, he knew he couldn't tell her only half-truths. But he wasn't ready for everything to come out. Not yet. He'd give her the watered-down version. His hand was still on her shoulder. Stepping back, he put some space between them.

"I was an interior electrician in the army, so I know what I'm doing. I also completed a training program a few months ago."

She looked skeptical. "If you have all that training, what are you doing here? Why aren't you working for your brother?"

"I plan to, eventually." He took a deep breath. Here went nothing. "The truth is, I just got out of prison and I'm not ready to face my family yet."

Stacy's eyes widened and she looked as if she was ready to run. "For what?"

Caden dropped his chin, unable to look her in the eye. "Negligent homicide."

She gasped. "What does that mean?"

This was what he'd feared. The look of distrust in her eyes. He gave her the textbook definition. "It means I was responsible for the death of someone due to criminal negligence."

She pressed her lips together and took a measured breath. "What happened?"

His gaze went to the floor and he clasped his hands to stop them from shaking. "I was driving under the influence."

"Of what?" Her voice was cold.

"Alcohol." He raised his head to look at her.

The glare she gave him crushed his soul. He'd come to Coronado knowing that she would be angry with him. Maybe even hate him. He deserved it, but he'd never expected to care as much as he did.

"Are you an alcoholic?"

"No."

"I can't risk my market for someone who's going to disappear every time they need a drink."

"I haven't had a drop since that night and I never will again."

"How can I believe you?"

His words came out in a rush. "If I stay here past the end of the month, I have to contact my parole officer and have my file transferred to the local law enforcement. Frank can give me a drug or alcohol test as often as he likes. Whenever he likes. You can have me tested every day if you want."

"What if you test positive?"

"You won't have to fire me, because I'll be back in prison." Caden could see the wheels turning in her head. "If you don't fix the wires, the fire marshal will shut you down, hopefully before the place burns to the ground. I'm willing to do the work in exchange for a roof over my head, a motorcycle and the opportunity to prove myself to my brother. This is a win-win for both of us, and I'll be out of your hair as soon as I'm done."

TAKING A DEEP BREATH, Stacy willed her heart rate back to normal. Was she crazy for considering his suggestion? Could she trust her market to an ex-con? And one who had caused someone's death?

The pain she saw in his eyes was enough to tell her that he'd known the person who'd died. Probably very well. Not that she didn't want to know more, but this wasn't the time. Keeping her market open and earning enough money to pay her mother's medical bills took precedence over everything else.

"You better not make me regret this," she said with a sigh. "I'll make prison seem like a walk in the park if you do."

Then something happened that rocked her world.

He smiled. Not the faint curve-on-the-edge-of-the-lips smile she'd seen before, but a full-fledged, white-teeth-showing smile. A rush of emotion flooded her chest. For all his dark broodiness, his smile was like someone had been drowning and he'd just tossed them a life preserver.

Caden extended his hand to her. "You've got a deal."

She reached out to shake his hand. His fingers clasped around hers and warmth shot through her, all the way to her toes. "What do we do now?"

"First, you better go save Millie. A crowd just walked in. I'll go talk to the sheriff and let my parole officer know what's going on. He may ask you to fill out an employment verification, though." His voice trailed off as if he expected her to refuse.

"Fine. As soon as things clear out, I'll go see Frank. What do we do about the fire marshal?"

Caden's brow furrowed. "All work has to be done by a licensed contractor, and since I haven't done that yet, I'll talk to Patrick to see if he'll let me work under his license."

She grinned. "I guess this means you aren't getting on that bus at the end of the month."

"I guess not."

"Good. I'm glad."

No matter the pain in those dark gray eyes of his, she would do anything to see that smile again.

They made their way to the front of the market, where a line was waiting at the deli counter. She grabbed her apron from the hook and walked around the counter.

Out of the corner of her eye, she saw Caden

at the door. "When are you going to talk to Frank?" she called.

"As soon as I check on Max."

"Tell him I need to talk to him," she said. "About my dad."

Caden picked up his bag of groceries and disappeared out the door.

Stacy felt hopeful for the first time in a long time. But could she trust him? Trust was something she wasn't good at. Her mother had said to trust her and everything would be all right. Her father had said to trust him because he'd take care of everything. So far, everyone in her life had let her down. The only person she could count on was herself.

The crowd of people, all in the White Mountains for a family reunion, paid for their food and supplies and disappeared. Millie finished cleaning up the deli and clocked out, leaving Stacy alone for the next few hours.

She pulled a sudoku book from underneath the counter. Puzzle books of all kinds were a habit for her. When her mother had first brought her home, she'd been shy and reserved. It was watching her new mother complete a puzzle that had finally got Stacy to open up. Learning a new language and moving to a new country had been overwhelming, especially for an eight-year-old girl. So, for several years after arriving in America, her mother had kept jigsaw puzzles stacked in every corner of the house. Every time Stacy had felt overwhelmed with all the new things she'd had to learn, she could retreat and work on a puzzle.

As she got older, she'd fallen in love with puzzle books. The harder, the better. It was her father who'd pointed out that people were the hardest puzzles of all. Together, they used to people-watch, trying to make up an outlandish story about different people they observed. It was a game she still played.

Stacy caught her breath.

Did Vince still play it, too?

Where was he and why was he visiting her mom?

CHAPTER ELEVEN

CADEN ALMOST RAN back to the cabin. Part of the dread he'd been carrying for the last two weeks had dissipated. She didn't know the whole truth, but she knew some of it and she hadn't shied away from him. Was there a chance she could forgive him? Maybe even accept him?

He hurried into the cabin to check on Max and give him some painkillers. He didn't exactly take the afternoon off, but he stayed close to the cabin. He got the lawn mower put back together and chopped more wood. Max woke up a few times. Once, Caden came into the cabin to see Max limping to the water dish. After a long drink, he went back to his blanket, and every time he opened his eyes, he lifted his head and searched the room until he spotted Caden.

Because of that, Caden spent the rest of the afternoon inside. He made a list of tools he'd need for the job at Stacy's market. He could get a few basic supplies at the hardware store next door to the market, but what he really needed were the meters and specialized equipment that were in his storage area back home.

Tapping his pencil on the table, he reread his list. He would need a permit, which could only be given to licensed contractors. Would his brother help him?

He opened the kitchen drawer where he'd put the cell phone and scrolled through the contacts. He stopped on the name of his older brother.

Knots twisted his stomach as he waited for Patrick to answer. "'Lo?"

His throat tightened. "Patrick. It's Caden."

Silence.

"Hello?" Caden held his breath, waiting for his brother to respond.

"Caden? Is it really you?" Patrick's voice shook. "How are you? Are you okay? Where are you?"

"I'm fine. Just taking your advice."

Patrick let out a shaky laugh. "What advice was that? Whatever it was, I'm pretty sure it involved you coming home."

"I'm working on it, Pat. I'm working on it."

"Mom said you sent her a letter that you

were out of prison, but you haven't called her. Why? Where are you at?"

He squelched the guilt rising in his chest. "Do you remember what you told me right before I went to prison? About coming home whole?"

"Yeah. I remember." His voice was quiet.

"There are some things I have to do before I can come home, but I need a favor."

Patrick didn't hesitate. "Whatever you need, little brother."

Caden took a deep breath, explained why he was in Coronado and what the market job entailed.

When he was done talking, Patrick let out a big sigh. "Sounds like my little brother has really grown up. I'll do it on one condition."

"Anything."

"Call Mom."

Caden swallowed the lump in his throat. "I'm mailing her another letter tomorrow."

"You really think a letter is enough? Come on, Caden. She wants to talk to you. Hug you. Spoil you rotten. You know you're her favorite."

His cheeks burned. "Not anymore. Not after what I've done. Do you think they can ever forgive me?"

Patrick's voice was hoarse. "They forgave you the moment it happened. Caden, it was an accident. Even Miranda knows that."

Caden's heart jumped out of his chest. "You talked to Grayson's mom?"

"All the time. She calls to check on you."

"She must hate me."

"No, she doesn't. When you come home, you'll find that out for yourself."

"As soon as I'm done here, I'll come home. I promise. Now, how is your family?"

Twenty minutes later, he disconnected the call.

Patrick had promised to overnight his tools to him and call the county to apply for a permit; Caden was officially an employee of Shamrock Construction.

He could hardly wait to get started. But he wanted to make sure everything was done correctly. He couldn't risk something going wrong and Stacy's market being fined because of him. Did the local library have computers? He'd finished the electrical program in prison just six months ago, but what if something had changed?

He added "library" to his list. Then he picked up the phone to call Lieutenant Erikson. His parole officer was thrilled that Caden had found a job working in the construction business, and assured him that he would contact Frank and take care of everything.

The small flip phone felt like lead in his hand. Guilt gnawed at his chest. He punched in his parents' number and held his breath until a familiar voice answered the line.

His throat tightened and he could barely swallow.

"Hi, Mom."

AT FIVE O'CLOCK, Donna arrived at the market to take over. Stacy usually went to the nursing home to see her mother, but since she'd already been there earlier, she decided to make her favorite meal.

She hummed as she finished all the layers for her homemade lasagna and slid it into the oven. Cooking was her escape. She enjoyed nothing more than serving her friends and family a good, home-cooked meal.

She set the timer on the oven and went to take a shower. An hour later, the lasagna was keeping warm in the oven while she tossed together a salad and made garlic bread. The smell of pasta filled the tiny apartment, and her mouth watered.

It was a shame she didn't have anyone

to share her meal with. She pulled a single plate out of the cabinet. Caden would probably enjoy her lasagna. No. She needed to stay away from him. And not because he had just got out of prison. She liked him, but he'd made it clear he was leaving when the job was done.

Before she could serve herself, she heard a knock on the door. Last time she'd had an unexpected visitor, it had been Vince. She peeked through the window and was relieved to see her uncle standing outside.

"Hi, Frank." She opened the door. "Hungry?"

He took a deep breath. "Smells great, but I'm afraid I can't stay. I'm actually here on official business." He pulled a paper out of his front shirt pocket. "I need to have you fill this out and sign it for me."

She scanned the document. "How'd you get this so fast?"

He grinned. "I had it drawn up last week."

"You knew he just got out of prison?"

"Since the day he got off the bus." Frank smoothed his bushy mustache. "I had a good feeling about him and hoped to convince him to stay for a while. You did that for me."

She put her hands on her hips. "Don't you

think I should've been told that I had a convicted felon working for me?"

Frank shot her a hard look. "Technically, he works for me, since I'm the owner of Whispering Pines."

"Still, you should have told me," she snapped. "I should know if a criminal is living close by."

"He's not a criminal." Frank shook his head. "Not in the way you're meaning, anyway. He was a young kid, fresh out of the military, and he made a mistake."

"I'd say." She arched one eyebrow. "Killing someone is a pretty big mistake."

"Yes. And he could have gotten off with little more than a slap on the wrist." Frank handed her a pen. "His father is a district attorney in Tucson. You don't think he could have worked out a deal to get him a reduced sentence? Maybe even probation?"

"Why didn't he?"

"Caden refused to let his father represent him and used the free counsel assigned by the court. According to his parole officer, even the judge tried to get him to accept a plea deal. But he refused because he wanted to accept the full responsibility of what he'd done. He could have served less than a year in prison, but he didn't. He served almost seven years."

It seemed Frank was Caden's biggest cheerleader. She took the pen from him and signed the work papers. "Why are you telling me this?"

"Because the man has served his time. He's living with a terrible guilt, and I don't want you to make it any harder for him."

Something in his tone made her suspicious. "Why would I do that?"

Frank opened his mouth to say something but stopped. "No reason."

Before he could get out the door, Stacy stopped him. "Did you know that Vince visits Mom every Saturday?"

He nodded. "Who do you think picked him up at rehab and brought him here every week?"

"Rehab? What are you talking about?"

Frank gave her a sad look. "When Missy checked herself into the nursing home, he checked himself into a rehab center."

She gritted her teeth. "Too bad it didn't help."

He frowned. "How would you know if it helped or not?" With that, he tucked the paper back in his pocket and left.

Had she been too quick to judge?

There was nothing she could do about her father. But she could do something about Caden.

She covered the lasagna pan with foil and did the same thing with the salad. She placed the food carefully in a tote, along with some paper plates, and locked the apartment door behind her.

Long shadows fell across the ground as the sun slipped behind the trees. It would be at least an hour or so before the daylight disappeared completely.

The campground was a hub of activity. Several families were enjoying the evening with a cookout in the common area, and Stacy could see Coy's horses grazing in the pasture behind the barn. She pulled her phone out of her back pocket and snapped a couple of pictures. These would look great on the website.

Caden's cabin was quiet, but she knocked and waited.

He swung the door wide, looking more relaxed than she'd ever seen him.

"Hi," he said. "What are you doing here?"

"I had to do some therapy this afternoon, so I thought I would share the spoils with you."

"Therapy?"

She held up the tote. "Food. My therapy is cooking. I hope you're hungry."

He stepped back to allow her to enter and she caught a whiff of him. She couldn't put her finger on exactly what it was. A combination of soap, shampoo and motorcycle. His gray T-shirt stretched tightly across his chest and shoulders.

"How's Max?" She placed the tote on the counter and walked over to check on the dog. Max wagged his tail as she petted him.

"I think he's sore, but that sad look is gone from his eyes now."

She washed her hands at the sink and pulled out the foil-covered dishes. "I hope you like lasagna."

"Love it."

"Is there anything you don't like?"

"Brussels sprouts."

His face was so solemn that she couldn't help but laugh. "No one likes brussels sprouts."

"My sister does. My mom made them for her every once in a while, so the rest of us had to choke them down."

"You have four siblings?"

"Yes. I'm the youngest."

A familiar ache squeezed her chest. She'd always wanted to be part of a large family.

She handed him two plates. "Will you put these on the table while I toast the garlic bread?"

He did as she asked while she placed the bread on the broiler pan. "Do all your siblings live in Tucson?"

He stood behind the wooden chair, grasping the back of it. "My parents still live there, but most of my siblings moved away."

His low voice carried a hint of sadness. Did he miss them? "Where to?"

"Sean still lives in Tucson, but Sarah lives in Phoenix. Beth's husband is in the air force, so she moves around a lot. Patrick lives in Prescott."

She slid the bread into the oven. "Have you seen them since you got out of prison?"

"No." He didn't look at her.

"And why not?"

Caden lifted his chin. "It's hard to stay in touch from prison."

A twinge of apprehension ran through her. What was his story? He had already admitted that someone died due to his carelessness. Was it a family member? Someone he didn't know? She shook her head. "There's no such thing as just losing touch. Someone made the decision to stop making an effort."

He didn't answer.

"So what was it?" She knew she shouldn't push him, but she had to know. "Who quit trying? You or your family?"

The questions hung in the air. He stared down at his hands, popping his knuckles. He let out a long sigh. "It's complicated."

Stacy bit the inside of her cheek. She could spend hours lecturing him on the importance of family, but the broken look on his face told her a speech wasn't necessary.

Was that why he'd got off the bus in Coronado? To get his life back together so he could make amends with his family? Or was he hiding from them?

She put their dinner on the table and waited for him so they could sit down. "What are you going to do about uncomplicating it?"

He looked up, his eyes the color of the sky on a stormy day. "I'm working on it."

"At least you haven't given up." Stacy pulled apart the garlic bread and handed him a slice. "Have you ever been married?"

"No." He gave her a puzzled look.

"Did you have a girlfriend before prison?"

"No."

They ate in silence for a moment. He was so hard to figure out. She wanted to ask him about his accident and time in prison, but she didn't want to blurt it out.

Before she could ask any more questions, he turned the tables on her. "How long has your mom been in the nursing home?"

"For the better part of four years."

"I always thought nursing homes were just for old people. Was she older when she adopted you?"

"They also provide long-term care for people with terminal illnesses. My mother is only forty-nine."

He shifted in his chair. "How long does she…? I mean…what is the life expectancy for someone with her disease?"

"It's different for everyone. She's lucky to have survived this long. Her mother died before she was forty and her two brothers died in their early thirties.

"That's why my mother refused to have children of her own, because of the likelihood of passing the disease on to her children, so she adopted me."

Caden bit his lip. "Wasn't that risky? Adopting a child, not knowing how long she would be around?"

She shrugged. "Most people looking to adopt children want babies, or at least toddlers. My mom knew if she left me there, I'd never get out of that orphanage."

He nodded. "Any time with a family was better than no family at all."

"Exactly." Talking about her past made her uncomfortable. But maybe that was the point. Hadn't she just done the same thing to him? She wasn't going to let him know it bothered her. If she did, he wasn't likely to answer any more of her questions. "My mom knew she might not have much time, so she lived life to the fullest. I guess she thought I needed to be exposed to all the things I missed out on while living in an orphanage, so she took me with her and we never looked back."

"Sounds like it wasn't as exciting for you as it was for her."

He was much too observant. "Okay, cowboy. Let's talk about something else."

Reaching to the center of the table, he picked up another piece of garlic bread. "This bread is excellent. Do you make it from scratch?"

"Sort of. I get a little help from my bread machine." She tried to hide a smile at the look of relief on his face. It seemed their game of cat and mouse was over.

At least for tonight.

CHAPTER TWELVE

"GOOD MORNING, MOM." Stacy waited for a reaction from the still figure on the bed. Nothing. She slid a chair close to the bed and sat before reaching over and squeezing one of the small, frail hands.

Missy squeezed back ever so slightly and Stacy breathed a sigh of relief. "Glad you're with me. Now, let's see if we can get you to eat some breakfast." She pushed the call button and waited for a nurse to come.

The door opened a few minutes later. "You're a little late this morning." The nurse carried a food tray to the counter and set it down.

"Sorry, Mrs. Abbott. I had a hard time sleeping last night." She blamed it on Caden. It was pretty late when she'd finally made it home. Then she'd spent several hours on bookkeeping. It'd been after 2:00 a.m. when she'd finally crawled into bed. Between the market and the campground, she would have enough to make this month's nursing home payment, as well as a small amount on the balance. Would it be sufficient?

The nurse checked Missy's vitals and recorded them in the chart hanging at the foot of the bed. "I don't want to add to your stress, but you need to start preparing for the worst. She's hardly eating anymore. I hope you can get something down her."

Stacy's shoulders tightened. "She'll be fine. It's just a slump. Her appetite will pick up soon. You'll see." She went across the room to her mother's food tray and stirred some sugar into the bowl of oatmeal.

The bed hummed as Mrs. Abbott raised it into a sitting position. "You need to face facts, honey. Your mother is dying. There is no cure for Huntington's disease."

"Not yet. It takes fifteen to twenty years for death to occur after the onset of symptoms. She still has at least five years." Stacy had read every book she could get her hands on about her mother's disease.

Mrs. Abbott shook her head sadly and left the room.

"They don't know what they're talking about, Mom. Don't listen to them." She pulled a chair next to the bed and patted Missy's cheek. The skin was softer than velvet and no longer stretched tightly across her high cheekbones. Her mother had lost so much weight. How had she not noticed before? Stacy smiled when Missy finally opened her eyes. "Morning, sleepyhead."

Missy's once-clear eyes were now cloudy. She blinked as if she was trying to recognize the face in front of her. The edges of her lips turned up in a smile that made Stacy's heart leap.

"Yes, Mom, it's me. I'm here." She held the spoon to her mother's mouth. "Open up and eat a little for me."

It took some coaxing, but Missy managed to swallow a few spoonfuls before turning her head away. Stacy pressed her lips together. She'd never understand why her mother had signed orders that not only prevented her from being resuscitated, but also prevented her from being placed on any type of life-sustaining machines, including a feeding tube.

"Why, Mom?" she whispered. "Why would you sign those orders? And why did you check yourself in here while you were still perfectly healthy?"

"Because she didn't want to burden you with her care."

She whipped her head around to see Vince

standing in the doorway. "How would you know what she wanted? You deserted us."

He stood, with his cowboy hat in his hands, and stared at her. "I know more about Missy than I know about myself."

She didn't want to believe anything he had to say, but curiosity won out. "Enlighten me."

Vince entered the room and bent over her mother's bed. He kissed her forehead. "Good morning, my love."

When he turned around, Stacy caught a glint of wetness in the corners of his eyes. He sat on a chair next to the bed.

"Your mother always hoped it would skip her." His voice was low. "It happens, you know. Not everyone in the family gets it."

"I know."

"She was officially diagnosed right after we brought you home." Vince's eyes held a faraway look. "That's when she started making plans."

Stacy shook her head. "I was fourteen when she was diagnosed."

"No, *siyvarulo*." He shook his head. "She didn't *tell* you until you were fourteen."

She calculated the years, and fear grew in her chest. Her mother really was at the end of the life expectancy. Deep down, Stacy knew it. She'd recognized all the signs, but she hadn't wanted to admit it.

"What kind of plans did she make?" The plans must not have included paying for long-term care. Or maybe they had and Vince had squandered it away.

Vince touched Missy's hair. "Did you know she took care of her mother until she died?"

"Yes."

"She took care of her brothers while watching her mother waste away to nothing. Then she watched the same thing happen to them. It terrified her to think about you being put in that position."

More than once, her mother had said she didn't want to be a burden to Stacy. That was why she'd chosen to go into a nursing home. "But she was still very healthy when she came here. Couldn't she have waited? Or given me instructions on when to bring her here?"

"Would you have done it? Or would you still be trying to take care of her at home?" He gave her a pointed look.

She lifted her chin. "It wouldn't have been too much if you were still around. But as soon as things got hard, you left. You abandoned her."

"No, Anastacia." He touched his wife's cheek. "I didn't. She abandoned me."

Stacy clutched her stomach. She couldn't listen to any more of his lies. "I think you'd better leave."

Vince didn't argue. "Someday maybe you'll let me tell you my side of the story. Then maybe you'll be able to forgive me."

Heat flushed through her. "How can I forgive you when you don't think you did anything wrong?"

"That's not true. I've done many things wrong."

"Just go, please."

She turned to get a washrag from the cabinet. By the time she ran it under warm water in the bathroom sink, he was gone.

Gently, she washed Missy's face.

"Morning, Stacy," Calvin, the physical therapist, called from the doorway. "How're things at the market?"

"Good." She stepped aside to allow Calvin access to her mother's bedside.

"You might as well go on home." Calvin glanced at Missy's chart. "We're going to be a while. I need to reevaluate her plan, considering the…" His voice trailed off.

Stacy lifted her chin. "Considering what?"

He scratched his bald head and grimaced. "There isn't an easy way to put this. She's sliding downhill fast. Physical therapy may not be necessary any longer."

"You're the second person today who's told me that. I'll ask that you not speak that way in front of my mother. I don't believe it, and I don't want her to believe it, either." She bent over and kissed Missy's forehead. "I'll be back tonight."

She faced Calvin. "I expect to see her new physical therapy plan in place by the end of the week."

Her hands were still shaking when she entered the common area. Her mind raced with bits and pieces of information she recalled from her research. There had to be some therapy that could help her mother. Even if she had to sell the market to pay for it, she would find it.

Something solid hit her shoulder and she glanced up. "Sorry," she mumbled to the person she'd just run into.

"It's okay, *sykhaara.*"

Stacy froze at the familiar term of endearment. "Nina!" She threw her arms around the stout woman who had been her mother's best friend. It was Nina who had helped Stacy to adjust to life in the United States.

"Come, come, dearest." The woman guided Stacy through the door toward the park benches in the small courtyard. "Tell Nina everything."

Tears welled in her eyes, but Stacy refused to allow them to fall. She'd promised Missy she'd be strong for her. She'd had to make that promise to two different mothers. Her birth mother had been so sick that Stacy had taken over the responsibility of running the household. When her four-year-old brother got sick, seven-year-old Stacy had done everything she could to make him better, but his little body couldn't hold out for long. Stacy had cried for days, sure it was her fault.

Finally, her father had put his foot down. "The strong are silent. Tears are for the weak," he'd said.

She'd never cried again. Not when her birth mother died. Not when social services took her baby sister away from them. And not when her father had dropped her off at the orphanage and told her it was her only chance for a better life. Three months later, she'd received word that her father had been killed in a factory accident.

When Missy had found her in the orphanage, Stacy hadn't wanted to leave without her baby sister. The nuns had finally admitted that the infant had been adopted less than two weeks after arriving at the home. So Stacy had left her tiny village in Georgia and made the long journey to America. A new land. A new family. Same promises.

Stacy told Nina about the nurse's prognosis, the physical therapist's grim comments and her father's revelation that Missy's disease had started years earlier than Stacy had thought. The words poured out of her so fast, she didn't realize she'd slipped back into her native tongue until Nina responded in Georgian.

"Why do you try to be so strong, little one?"

"Because I have to be. If I'm not strong, I'll break."

"No, sweetness." Nina pressed her hand to Stacy's cheek. "Trees survive the worst storms because they bend. Sometimes bending makes you stronger."

She reverted back to English. "Another one of your Georgian proverbs?"

"No. Just good ol' common sense." Nina smiled. "Now, go home. Don't worry about your mother. Not today. And tonight, when you crawl into bed, it's okay to cry for her. It doesn't make you weak."

But it does. Because she knew if she ever let the tears flow, they would never stop.

It was Saturday. The weekends were the busiest time at the campground for everyone except Caden. Many families checked in on Friday night and left Sunday afternoon, so Caden made sure all the cabins were ready before they arrived. He'd chopped so much wood, there was no place left to stack it. Now that the riding lawn mower was running, it only took an hour to have the common areas mowed and looking good, and there wasn't one weed to be pulled.

Caden kept a close watch on the time. Partly because he didn't want to forget to give Max his medicine, but mostly because he needed to go to the market to make a list of everything he would need for repairing the store. He didn't want to be in the way, so he would wait until after lunchtime.

To keep his mind occupied, he finished taking the motorcycle apart. As he worked, he hummed. He sat on the floor and removed parts from the engine. There was something therapeutic about disconnecting old, greasy parts, cleaning them up and replacing them. The bike would never be as good as it was when it had been brand-new, but it would run. It would function. Just like him.

Shadows crept up to shade the windows of the cabin. Caden wiped his hands off with a rag and gave Max his medicine. Once the dog settled himself on the blanket, Caden gathered up his notebook and a few tools. Hopefully, he could be done before the market got busy again. And before Stacy returned from her afternoon visit with her mother.

Last night's dinner had been…nice. For a little while, he'd forgotten himself and just enjoyed her company. But he couldn't let that happen again. He liked her more than he should, but she wasn't his and she never could be. For his own sanity, he needed to stay away from her.

Donna, the lady who worked the afternoon shift, was chopping lettuce in the deli section when he walked in. "Hello, Caden. Want lunch?"

"No, thanks." He nodded toward the storeroom. "I need to look at some stuff in the back. Is that okay?"

"Suit yourself," she said. "Holler if you need something."

He made his way down one of the aisles. The refrigerated section was at the very back of the store. He walked through, counting the number of coolers and noting that two of the five were empty.

He opened the door to the storeroom and looked around. He found the breaker box and made some notes. He would have to climb into the attic crawl space to see what the electrician had seen, but to do that, he needed a ladder. Did he have time to run back to the cabin and get one?

"I was told I could find a red-haired pip-squeak back here," a voice boomed through the storeroom.

Caden froze. It couldn't be.

He closed the breaker box and hurried to the front of the storeroom. A man stood in the open doorway. His heart swelled with recognition. "Patrick?" He couldn't believe it.

His older brother grinned at him. As soon as he got close enough, Patrick pulled him in and hugged him.

Such a display of affection was unusual for Patrick, but Caden was so happy to see him, he didn't question it. He just hugged him back. The hug broke the dam of emotions Caden had been holding in for seven years.

"It's good to see you, little brother." Patrick's voice was thick.

Caden stepped away and tried to regain his composure. "What are you doing here?"

"Company policy. I have to interview all potential employees." Patrick grinned. "Show me what's going on."

It was just like Patrick to get right to work.

Caden gave Patrick a quick rundown of what was going on. "I really need to get into the attic and look at those wires, but I don't have a ladder. I was just about to run back to the cabins and get one."

"No need. I brought my work truck. I'll pull around to the back and bring it in." Patrick gestured at the back door.

The door made Caden think of Stacy. He could still remember the smell of her hair when the ladder had knocked her off balance and into his arms.

For the next half hour, they talked of only the job. Patrick mostly listened while Caden told him what his plans were. When they finally emerged from the attic, Caden waited nervously for Patrick's opinion.

Then the questions began. Patrick made it clear that his business's reputation was on the line and he wasn't going to let Caden work under his license if he didn't know what he was doing, brother or not.

Caden wasn't insulted. The last time he'd worked for Patrick, he'd been fresh out of high school and more interested in partying than in working. He didn't blame Patrick for firing him then. Or for presenting him with a bill for the tuition he'd paid for Caden to go to school.

"Welcome to Shamrock Construction," Patrick said, holding his hand out to Caden. "I can hardly wait for you to get finished here so you can come work with me."

Caden shook his hand. "Don't rush me."

"Excuse me, you can't be back here." Stacy entered the storeroom. When her gaze landed on Caden, she smiled. "Sorry, I didn't know it was you."

Caden's heart skipped a beat when he saw her. "Stacy, this is my brother Patrick."

"Oh—" she flashed one of her brilliant smiles "—it's nice to meet you."

Patrick shook her hand. "I've heard a lot about you."

"Will you be staying in Coronado long?"

"I only came to interview my newest employee and deliver some work tools for him."

Stacy glanced at Caden, confusion marring her features. "Are you leaving?"

"No. Patrick is letting me work as an employee under his license so that everything is on the up-and-up for your insurance."

She smiled. "Oh, I see."

Caden liked the look of relief on her face that he was staying. Immediately, he felt guilty. He shouldn't want her to want him to stay. Most of all, he shouldn't want to stay.

Patrick clapped his hands together and rubbed them. "This calls for a celebration. Let's all go to dinner tonight. Where's the closest steak house?"

Caden stiffened. The only restaurants he'd seen in Coronado were the café across the street and a barbecue place. He wasn't ready for another vehicle ride, even if it was close by.

"Springerville," Stacy said. She glanced at Caden. "But I have a better idea. Let's grill a couple of steaks at the cabin. I'm sure Caden doesn't want to leave Max alone for that long."

"Max?"

Caden nodded a thank-you to Stacy before explaining, "My dog. He needs medicine every few hours, so I really couldn't go to Springerville."

"Okay." Patrick clapped Caden on the back. "Where can I buy some good steaks?"

"Follow me," Stacy said. "We just got some beauties in."

This would be a good time for him to make a getaway. "I need to get back to the cabin to check on Max. Stacy can tell you how to get to the campground."

Patrick asked, "Should I leave your tools here or take them to the cabin?"

Relief flooded Caden. His brother hadn't picked up on his apprehension about going out of town, or the silent messages he and Stacy had exchanged. "Leave them. The cabin is within walking distance, but I don't want to lug them back and forth every day."

Patrick made an exaggerated bow and offered her his arm. "Lead on, my lady."

Stacy laced her arm through his and led him out of the storeroom.

Caden cleaned up the area and locked the back door. He stepped from the storage room to the rear area of the market and spotted Patrick and Stacy in the very limited meat section. He couldn't hear what they were saying, but their heads leaned toward each other.

Patrick was a newlywed and madly in love with his wife, but it didn't stop a twinge of jealousy from hitting Caden when Stacy's laughter floated through the air.

Of all his siblings, Patrick was the most laid-back and charming. Probably because he'd escaped the pressure of being the oldest and the attention of being the youngest. Caden wished he could be as relaxed as his brother. Maybe then he could make Stacy laugh like that.

CHAPTER THIRTEEN

THE ALARM CLOCK buzzed and Stacy took great delight in turning it off. It was Sunday, the one day she could sleep in since the market didn't open until after church. Rolling over, she snuggled back into the pillows and quickly fell back asleep.

It was almost seven thirty the next time she looked at the clock. Not as late as she'd wanted to sleep, but she'd take it. Ever since she was little, she'd woken up early, no matter what time she went to bed the night before. It didn't matter that she hadn't got home from Caden's until midnight.

She couldn't remember how many times his face had turned bright red from his brother's teasing. There was an awkwardness between the two brothers, although it was obvious they held a great affection for each other. Several times, they'd exchanged glances and Stacy knew they'd spoken a secret language only siblings could understand. Would she and her sister have shared the same kind of relationship if they'd grown up together?

With a groan, she tossed the blanket back. She would not let herself dwell. Might as well get ready for church. Up until a year ago, she'd picked her mother up and taken her to the service. Now her mother couldn't leave the nursing home.

She timed her arrival at church so that everyone was seated and the music had already begun. Halfway through the sermon, Stacy let her gaze wander over the congregation. She'd known most of these people her whole life. A few rows up, she saw three former classmates whispering and giggling like they were back in high school. She shook her head. They were nice enough, but they were the biggest flirts in town. Every few seconds, they'd glance toward the back of the room.

Who were they staring at? There wasn't anyone new in town except Caden. Her eyes narrowed as the women glanced back again and again. It couldn't be. Slowly, she turned and looked over her shoulder. There, on the very last row, sat Caden, listening intently to the pastor and not paying the slightest attention to the women in front of him. He was wearing darker jeans than usual and a light blue dress shirt that made his gray eyes appear even lighter. He'd shaved for the occasion, and with his scruffy beard gone, he looked years younger. No wonder the women couldn't keep their eyes off him. Before she could turn around, his gaze found hers. He shot her a hint of a smile and nodded.

She smiled and turned back to the front of the room. A few rows up, Kelsey glared at her, which made her feel even more smug.

After the service, Millie came to stand beside her as they all filed outside. "Did you see Caden?" she whispered.

"Yes. So did every single woman in the county." She searched the line ahead of her. She knew it wouldn't do much good. Caden had been the first one to sneak out when the sermon was over. Not that she had been watching. "Did you see anyone else with him?"

"No. Why?"

"His brother was in town yesterday. I'm pretty sure he stayed the night."

Millie's eyes widened. "He has a brother? Is he younger? What does he look like?"

"You're as bad as Kelsey and her crew." Stacy laughed. "Patrick is older. And they don't look anything alike."

"We're going to the Bear's Den for lunch," Millie said. "Do you want to join us?"

She wouldn't mind going to lunch with Millie, but the small café would be full of people from town. She could only answer the question "How is your mom?" so many times before it got to her. "I can't. I need to update the websites for the market and the cabins."

Behind Millie, two young soldiers waited patiently. Stacy grinned. "Brian. I didn't know you were home."

The young man nodded. "Just for a few days. We ship out next week for Afghanistan."

"Your family must be thrilled you got to come home for a while first." Stacy turned her attention to the man standing next to Millie's brother. "Hi, Randon. Are you going to Afghanistan, too?"

"Yes, ma'am. Where Brian goes, I go."

His answer didn't surprise her. Brian and Randon had been inseparable since they were kids. Although, Stacy often wondered if the reason Randon spent so much time at the Gibson house was that he was in love with Millie. Everyone could see it, except Millie.

It took her almost a half hour to get out of the church. Every few steps, someone stopped her to ask how her mother was. Stacy smiled and repeated the same answer every time.

Donna opened the market for her at one o'clock on Sundays, so she wasn't in a hurry to go home. Her normal routine was to visit her mother for a while and spend the rest of the afternoon doing paperwork. She wasn't in a hurry to sit in front of her computer for hours.

Coy's horses were still at the barn. Maybe she could convince Caden to go for a horseback ride. Her pulse quickened at the thought. She hadn't been horseback riding since she'd been forced to sell Maze a few years ago.

She bypassed the turn to the market and headed for the campground. She wasn't sure if she was more eager to see Caden or go riding, but the dirt road seemed longer than normal. She rolled the windows down and let the pine-infused air fill the truck.

A large sign welcomed her to Whispering Pines Campground. The barn was the first building she passed and the sight of horses grazing in the pasture once again filled her with satisfaction. The way the cabins were nestled in the valley meadow reminded her of a town in the Old West.

Once upon a time, she'd wanted to build a replica of a Western town across the road from the barn. That was a funny phrase… *once upon a time*. She'd had big plans for the campground that she'd hoped would be hers someday, but that was before her mother's disease.

She blamed Vince for everything. Well, almost everything. She couldn't blame him for her mother's Huntington's disease, of course. But how different would things be now if he had been the supportive, loving father and husband he should've been?

The campground was quiet as she drove through. A few families were outside, but most of the cabins appeared empty, which wasn't surprising for a Sunday afternoon, when most families had to drive several hours to get back to their homes.

Caden's cabin was the very last one, hidden off the main road that looped through the camp.

She pressed a hand to her stomach to calm the butterflies as she knocked on the door. No answer. The shortcut over the ridge was faster than it had taken her to drive over, so he should have had time to get home. But what if he hadn't come straight home? What if Kelsey and her friends had caught him and invited him to lunch?

She bit her bottom lip. It wasn't any of her business what Caden did on his off time. Or who he did it with. But that didn't stop jealousy from clawing at her chest.

PATRICK HAD LEFT EARLY this morning, anxious to get back to his new wife. Before he'd left, he'd made sure all the numbers in Caden's cell phone were updated, and made him promise to call their parents later in the week.

It had been nice having his brother there. They had sat up late into the night and he'd explained to Patrick why he had come to Coronado. His goal had turned from confessing what he'd done to doing something to help Stacy. Now she was the one helping him.

Working in the market had given him the opportunity to reconnect with his brother, and for the first time in a long time, he had something to look forward to. Not that he wanted to work for his brother forever, but at least he had options.

When he was a kid, Sunday mornings meant church, whether you wanted to go or not. He'd never attended one service when he was in the military. He'd never missed one service when he was in prison.

There was a small community church just down the road from the store. He'd seen it on his way to talk to Frank. He timed it so he arrived a few minutes late and slipped into a back pew unnoticed. Or so he'd thought. A group of women kept glancing over their shoulders at him.

Caden stared at the back of Stacy's head throughout the entire service. He hadn't known it was the same church she attended, but he was glad it was. When Stacy turned and spotted him, his heart swelled. There was no way she'd been looking for him, but when her gaze had fallen on him, she'd smiled. Her smile had been genuine, unlike the smiles of the ladies sitting several rows ahead of Stacy.

As much as he wanted to find an excuse to talk to Stacy after church, he had the feeling he would get cornered if he didn't make a quick escape. Just before the service wrapped up, he ducked out and ran straight into the elderly women from the post office.

"Excuse me," he murmured and tried to step around them.

"Cutting out a little early, aren't you, dear?" The sister with bright blue hair frowned at him.

"Just trying to beat the rush," he said.

The one with pink hair giggled. "The rush? Or the singles welcoming committee?"

He shook his head. "I don't know anything about a committee. Excuse me."

She looped her arm through Caden's. "Come on, son. Walk us two old ladies home and we'll tell you all about it."

They sandwiched him between them, and there was no getting away. But at least they were clear of the church when the crowd emerged. He glanced back at the people leaving the chapel. Did Stacy look for him?

The two women dragged him down the street, heading away from the main road, and made several other turns, all the while chatting and asking him questions. Not that they ever stopped talking long enough to hear his answers.

Finally, they arrived at a bright purple house. "Here we are. Would you like to come in for tea?"

"No, ma'am. Thank you, though, but I better get back to the campground. I have work to do."

One of them squeezed his arm. "Monday is baking day. Edith makes the best tarts. You must come for tea on Monday."

Tarts had been his grandmother's specialty before she passed away. Being around the two women reminded him of how much he missed her. "I look forward to it."

"Don't you let Stacy work you too hard." Edith pressed a kiss to his cheek.

"Nonsense." Margaret kissed his other cheek. "That's what big, strong men like you are here for. You'll take good care of our girl."

Caden's steps felt lighter as he found his way back to the road leading to the store. How was it that he felt more at home in Coronado in three weeks than he ever had in Tucson?

The market was open, so he stopped and went inside. He might as well start as soon as he could.

Donna was behind the counter. She glanced up from the book she was reading. "Hey, Caden. What's up?"

He didn't think he'd ever get used to being accepted so easily by the people around here. Only because they didn't know the real him. He could never let himself forget that.

"Is Stacy around?"

"Haven't seen her." Donna laid the book on the counter. "She usually goes to the nursing home after church and visits her mother. I don't expect her to be back until later this afternoon."

"Okay, I'll be back then." He needed to check on Max anyway.

All the way back to the cabin, he told himself the heavy feeling in his chest was because he was anxious to get to work and not disappointment over not seeing Stacy.

The path between the market and the cabins was worn. The motorcycle would be repaired soon, but he wouldn't give up this short walk for anything. As he approached the cabin, he heard Max whining inside. He hated to leave the dog cooped up in the house, but he was still recovering.

Max was waiting by the door when he opened it. Caden bent to pet him. The swelling around the dog's face had gone down and he could now open both eyes. It was too early to know if his sight was damaged in his injured eye, but Caden was relieved to see that Max tracked him with both eyes when he moved across the kitchen to get his medicine.

The motorcycle stood on its kickstand in the middle of the living room. It might as well go outside, too. He opened the cabin door and rolled the bike outside. Max followed him and rested on his haunches when they reached the toolshed.

"Stay." He went back inside to get his tools. Max was in the same place when he emerged from the cabin.

"Max, you've kind of thrown a wrench in things," he told the dog as he sat next to the bike. "I thought I could leave as soon as I got the bike fixed, but what am I supposed to do with you?"

Max cocked his head, listening to Caden's voice.

"I'm not real good at sticking with my plans, am I?" He continued to talk as he worked on the bike. "I was only supposed to be here for a week. Now I've been here three weeks and I still haven't accomplished what I came to do."

He kept talking as he worked. After seven years of keeping to himself, it was kind of nice to say whatever came to his mind. In prison, he'd never blurted out anything. That kind of reckless behavior could get someone in big trouble. He felt the same way every time he was around Stacy, too. Maybe even more.

WITH CADEN NOWHERE to be found, Stacy left the cabin and drove to the nursing home. She doubted if her mother would be looking for her, but she wanted to check the schedule and make sure physical therapy would be offered this week.

As she pulled into the parking lot, her father was walking out of the building, carrying a briefcase. She waited in her vehicle until he got into a beat-up Chevy truck and pulled away.

She stopped at the nurses' station. "I thought Vince only came on Saturdays."

"He used to. For the last several months, he's here every day," one of the nurses said. "Usually twice a day. He comes in the mornings and then again in the evenings, right after you leave."

Stacy frowned as the nurse hurried away. It didn't make sense. Why was he checking on her mother so often? He was the one who'd left, despite his claim that Missy had abandoned him.

After checking on her mother, she verified the schedule for the week and was relieved to see that her mother hadn't been removed from the physical therapy sessions.

Her visit was shorter than usual. Mostly because she'd spent so much time there the day before, but also because she wanted to talk to Frank to find out what he knew about Vince.

When she got home, Caden was sitting on a bench outside her door, petting a much-better-looking Max behind his ears. He'd traded his church clothes in for faded jeans and a long-sleeved work shirt.

Her heart stuttered at the sight of him. Was he waiting for her? "Hi. Are you here for lunch?"

He shook his head and stood. "No. I can't do much at the campground right now, so I thought I'd get started on the wiring."

Of course. He wasn't there to see her, but to get started working. "Where's Patrick?"

Something flashed in his gray eyes. Jealousy?

He averted his gaze from hers. "He left early this morning."

"Why so soon?" After seven years of not seeing each other, one day hardly seemed like enough time to catch up.

Caden shoved his hands in the pockets of his jeans. He looked at the ground and mumbled. "He doesn't like to be away from his wife for too long."

Stacy cocked her head. "Didn't your visit go well?"

Caden shrugged. "Yeah. It went fine. We just disagree on things sometimes."

"Like what? How to do the job?"

"Not exactly." He looked at her, his face pinched.

"Family can be like that. They want one thing and you want something else." She unlocked the door and motioned for him to come inside. "Coffee?"

He hesitated before entering with Max on his heels.

"So what did you disagree on?"

"Everything."

She slipped off the high heels she'd worn to church. "When I was young, my mother wanted to travel the world. She thought she was doing me a big favor by taking me with her."

"You don't like to travel?"

"No." Stacy poured water into the carafe. "After most of my birth family died and my sister was taken away, all I wanted was a home. I wanted security. My new mother thrived on change and adventure, and I hated it."

"Did you tell her?"

Stacy bit her lip. "I was too afraid I would

make her unhappy and she wouldn't want me anymore."

"But you did tell her eventually?"

"Actually, Vince did." Her stomach tied itself into a knot and she busied herself with the coffee maker. Vince had always understood her better than her mother had. Maybe that was why she felt so betrayed.

Caden sat on a bar stool, shifting every few seconds. "Is that all?"

"Goodness, no." The coffee was done and she placed two neon-green mugs on the counter. "We disagreed on where I would go to high school. Where I would go to college. What my major would be. Me quitting college to come home."

"Who won?"

"Me." Her brow crinkled. "Except for the most important one."

"Which one was that?"

She tried to push down the lump that formed in her throat whenever she thought about her mother. "I didn't want my mother in a nursing home."

Caden nodded. "Did your father put her in? Is that why you two don't talk?"

"No. She put herself in there. Something

about not wanting to put me through what she'd had to go through with her family."

He frowned. "That was a very selfless thing to do."

"It was a stupid thing to do." She poured their coffee, not looking at him. "I mean, I could take care of her. She didn't need to do that."

"Could you really?" He rubbed the back of his neck with one hand. "From what I've seen, you have your hands full now, trying to manage both the market and the campground. How would you take care of her, too?"

"I would manage. I always do."

"Speaking of manage, I need to manage my time better today and get started on the store." Caden stood to leave and Max jumped up from beside him.

"Um…" She hesitated. "Max can go in the storeroom, but not through the inside of the store. It's against the health code. He'll have to go around the back."

Caden glanced down at him. "Maybe I should just take him home."

"He can stay with me. Donna works the front while I do paperwork on Sundays."

"Okay, as long as you don't mind." He

opened the door from the apartment to the store.

Max tried to follow. Stacy snapped her fingers. "No, Max. You stay with me."

The dog stopped and gave her a long look before turning in the direction Caden had gone. He whined.

She rinsed the coffee cups out. She'd better hurry up with the paperwork. Sunday evenings were usually busy. Families who'd been out hiking or fishing all weekend often stopped by to get something to eat. Since the Bear's Den closed early on Sunday afternoon, her deli was the only place in town to get food. She usually ended up working all evening.

An ear-piercing howl echoed through the store. Stacy jumped up from the table. Where was Max? The door was slightly ajar. Caden must not have shut it all the way. She heard another howl and dashed to the storeroom. There was no sign of Caden. Only the ladder standing beneath the open entrance to the attic. At the bottom of the ladder, Max stared at the ceiling, his paws scratching the ladder.

Caden's head emerged from the hole. His gaze fell on Stacy. "What's wrong?"

Max whined when he saw Caden. Stacy

laughed. "I think Max thought you'd disappeared."

"Sorry, boy," Caden told the dog. "You can't come up here."

His head disappeared again, causing Max to start barking and pawing at the ladder.

Caden peered through the hole. "Max, sit."

The firmness of his voice caught the dog's attention and he stopped whining and sat.

"Good boy. Stay." He ducked back into the attic.

This time Max didn't whine, although his eyes stayed fixed on the attic. Stacy reached down to pat him. "Come on, boy. He'll be out in a little while. Come with me."

Max refused to move. Stacy put her hands on her hips. "Stop being stubborn." As long as he didn't enter the store, she wasn't violating any health codes.

The dog cocked his head and looked at her. "I can't force you, so if you won't move, I'll stay with you."

Almost an hour later, Caden emerged from the attic. Stacy stood. "All done for now?"

"Yes. What are you doing down here?"

"Max wouldn't leave, so I stayed with him."

"I'm really sorry. I know you have a lot to do."

"That's okay. You'll make it up to me on Tuesday."

He looked startled. "What's on Tuesday?"

"You're taking me on a picnic."

CHAPTER FOURTEEN

ONCE CADEN EXAMINED the wiring, he could see why the electrician had been so concerned. The electrical mess in a dry wooden market was a tinderbox waiting for a spark. He couldn't walk away from it.

After returning Max to the cabin, he went back to the market and refused to climb out of the attic until he was reasonably sure the building would make it through the night without bursting into flames. Over the next few weeks, he'd have to do most of his work at night, when there weren't any customers. The electricity would have to be off for a short time and, if things went right, it would be back on before the market reopened each morning.

It was almost dark when Caden made it back to the small cabin. A layer of dust covered him and one arm was red and itchy from contact with fiberglass insulation. Scratching his arm, he headed for the bathroom. The

smell of coconut and vanilla filled the tiny
room when he opened the cabinet to grab a
towel. Pressing the cloth to his face, he inhaled. Stacy. All the towels she'd loaned him
smelled like her. He really needed to go to
the Laundromat and wash her smell out of
everything, for his own sanity.

He'd meant to take a quick shower, but the
hot water beating down on him felt so good,
he lingered. Only the growling of his stomach forced him out of the soothing spray.

Stacy had invited him to dinner, but he
wasn't ready to be alone with her again. She'd
been nowhere to be found when he'd descended the ladder at the store, so he'd asked
Donna to give her a message.

Tucking a towel around his waist, he ambled up the stairs. He pulled a T-shirt over
his head and slid on a pair of pajama bottoms. What he wouldn't give for a pair of soft
flannel pants. He'd had some of every color
folded neatly in his dresser at home. Home?
He didn't have a home anymore. Everything
he owned had been packed up and put in storage when he'd gone to prison.

He took a few steps out of the loft and
stopped. Stacy smiled up at him.

"You left without food." She held up two plates wrapped in aluminum foil.

Hunger won out over pride. Taking the steps two at a time, he joined her in the kitchen. "Thanks. I hope you didn't go to any trouble."

"I can't have my own personal electrician starve before the job is done." She leaned on the counter. "Donna said you were too tired for dinner."

"I wasn't sure if she heard me."

Stacy's musical laughter filled the air. "I'm pretty sure she pays attention to everything you do and say."

He puckered his eyebrows together. "What does that mean?"

Her laughter rang out again. He couldn't recall a time when anyone's laughter had lightened his spirits like hers did. She was so easy to be around.

"Let's see…" She tapped her chin, pretending to think. "She said if she was twenty years younger, she'd snatch you up."

Caden's ears burned and he knew he was blushing. He ignored the comment and walked over to the counter. "What's for dinner?"

"Chicken enchiladas."

"My favorite." He carried the plates to the table.

"I know," she said. "Your brother told me."

He stiffened. "Why?"

She chuckled. "Because I asked him."

"Why?" And what else had Patrick told her? His brother had never been good at keeping secrets.

"For ammunition." She wrinkled her nose. "I need a favor."

There was nothing in the world he wouldn't do for her. But she could never know that. He crossed his arms and waited.

"Years ago, my parents ran the market and my grandfather ran the campground, with the help of Coy and me. We offered trail rides, horse boarding, all kinds of stuff."

She wasn't telling him anything he didn't already know. What was the favor she needed?

"After Pap died and Mom got sick, I had to sell off the horses and focus only on the store."

Caden knew that, too. "Because Coy joined the rodeo circuit and wasn't around to help you out anymore."

"Right." She rocked on her feet. "One of our regulars bought my favorite horse. Every year he and his family stay at the campground and bring their horses. I offer him a huge discount because it's the only way I get to see Maze. This year, they are bringing two other families. It could mean a lot of money and great reviews."

It always came back to money. How much trouble was she in financially? And how much of it was his fault? If Grayson were still alive, he'd be here to help her and none of her problems would exist. Caden sighed. "I'll make sure the barn and stalls are clean and ready."

"It's more than that." She rubbed her hands together. "You see, I made a deal with Coy. He would come home while the Mitchells were here and keep them entertained. Take them on trail rides, exercise their horses, stuff like that."

"I'm still waiting to find out the favor." Coy was already in town. He came by every day to feed the horses in the barn, and he and Becky exercised the horses every day.

"Turns out, Becky can't take as much time off the circuit as she wanted if she wants to qualify for the finals. So, Coy and Becky are going to Reno."

He must be missing something. "Just spit it out, Sunshine. It can't be that bad."

"Maybe not to most people, but I'm afraid you might think so."

Now she had him worried. "Why?"

"I know you're not really a people person."

Caden frowned. Was that really how she saw him? There was a time he'd considered himself the life of the party. Look where that had landed him. "I think I can manage to take them on a trail ride, if that's what you need."

Her face brightened. "Really? You don't mind?"

"I just need a layout of the area. It wouldn't look good to get them lost."

"What if we turn our picnic Tuesday into a trail ride? I can show you all the best areas."

A picnic and a trail ride with Stacy. Alone. His heart pounded at the thought. So much for not spending time alone with her. "You have a deal, but I'm going to need a lot more enchiladas."

She laughed, and it was the most wonderful sound Caden had ever heard. He removed the foil from the plates, and the heavenly smell of the spicy food filled the cabin. Then he noticed the contents of the plates. One held enchiladas, the other beans and rice.

"Aren't you going to eat, too?"

She yawned. "Not this time. I've still got a lot of paperwork to do at the store."

Caden took a deep breath as she disappeared out the door. What if she ran into a bear on the way back to the store? As hungry as he was, he couldn't let her walk home in the dark alone. He hurried out behind her, careful not to let her see him.

With each step, guilt weighed on him. He hadn't outright lied to her, but he was certainly deceiving her. It didn't feel right. The urge to stop her and tell her the truth increased. Would she believe him if he told her he just wanted to help? Did she know what she'd really lost when Grayson died?

Stacy was the most amazing person Caden had ever met. From what he'd seen, she made a habit of sacrificing her own wants to make others happy. She deserved so much more than what she had.

Would his being here give her some answers or make things worse?

Stacy paused at the door. "Dinner will be waiting for you when you get done working tomorrow night. Don't make me bring it to you again."

He froze. How long had she known he was there? "I won't."

She turned to look at him in the shadows. "Why are you following me?"

"I just wanted to make sure you got back safe." He emerged from the trees.

"I've lived in the mountains most of my life. You'll need saving before I do."

He nodded. "Probably. There's not much that scares you."

"There are a couple of things." Within a few steps, she was in front of him. "What about you? What are you scared of?"

His pulse rocketed. "Cars."

She cocked her head. "I think you're scared of me."

Scared? She terrified him. "I better get back."

"You sure go out of your way to help someone you don't want to be friends with."

He swallowed. "I never said I didn't want to be friends. I said you didn't know me well enough for us to be friends. If you did, you wouldn't want to be."

"You don't make any sense. What's wrong with having a friend?" She stepped even closer and rested her hands lightly on his chest.

Between the moon's illumination and light coming from the porch, he could see the intensity in her eyes. His heart raced and he was sure she could feel it beneath her fingers.

Standing on her tiptoes, she brushed her lips across his, sending a firestorm of emotions through him. He froze, forbidding his body to respond, but when her hands traveled from his chest to the back of his neck, his arms snaked around her waist, pulling her even closer to him.

She kissed him back and emotion swirled around him. He caught himself before he could deepen the kiss.

What was he doing? How could he betray Grayson like this? Resting his hands on her biceps, he gently pushed her away. His chest heaved. "That's why we can't be friends." Turning on his heels, he disappeared into the night.

The trail between the market and the cabins was well marked and easy to follow, even in the dark. He scrubbed his mouth, trying to wipe away the memory of her sweet kiss. Of his betrayal.

His steps were heavy when the cabin came into sight. He was so tired. He was tired of feeling tired, and he was tired of the guilt that pressed on him every day. Grayson was gone and nothing he could do would change it.

In the morning, he would tell Stacy the truth and hope she would let him finish the wiring on the store. He would even stay long enough to entertain the Mitchells, if she would let him.

Then he'd be out of her life forever.

STACY SLEPT THROUGH her alarm for the first time ever. Between trying to do bookkeeping and trying to forget the kiss that was burned into her memory, it was well after midnight before she'd gone to bed. And even then, she couldn't sleep.

After a quick shower, she tossed her hair into a ponytail and hurried into the store. She stopped to press the brew button on the coffee machines before unlocking the door.

Margaret and Edith were waiting patiently on the sidewalk. She held the door open for them. "Good morning, ladies. Sorry I'm late. The coffee will be ready in a couple of minutes."

The elderly women smiled at her. Margaret patted her puffed-up hair. "We were starting to worry. Everything okay?"

"Yes. I just overslept."

The women selected their bear claws and wandered through the market until the coffee was done. Then they made a beeline for one of the machines. Stacy followed and poured herself a cup.

Edith waddled over to the counter. "No wonder you overslept. You work much too hard for such a young woman. You should be enjoying the summer weather. You should hire some extra help around here."

Stacy smiled. "I have plenty of help."

Most of the time, the sisters took their coffee and treats to go, but this morning they sat in the deli section. That could only mean one thing. They had some juicy gossip to share and couldn't wait for the café across the street to open.

Stacy put her apron on and started making breakfast burritos. If she was lucky, the women would be content to talk to each other until the Bear's Den opened. Then they would go across the street to gossip to their hearts' content.

"Stacy," Margaret called from the table, "I hear you hired a handsome groundskeeper for the cabins."

It appeared she was not to be lucky today. They weren't waiting to share gossip—they were looking for some. "Frank hired someone. Not me."

Edith giggled. "What do you think of him? He's single, you know."

Stacy started to ignore the question, but she knew it would add fuel to the fire. "I don't know that much about him. Sorry."

That was true. Except she knew he was an early riser. And a hard worker. He loved dogs and liked to keep to himself. He also had a good sense of humor and a rare, killer smile. And his kisses were like nothing she'd ever experienced before.

"Well, you should ask him out," Edith said.

Margaret squealed. "Oh, yes, Edith. That's an excellent idea. Our Stacy has been alone for far too long."

The bell on the door saved Stacy from listening to the women's matchmaking plans.

Her heart stopped in her chest. Bryce hadn't been kidding when he'd said he would report her to the fire marshal. Her hands began to shake. She knew it was too much to hope that he wouldn't bother coming all the way to Coronado.

"C-can I help you?"

The man pulled out a clipboard and scanned it. "I'm looking for Anastacia Tedford."

"You've found her."

"There are some concerns about the safety

of your store. I need to have a look at the wiring. I'll need access to the attic."

"I have someone working on correcting the problem now. He'll be in soon." What were the chances that he'd take her at her word and leave?

"Great. I'll need to speak with him."

"I'm right here." Standing at the door was the man who had the two elderly women in a tizzy.

Caden stepped forward to introduce himself and shake the fire marshal's hand. "Come on back and let me show you what's going on."

The confidence in Caden's voice sent a rush of relief through her. Caden wouldn't be so eager to show the man his work if he didn't think it would pass inspection. She hoped so, because her future, and her mom's, depended on it.

"Good morning, ladies. You both look beautiful today," Caden greeted the two women sitting at a table and enjoying their coffee.

Margaret's face turned the same shade of pink as her hair. "Will we see you for tea this afternoon? Two o'clock."

"I'll be there."

A fit of giggles erupted from the sisters as soon as he disappeared.

Edith sipped her coffee. "Margaret, I do believe this is going to be an entertaining summer."

"Interesting, at least."

Tea? Stacy approached their table. "Am I missing something here? How do you know Caden?"

"Oh, goodness—" Margaret placed her hand on her chest "—we met him yesterday at church. Delightful young man, don't you think?"

Edith placed her hand over Margaret's. "No, dear, we first met him when he came to the post office, remember?"

"Oh, that's right. He was mailing a letter to someone and he wouldn't put a return address on it." Margaret gave Stacy a wink. "Don't you worry. I took care of that for him. He's very sweet, don't you think?"

"And so handsome," Edith added.

Stacy gave them the sternest look she could manage. "I can see the wheels spinning in your diabolical heads, ladies, and I'm telling you right now to forget it."

"Why, Anastacia, I have no idea what you're talking about." Margaret gave Edith a wide-eyed look. "Do you know what she's talking about?"

Edith shook her head. "I have no idea. Stacy, you work much too hard. You really need to take a day off."

Throwing her hands in the air, Stacy stomped back to the cash register. She was going to have to warn Caden about those two.

She found Caden and the fire marshal strolling down the aisle. Whatever they were chatting about, both men seemed in good spirits. "Everything okay?"

The marshal nodded. "You made an excellent choice hiring Caden. He's really got a handle on what he's doing." He made a few notes on the clipboard and pulled off the top copy to hand to her.

Her mouth dropped open. "This is a warning. I thought you said everything was fine." She read some more. "I have to post this in the store?"

"Standard procedure. As soon as the work is complete, the notice can be removed. Just be glad it's a warning and not a ticket." He shook Caden's hand and walked out the door.

She held the paper out to Caden. "What exactly does this mean?"

He took the notice from her. "It means you get to keep the market open while I finish the repairs. And you don't have to post this in the front where customers can see it. I'll hang it up in the storeroom."

"How long will it take?" As anxious as she was to have this mess behind her, she had the feeling Caden would be leaving as soon as the job was done.

His eyes darkened. "It depends. I kind of wanted to talk to you about that."

Stacy sucked in her breath. "I know. It's going to depend on money, isn't it? I'll talk to Denny about setting up an account for you."

"No. That's not— Who's Denny?"

"He owns the hardware store. He'll order whatever you need."

Caden frowned. "I was hoping to talk to you this morning," he said, casting a sideways glance at the elderly women who were pretending they weren't listening. "Alone."

Her heart leaped to her throat. "Okay." Her voice wasn't as strong as she wanted it to be. Was this where he told her what a mistake the kiss had been? He couldn't tell her he hadn't felt something, too. No one could kiss like that and feel nothing.

As soon as she was out of hearing range, she turned to face him.

He looked like he was heading for a funeral. Had kissing her been that bad? She could handle rejection, but it was easier to avoid it.

She flashed him her brightest smile. "Let's cut to the chase. I like you. And I think you like me, too. But we are both dealing with a lot of stuff right now and I just don't have the time or energy to invest in a relationship. And, honestly, if I had to choose between you and my store, the market is going to win. I'm out of options and I can't afford to lose your help just because I find you attractive."

Caden's brow wrinkled. He ran a hand through his auburn hair. "That's not what I wanted to talk to you about."

"It's not?" Her heart fluttered.

"I need to tell you about the accident." His stormy gray eyes bored into hers.

The release of air brakes outside reverberated through the store. "Oh, no! I forgot about the bus."

She hurried to the front of the market as a crowd of people entered. Funny. Just three weeks ago, her entire future had been pinned on increased profits from moving the bus stop to her store. Now her entire future was pinned on the man that bus had dropped off.

CHAPTER FIFTEEN

CADEN RINSED HIS coffee cup out in the sink and went upstairs to get his flashlight. It was small and the beam was weak, but it had been enough to read by after lights-out without drawing attention. How well it would help him in the attic was debatable. He added "good flashlight" to his hardware list.

He reached into his pocket to make sure the key was still there. It was. Stacy had given him the key so he could come and go when he wanted. After the fire marshal's visit yesterday, he'd chickened out on telling her the truth. He could tell her as soon as he was finished. If he worked before the market opened and after it closed, he'd get done that much faster.

He left Max in the cabin. The dog whined and scratched at the door, but Caden would only be gone for an hour or so. He stopped at the toolshed to pick up more electrical tape.

He'd already used three rolls securing all the loose and frayed wires.

The market was dark when he slipped up to the front door. He turned on the flashlight so he could see where to insert the key in the lock. Safe inside, he locked the door and made his way through the narrow aisles to the storeroom at the back.

Once he got into the attic and started working, he forgot about everything else. He lost himself in the middle of the tangled mess of multicolored wires.

A beam of light cut through the attic and into his face. "I've got a gun on you, so back out of there real slow. Let me see your hands."

He recognized Sheriff Frank Tedford's gruff voice. "It's me. Caden Murphy. I'm coming out."

"What're you doing sneaking around in the middle of the night?"

Fresh air hit Caden's face as he stepped onto the ladder and descended. "It's five in the morning and I'm not sneaking. I'm working."

Frank holstered his sidearm. "Goodness, boy. You scared the dickens out of old man Morgan. He saw your flashlight and was sure a robber was in here. Why are you doing this so early?"

"Did you catch 'em?" a voice hollered from across the store.

"It's okay, Denny. It's just the electrician."

Caden's breath caught. Electrician. Not prisoner. Or convict. Electrician. It sounded nice.

A hunched old man appeared at the door to the storage room. "I'm Dennis Morgan. I own the hardware store next door. You scared ten years off my life and those are ten years I can't afford to lose."

Caden accepted the gnarled hand offered to him. "Sorry about that. I didn't want to bother customers, so I'll be doing most of my work early in the morning. I didn't mean to disturb you."

The lights flipped on and both men blinked at the sudden brightness.

"Sorry," Frank said. "Should've warned you I was turning the lights on. No sense standing around in the dark."

Denny gave Caden a toothless grin. "I didn't see a truck outside. What company you with?"

Caden shot Frank a sideways glance. "I'm more of an independent contractor."

"He's the new maintenance man for us

at Whispering Pines for the summer, and agreed to take on the market as a favor." Frank walked up to Caden and put his hand on his shoulder. "We were sure lucky he decided to vacation in Coronado."

He'd asked Frank not to reveal who he was to Stacy. It hadn't occurred to him that he'd have to lie to the whole town. Still, it didn't stop the swell of pride at Frank's praise. How he wished he'd earned it.

"What's your rate?" Denny asked.

"Rate?"

The old man shoved his hands into the front pockets of the jeans that were two sizes too large. "I've got a couple of faulty breakers that need fixed. I've got arthritis so bad, I can't do it anymore, and I'm too stubborn to pay the outrageous fees they charge to come from out of town."

His heart went out to Denny. Changing a breaker was a ten-minute job. Admitting he could no longer do it had to have been hard for the elderly man. "I don't have a lot of experience with breakers, but if you're willing to offer your expertise to teach me, I'll be glad to come by and take care of it for you."

Denny's hunched shoulders lifted and his

chest puffed out just a bit. "Oh, it's easy. Nothing to it."

"I'll come over there as soon as I finish up here."

"I'll be looking for you." Denny nodded and left the room.

Frank gave Caden a strange look. "There's a lot more to you than you let on, Caden Murphy." Whistling, he walked out the door, pausing only long enough to lock it with his own key.

Caden crawled back up into the attic and finished tracing wires. By the time he came back out, he'd decided that it would be easier to run new wire down the walls than to try to figure out where the old wiring went. It would probably be faster, too.

He stashed his supplies in the storeroom and walked to the hardware store. An hour and a half later, the job was done. The breakers had taken less than ten minutes to change, but Mr. Morgan had wanted to talk. And talk. By the time Caden had finished purchasing the things on his list, he'd known more about Denny Morgan than he did his own grandfather. Of course, his grandfather had always been too busy to tell stories.

As long as he was so close to the market,

he might as well grab breakfast. He went into the deli area, but Stacy wasn't there. He remembered it was her day off. They were supposed to go on a trail ride today so she could show him around the area.

He wasn't sure what he was more excited about, spending the morning with Stacy or getting on a horse again.

His burrito was gone by the time he topped the ridge going back to the campground. He looked down the hill, searching for Stacy. He didn't see her, but he did see two horses grazing in front of his cabin.

"It's about time," Stacy greeted him from the stump he usually sat on in the mornings. "Did you forget we had plans today?"

"How long have you been here?"

"Not long. You ready? Do you need to give Max medicine before we leave? We'll probably be gone most of the day." Stacy walked over to the chestnut mare and swung herself into the saddle.

Caden opened the door and let Max out. "Max is coming."

He watched the dog's reaction to the horses. He'd feared that Max would bark at the larger animals, but the dog ignored them. He then adjusted the stirrups on his saddle before putting one foot in the stirrup and lifting himself up.

The leather creaked underneath him. He took the reins in his hand and urged the horse forward. The black gelding responded almost immediately.

"Does Coy rope with these horses?" He followed Stacy down the road, toward the barn.

"No," she said over her shoulder. "He concentrates mostly on bull riding now, but he also steer wrestles. These are his cutting horses."

Caden nodded. That explained why the horse responded so well. The job of a cutting horse was to separate one animal from the rest of the herd. The horse had to be quick on its feet and respond to the slightest touch of the reins.

"Where are we going?"

Stacy pointed to a trail that cut into the trees behind the pasture. "There are three main trails. This one leads down to Elk Wallow Meadow."

She pointed out a trail on the opposite side of the road. "That one leads all the way to Black Fork River. It's a beautiful trail, but it's really long. I wouldn't suggest taking the Mitchells on it unless they want to be gone for the entire day. The other one is used mostly for hiking now. The beginning of that trail starts closer to the campground."

They rode in silence for a while. He knew it wouldn't last long. Stacy was always full of questions about him. But this time, he had questions for her, too.

THE TRAIL WAS more overgrown than Stacy had ever seen it. The grass brushed Max's belly as he trotted ahead of the horses. A few times, she could just make out his tail above the waving grass. "Maze and I used to keep this trail pretty worn. I didn't realize it was this bad."

"Maze?"

"My horse," Stacy said. "A beautiful palomino mare. I raised her from a foal, and Coy broke her for me. She was a great horse."

"What happened to her?"

Stacy paused. Even after all this time, it was hard to talk about. "The Mitchells bought her. I had to sell her and all the other horses to keep the bank from taking the store."

Caden let out a whistle. "Wow. I'm sorry. That had to be rough."

"Not as rough as discovering your father

betrayed his family for a bottle." The pain was still raw, but she kept it at bay with anger.

"I'm guessing your grandfather owned the campground and your parents owned the store."

"No. Pap owned both of them. Originally, the campground was more like a dude ranch and the market was part of it. But as Coronado grew, it grew in the opposite direction of the campground, so Pap moved the market to the main road in the early 1950s." She was thankful for a chance to change the subject.

"Smart move, although it would be nice to have the market closer to the campground."

"Pap's idea was to turn the trail that we use to walk between the two into a road and have that be the main entrance to the campground."

Caden frowned. "That makes sense. But it would be a shame to ruin that beautiful trail with a road."

She nodded. "That's what I thought, too. Coy and I were supposed to take over the campground. We had big plans to turn it into the best dude ranch in Arizona. I wanted to build a Western town at the entrance we use now. That kept Pap from building the new road."

Caden's eyebrows pulled together. "A whole town?"

"Yes." Excitement bubbled up every time she thought about it. "A general store, a restaurant, a post office, a saloon. Of course, the saloon would only serve things like sarsaparilla, ginger beer and sodas. Maybe even some ice cream."

"Sounds great."

"It would've been." A soft sigh escaped her lips. "Except somehow my dad convinced Pap to sign the market over to him. It wasn't until after Pap died and my mother went into the nursing home that I found out Vince had taken out so many loans using the market for collateral that we were about to lose everything."

All talking stopped as they approached a part of the trail that had been washed out. She concentrated on navigating the path. Talking about the campground and Vince gave her a sick feeling in her stomach. Why had she even volunteered the information? It wasn't like Caden was prodding her for answers.

"I guess this trail is out of the question," she said. "I wouldn't chance bringing inexperienced riders through that."

They rode in silence for a little longer. It

wasn't an uncomfortable silence. She glanced at him. Looking at home on his horse, he was taking in the scenery. How had she ever mistaken him for a city boy?

The meadow could be seen through the trees, the sound of trickling water filtering through. Stacy ached to urge her horse into a run. Without knowing the condition of the trail ahead, it was too risky to try. Craggy cliffs jutted out of the mountains on the far side of the meadow.

Now that the trail was broader, Caden guided his horse up next to hers. "What happened to you and Coy taking over the campground? Why does Frank have it? And how did you end up solely responsible for the store?"

Stacy cast a sideways glance at Caden. *He finally decides to get chatty and it's a subject I don't like to discuss.*

It was her own fault for bringing it up to begin with. She swallowed the bitterness.

"The bank was about to foreclose on the store. The only way I could come up with enough money to stop it from happening was to sell the horses. So, Coy agreed to let me sell them if I would sign my part of the campground to him. And I only agreed to save the market if Vince signed the market over to me."

He nodded. "Coy doesn't seem to have much to do with the campground."

"Coy is more interested in chasing a buckle. He needed money to get started on the circuit, so he sold the campground to Frank with a stipulation that if Frank ever wants to sell it, Coy and I both have to agree to it, and I get first dibs."

He let out a whistle. "That's a lot of wheeling and dealing."

She shrugged. "I never thought about it before, but I guess you're right."

"Maybe you can buy the campground from Frank after I've finished the repairs on the market and—" He stopped abruptly.

She took a deep breath. "And my mother dies so I don't have to worry about her anymore."

Caden's face turned red. "That's not what I was going to say. I was going to say, when your dad starts helping you out."

"That'll never happen."

Caden frowned. "What if Frank is right? What if Vince really has stopped drinking?"

Stacy shot him a look. "Maybe he quit drinking and maybe he didn't. But he lied to me. He went behind my back and, because of him, I almost lost the market *and* my mother." She pushed down the anger. "Let's talk about something else."

He nodded and they rode along quietly. This time, the silence wasn't as comfortable.

They came to a stream that cut through the middle of the meadow, giving her the perfect opportunity to lighten the atmosphere. "There used to be a lot of trout in this stream. Pap, Dad and I used to fish here every Sunday after church."

Caden pointed to a grove of trees on the side of the mountain. "Look."

It took a moment for her to locate the elk bedded down under the trees. She pulled a pair of binoculars from her backpack.

"How many do you think there are?"

"At least twenty. It looks like they're all cows and their calves." She handed the binoculars to him so he could look, too.

"I would sure like to see a group of bulls running together like that," he breathed.

"They will be, just before the rut starts. We should see some rubs in another month or so."

He just nodded. "I imagine this meadow

will be full of them then. I saw some old rubs in those little trees on the edge of the trail."

Even though he was from the desert part of the state, he knew about the scars left on young trees when bull elk scraped the velvet off their horns. It shouldn't make her happy that he was familiar with something so commonplace to her, but it did. "Are you an elk hunter?"

"I used to be." Caden avoided her gaze.

Stacy cringed. He probably couldn't hunt anymore. As a felon, he wasn't allowed to own a weapon. "Sorry," she mumbled. "I wasn't thinking."

He shook his head. "It's okay. I can apply to have my rights restored in a couple of years."

The trees grew closer together as the forest began to sprout up around them again. At the first grove, she pulled her horse to a halt and dismounted. "We'll let the horses get some water while we eat lunch."

Caden dismounted his horse as she removed the blanket that was rolled up and tied behind her saddle. She spread it out and slipped the backpack off her shoulders.

"Hope you like tuna salad sandwiches."

She pulled an insulated fabric cooler from

inside the backpack. Opening it up, she handed him a sandwich and a bag of chips.

He sat on the far corner of the blanket.

"I'm not going to bite you."

His face turned red and he called for Max. The dog came running and curled up next to him on the blanket. "What can you tell me about the Mitchells? Are trail rides the only thing I need to do to entertain them?"

It shouldn't surprise her that he was back to business. She'd hoped that he would enjoy the trail ride simply for the sake of it, but he never seemed to do anything for his pleasure. It was always about business.

"We used to have a barbecue on Friday night at the campground, but we haven't done that in a long time."

"Why not?"

"I don't have time to plan it or the money to buy the food, and Frank isn't interested in doing it. He's perfectly happy being the sheriff and only keeps the campgrounds because of Coy and me. He never liked the dude ranch idea, so he's okay just renting cabins out."

"That's too bad." Caden scratched Max behind the ears. "Sounds like it could be a lot of fun."

After he finished his sandwich, he asked,

"Why do the Mitchells come back every year if you don't offer them anything other than a place to put their horses and a couple of trail rides?"

Stacy crumpled her potato chip bag into a ball. "Mrs. Mitchell is from Coronado and still has a lot of friends here. They're the ones who bought Maze, and I offered them a discount if they would bring her back with them."

As soon as she had everything packed away, Caden stood, picked up the blanket and shook it out. "I'm looking forward to meeting them."

"We better head back. I'd really like to go see Mom before it gets too late."

CHAPTER SIXTEEN

"YOU'LL TELL HIM, won't you?" Jason Peterson asked as he peered over the counter at Stacy.

"Yes, as soon as I see him." She twisted her hair into a bun and slid the ponytail holder over it. "I promise."

Stacy slipped on plastic gloves and turned her attention back to the sandwiches she'd been making a few moments before. The bell on the door clanged, signaling the man's departure.

"That's the third person this week." Millie crossed her arms. "I don't get it. Caden's been in town less than a month and knows more people than I do."

"You know more than three people." Stacy wrapped the sandwiches for a customer who'd called in a to-go order.

"You know what I mean." Millie gave her a pointed look. "And how do they all know him? You're the only one in town he speaks to."

"After the way all the women in church

fawned over him for the last two Sundays, what do you expect? They probably scared the dickens out of him." It irked her that every unmarried woman in town between the ages of twenty and forty had suddenly set their sights on Caden. Not that she was jealous.

"Here he comes."

Stacy turned just in time to see Millie disappear to the back of the store. If only the rest of the women in town were as shy.

Caden strolled through the door, clutching a box from the hardware store next door. Max followed on his heels. She'd given up trying to keep Max out of the store. The dog wasn't happy unless he could see Caden. As far as she was concerned, he was a service dog. Although, she wasn't sure if Max took care of Caden or if it was the other way around.

She shook her head at the dog. "Good morning, Caden. How is Max this morning?"

He shook his head. "Much better. He's finally starting to gain some weight. Any luck on the flyers?"

"No. Nothing. I think you're stuck with him." She suspected Caden had only hung flyers up around town out of obligation. He was as attached to Max as Max was to him.

He lifted the box in his hand slightly. "Can I leave this behind the counter for a while?"

"More parts for your motorcycle?" Between what he'd bought in town and what he'd ordered online, it would probably have been cheaper to buy a new motorcycle.

"Yep. It's almost done." Pride laced his voice.

"How much longer?"

He ambled around the counter and placed the box on an empty shelf underneath the register. "This weekend, I hope. I want to take a ride up to Big Lake. Put some of those fishing poles in the shed to use."

Stacy smiled. "I happen to know where you can get some bait. It'll cost you, though."

Caden gave her one of his rare smiles. "I work cheap."

She grinned. "Sorry. I only pay with home-cooked meals." One thing she'd learned about him in the last couple of weeks was that he couldn't boil water. If she didn't feed him every day, he'd probably starve.

"I was counting on it."

She pointed to the rear of the store, loving their easy banter. "But you're going to earn every bite. Get to work, cowboy."

He snapped to attention and threw her a salute. "Yes, ma'am."

Stacy moved out of the way as he strolled past her.

Millie stared at her with wide eyes. "I've never heard him talk that much."

The comment stopped her. It was true. Except on their trail ride, he rarely exchanged more than a few words with people around town. He never spoke to anyone unless they spoke to him first. Those brief exchanges weren't really conversations, though. The surge of satisfaction she felt was unwarranted. She shouldn't like that he was more comfortable with her than anyone else.

"Where does he get all his money?" Millie peered into the box Caden had left under the counter. She examined a few of the mechanical parts.

"I don't know." She'd wondered the same thing. Glancing toward the back of the market to make sure Caden couldn't overhear, she leaned into Millie. "I think his family is rich. I bet he has a trust fund or something."

"Really? That would explain why he mails his mom a letter every week. He's probably asking for money."

That was news to her. So much for her knowing more about him than anyone else in town. "Where'd you hear that?"

"Edith told me."

Of course. Edith and Margaret managed to stir up gossip wherever they went. Still, she was willing to bet they didn't know he'd been in prison. She doubted Caden would tell anyone else. But why hadn't he mentioned that he'd been in contact with his mother?

She was just about to start making sandwiches when she remembered the message for Caden. She hung her apron up and went to the back, where she found him kneeling in the storeroom, sorting through his toolbox. Max sat dutifully beside him.

"Jason Peterson was looking for you."

Caden looked up from his task. "Thanks."

She waited. He didn't volunteer any information and she wasn't going to ask. He'd tell her if he wanted.

Who was she kidding? She'd break down at dinner and grill him.

"Can I ask you a personal question? You don't have to answer, because it's none of my business."

His face hardened. "What is it?"

"You've been in town for almost a month.

You work in exchange for free rent, and you haven't let me give you a dime. How do you pay for all this stuff?"

He stiffened. "I'm not doing anything illegal. I didn't think you, of all people, would think otherwise."

Stacy's mouth dropped open. Turning her back on him, she stormed out of the storeroom. Why would he say something like that? Not once had she treated him like an ex-con. She'd trusted him with the key to her store, for goodness' sake.

She marched into her apartment. A foot stopped her from slamming the door like she wanted to.

Caden stood in the doorway.

She clenched her teeth. "What do you want?"

"You're angry." He leaned his shoulder against the wall.

"Of course I'm angry," she snapped. "Have I ever once treated you like a criminal?"

His eyes dropped to the floor. "No."

"Have I even given you a reason to think I don't trust you?"

"No." His voice was soft.

"Then what's with the attitude?" She put

her hands on her hips. "We're friends whether you like it or not."

He rubbed the back of his neck. "I'm sorry. I'm not used to having friends."

"Friends tell each other things. I talk about myself with you all the time. You never talk about anything. Ever."

His gray eyes were as dark as storm clouds. "I got extra pay for overseas duty in Afghanistan. I put it away and never touched it. And I've been doing a lot of side jobs around town. That's how I have money."

She sucked her breath in. "That wasn't so hard, was it? And I'm sorry. I could have phrased it a little better."

He let out a long, slow breath. "That's okay. I shouldn't have gotten so defensive."

She smiled. "Now, can I ask you something else?"

He nodded.

She lifted her face to look at him. "When are you going to kiss me again?"

Caden stepped back as if she'd burned him. He shook his head. "That was a mistake. It won't happen again."

"I don't believe you." She stepped closer to him and he swallowed.

"I have to get back to work." He disappeared.

Stacy tried not to smile, but he flustered so easily that she couldn't help it. As tempting as it was to keep teasing him, she returned to the deli counter and left him to his work.

Several hours later, the FedEx truck delivered a box for Caden.

Unlike most of the deliveries, this one wasn't marked from a motorcycle parts company. The return address, scrawled in feminine handwriting, was in Tucson.

She sent Millie to the back to get Caden, but he had already left. She placed the large box in the back of her truck. She would take it to him this afternoon. Maybe she'd ask him why he was so scared of her.

THE SUN WAS setting over the mountains. Caden didn't need to look at his watch to know that it was well past Stacy's appointed dinnertime.

Somehow, he didn't think he'd be welcome tonight. He'd hurt her feelings this morning. The look in her eyes had haunted him all day. He'd broken his own rule and allowed himself to get too close to her. To get to know her. The more he was around her, the more he liked her. And that wasn't allowed. What would Grayson say?

He'd spent more time at Jason Peterson's than necessary. In no hurry to face Stacy again, he'd waited until it was almost dark before cleaning up his tools and heading home.

"Thank you!" Jason's wife waved to him as he closed the gate to their backyard. "I'm sorry Jason wasn't here to help you."

Caden nodded to her and started down the road. It hadn't taken long to change the thermocouple on the Petersons' water heater. He almost felt guilty taking money for doing a job that was so easy. Word of his repair skills had spread fast through the little town. He'd done side jobs almost every day for the last week. If he had been looking for a place to open his own business, Coronado would be the ideal location. The townspeople were tired of having to wait until larger companies could fit them into their schedule and pay exorbitant fees for them to travel to the small mountain community.

He patted the front pocket of his work shirt. Thanks to his side jobs, he'd been able to pay cash for most of the parts he needed for the motorcycle, as well as some of the supplies for the store. Why hadn't he just told Stacy when she'd asked? Why'd he have to go and get defensive?

He walked by the RV park and saw Vince working on his truck. The man waved him over.

Caden stopped in front of him. "Evening. How'd it go at the bank?"

Vince shrugged. "I couldn't get the loan."

"I could loan you the money."

"You're an ex-con working in exchange for room and board." Vince lit a cigarette. "You aren't much better off than I am."

Caden shook his head. "I put a lot of money away while I was in the military."

Vince took a drag from his cigarette. "Won't you need that when you leave here?"

"I have enough for that, too." He didn't need to tell Vince about the savings account or the trust fund he was entitled to.

"I'll think about it." Vince tossed his cigarette on the ground. "How're the repairs going on the store?"

"I have the wires ready to run down the walls. I'm waiting until after the weekend to start on that." The next part of the job would require working out in the market and tearing into some of the walls. Stacy didn't want the market to be a mess during Fourth of July weekend, her busiest time of the year.

"You replaced the breaker panel?"

"Did that last week." Caden knew the small talk was more than interest in the store. It was Vince's way of checking up on Stacy. "I better get going."

His steps were light as he walked toward the store. If Vince was able to get the nursing home account caught up, it would remove a huge strain from Stacy.

He was walking past the bar when he noticed a man stumbling toward a car. Even in the dim light, he recognized Jason Peterson.

Caden stopped him before he could get in the vehicle. "What are you doing?"

"Going home."

"Jason, you're in no condition to drive." He held up his hand. "Let me call someone to come get you."

"No. I'm fine." Jason tried to step around him. "Come on, man. It's just down the street."

Another man came out of the bar. "Listen to him. You've already had one DUI. If you get another one, you'll lose your job."

Forget the job. What if he crashed his car or hit someone? Caden's heart rate doubled and his stomach twisted into knots. "You can't drive."

"Sure I can." Jason's words were slurred. "It's not that far. I'll be fine."

Jason tried to open his car door, but the other man blocked the path. "Let me make some calls. I'll find someone to drive you home."

Jason stood up straight. "I said I'm fine."

"You get in that car and you're eighty-sixed for good." The man's voice was stern. "I mean it. You'll never set foot in there again."

"Aw, come on, Freddy." Jason slapped the hood of the car and squared off against the man.

Caden stepped between them. "Come on, Jason. Let me drive you home."

Jason's gaze darted back and forth between Freddy and Caden. Finally, he rolled his eyes, but he handed the keys to Caden. "Suit yourself." He walked around to the passenger side of the car.

Freddy clapped his hand on Caden's shoulder. "Thank you. If he gets in trouble again, he'll lose everything."

"I'm more worried about him losing his life than his job." He looked down at the keys in his hand and tried to stop the quivering in his stomach.

"You okay?" Freddy asked. "You look like you're going to be sick."

His mouth was too dry to answer, so he nodded. He opened the car's back door for Max to jump inside and then slid into the driver's seat. For a full minute, he stared at the steering wheel, sweat gathering on his forehead.

"Are we going or what?" Jason leaned back against the seat.

Caden's hands shook so badly, it took him two tries to get the key into the ignition. He closed his eyes and inhaled slowly through his nose. The last time he'd got behind the wheel of a car, he'd killed his best friend. Driving was the one thing he'd sworn he'd never do again. But here he was. His gaze strayed to the man in the seat next to him.

He could do this.

The car roared to life and the quivers in his body turned to full-blown shakes. Putting the car into Drive, he gripped the steering wheel with both hands and took his foot off the brake.

"I can walk faster than this," Jason complained.

"Shut up." Caden turned the blinker on and eased around the corner onto Oak Street. A few seconds later, he stopped in front of Jason's house.

"Thanks." Jason got out and met Caden in front of the car. He held out his hand for the keys.

"You're not going to hop in the car and go anywhere if I give you these, are you?" He hesitated to give him the keys.

"I'll be good." Jason's voice had a sarcastic ring to it. "I'm going to bed."

Caden handed him the keys and waited until Jason was inside and all the lights were off. His legs felt like jelly as he and Max started walking. But he'd done it. He'd managed to get the man home without incident.

He stopped a couple of times to wait for Max to investigate a new smell. "Hurry up, boy. We're late for Stacy's."

He better let her know he was running late. He reached into his shirt pocket to get his phone. It wasn't there. He checked all his pockets. Nowhere.

He jogged all the way back to the bar. After a thorough search of the parking lot, he still couldn't find it.

What if someone had found it in front of

the bar? It was against his parole to be inside a bar. They couldn't send him back to prison for being in the parking lot, could they? Maybe he'd left it at the cabin. He broke into a run.

He burst into the cabin. His phone sat on the kitchen counter. He bent over, his hands on his knees, and tried to catch his breath. Relief flooded through him as he sank onto the couch, feeling like a deflated balloon.

STACY FILLED TUPPERWARE with leftovers and threw them in the refrigerator. Where was Caden? It was one thing if he'd been too tired to come over for dinner—that wasn't unusual. But he hadn't answered his phone, and when she'd gone to the cabin, he wasn't there.

For a moment, she'd thought he'd skipped town, but all of his stuff was still in the cabin. And how would he get anywhere? It didn't make any sense. She'd gone past angry and now she was just worried.

She pulled the trash bag out of the can and went outside to throw it in the dumpster.

Max was lying on the ground in front of her apartment. She dropped the bag and hunkered next to him. "What are you doing here?" She ran her hands over him to see if he was okay.

Now she was really worried. Caden never

went anywhere without Max. She gave the dog a bowl of water.

While he was drinking, she called Caden again. No answer. Maybe he just didn't want to talk to her. She texted him.

I found Max out by himself. Where are you?

She grabbed her phone and keys and headed for Caden's cabin. Max still had a limp, and she stopped every so often to wait for him.

A light was on in the cabin. Stacy picked up speed going down the hill. Just as she got to the door, she heard a muffled scream.

Her pulse thundered in her ears and she pushed the door open to run inside. She froze.

Caden lay on the sofa, his body drenched in sweat. His face was contorted in agony and he shook his head over and over. "No. No. No."

"Caden," she whispered, kneeling next to the sofa. She stroked his hair. "It's okay. Caden. Wake up."

He awoke with a start. His eyes darted around the room, trying to focus. Stacy cupped his cheek with one hand and his gaze zeroed in on her. He rubbed his eyes and sat up. "I'm sorry."

She moved to sit next to him on the sofa, wrapping one arm around his shoulders. For once, he didn't push her away. He hugged her back. His lips brushed the side of her neck, then found her mouth. He buried his hands in her hair and kissed her like he was drowning and she was his life raft.

The kiss ended, but she clung to him to catch her breath.

"I'm sorry," he whispered into her hair. "I shouldn't have done that."

"Stop apologizing for kissing me."

He put some distance between them, his hands folded in his lap. They were shaking.

"It was just a bad dream." She placed her hands over his.

"No." He shook his head. "It's much more than that. They've gotten worse since I came here."

"Maybe if you talk about it, it'll help." She wanted to touch him. Comfort him. But he had retreated behind a wall and she didn't know how to get through. "I know you feel guilty because someone you love died in that accident. But it was an *accident*, Caden. You can't continue to punish yourself for something you had no control over."

He squeezed his eyes shut. "It was my fault. We'd both had too much to drink, but I thought I was okay to drive. I could've called my sister to come get us. Or a cab. But I thought I was invincible. I thought I could handle it. We were only going a few miles down the road."

Stacy wrapped her arms around him. "You need to forgive yourself. You're still here. You can't shut yourself off from the world."

"You don't know the truth."

"Then tell me."

Reaching into his back pocket, he pulled his wallet out. His hands shook as he pulled out a picture and handed it to her.

She gasped. "That's Grayson."

He nodded. "He was my best friend."

Her hand came up to cover her mouth. "That's why you looked familiar. Grayson had a picture of the two of you in his apartment."

After Grayson's death, she had read the articles in the paper, but she couldn't remember ever reading Caden's name. "You were driving?"

He nodded. "I had just gotten out of the army and he'd just graduated. He invited me out to tell me about this great girl he'd fallen in love with." His voice matched the shaking in his hands.

Stacy handed the picture back. "He wasn't

talking about me. We broke up almost a year before he died."

"It was you," he whispered. "He had just graduated from college and was coming to find you. He wanted to tell you he was sorry for letting you walk away. If he couldn't convince you to come back to Tucson, he was ready to move to Coronado because he loved you that much."

"Then why didn't he ever call me?" She hadn't heard a word from Grayson after the breakup.

"I don't know." His stormy gray eyes searched hers. "I just know that he loved you."

She remembered something he'd said when he'd first arrived in Coronado. "I'm the unfinished business you came to take care of."

He nodded.

Tears filled her eyes as realization of what he hadn't said dawned on her. She lifted her chin. "How come I never read about you in the paper? I never even heard about your trial."

His breath came in ragged gasps. "There was no trial. I pleaded guilty."

She needed space. She stood and walked over to the mantel. "It happened almost a decade ago. Why didn't you write to tell me sooner?"

"I wrote you a dozen letters. But the words wouldn't come out right on paper. I wanted to apologize to you face-to-face. I wanted to tell you how much he loved you. And I wanted to try to make things right."

"By lying to me?"

"I never lied to you."

"Then why does it feel like it?" She turned to face him. "Don't come to the market tomorrow. I need some time."

She fought the tears back as she fled from the cabin. Once she arrived at her apartment, she dug through her closet until she found a box marked College Memories.

She dumped the contents on her bed and sorted through the pictures. There were several photographs of Grayson. Since she'd taken most of the pictures, there were only a few of them together. She finally found one where she stood next to him, and stared at it for a long time.

Was Caden telling the truth? What would she have done if Grayson had arrived in Coronado declaring he loved her? Would things be different now?

While she'd grieved when she'd first heard

about Grayson's death, she'd never allowed herself to dwell on what-ifs. Mostly because she hadn't realized there could've been some what-ifs.

But it seemed Caden had spent seven years in prison considering the what-ifs.

And there it was. The source of the pain in her chest. Caden wasn't here for her. He hadn't stayed for her. Nothing he'd done was for her. Rather, he was trying to redeem himself.

She looked at Grayson's picture again. Closing her eyes, she tried to imagine a life with him. She'd been drawn to him because he was a lot like her mother. He laughed and joked a lot. He had a thirst for adventure and never liked to stay in one place for very long. All the things that attracted her to him were the same things that would have driven them apart eventually.

But every time she closed her eyes, all she could see were red hair, a scruffy beard and steel-gray eyes.

CHAPTER SEVENTEEN

IT HAD ONLY been two days since Caden had seen Stacy, but it felt like a lifetime. He was running out of things to do. The grounds around the cabins were immaculate. He'd chopped enough firewood for three winters. And if anything needed repaired inside a cabin, it was only because he didn't know about it.

The campground had been full that weekend, a good sign. Most of the guests had checked out by the time he got back from church, so he'd cleaned the cabins, too. Knowing Stacy, she probably cleaned the cabins herself instead of hiring someone to do it, and he'd needed something to do.

Now he paced around the cabin, Max trailing at his heels. The dog's eyes followed every movement Caden made, almost as if he was afraid to let Caden out of his sight. He'd left Max behind in his panic over losing his phone, and Caden wasn't going to let him out of his sight again.

Caden sat on the sofa and picked up a novel, Max at his feet. But he couldn't concentrate on the book. He kept wondering how Stacy's weekend was. Did the market do well? The town was certainly full of tourists. After a couple of trips to the hardware store, he'd avoided town altogether.

He kept replaying their conversation, when he'd finally told her the truth, over and over. He'd been prepared for her anger. That was an emotion he could understand. He'd expected tears over the man who'd left her behind. But the pain in her eyes wasn't because she was missing what could've been. The pain was because of Caden himself. She was disappointed in him. That was a reaction he hadn't been expecting at all and it shattered what was left of his heart. But could she forgive him?

She hadn't told him to leave town. She'd asked for time. He would give her all the time in the world.

It was easy to see why Grayson had fallen in love with her. She was beautiful, independent, smart. If they'd met at a different time and under different circumstances, he'd fall in love with her himself. But he couldn't, no matter how much his heart ached. Unless she asked him to leave, he'd stick around long enough to finish the work on the store. Then he could leave knowing he'd done everything he could to help her.

He gave up on reading. The last part for his motorcycle had come in. It was time to see if his work had paid off.

The Kawasaki was parked under a large juniper tree in the yard. It only took him a few minutes to install the hose clamps. He retrieved the gas can from the storage room and filled the tank. He sat on the bike, feeling the metal underneath him and hoping it would run. With his right foot, he pushed the kick start and the engine came to life. Max ran in circles around him.

"Stay here, boy. I'm going to take it for a test-drive."

But Max didn't stay. He chased Caden down the dirt road.

Caden pulled back in at the front of the cabin and shut the engine off.

"Do you want to go for a ride, too?" He scratched the dog's chin. "Let's see what we can come up with."

Caden walked around the bike, trying to figure out how to help Max stay safely on it with him. Dogs rode in the back of pickup trucks all the time, but motorcycles were different. "What we need is some type of seat belt. A way to hold you close to me."

A few minutes later, he had an idea.

Running up the cabin stairs, he pulled an oversize shirt out of his dresser and returned to find Max by the motorcycle. Sliding his arms into the sleeves, Caden sat on the bike and reached down to pick up Max and sit him in front of him on the seat. He pulled the dog close to his chest and tugged the front panels over Max until his head poked out of the top of the shirt. "Let's see if this works."

He started the engine and pulled slowly out of the driveway, bracing himself to stop if Max showed signs of panicking. After three trips around the campground, he was convinced that Max liked the motorcycle as much as he did.

His heart swelled with a mixture of joy and sadness. Now he could leave when he wanted to. Problem was, he didn't want to leave town. But he knew he couldn't stay.

The shadows were lengthening and a chill had settled in the air, so Caden parked the bike and he and Max went inside. When he opened the door to the cabin, his phone was ringing. Stacy? He glanced at the caller ID. It was a local number, but not one he recognized. "Hello?"

"Is this the guy that drove Jason home a few days ago?"

Caden didn't recognize the voice. "Who is this?"

"This is Freddy Macias. I own the Watering Hole."

Why was the owner of the local bar calling him? "What do you want?"

"I got your number from Jason," the man explained. "Anyway, you really did me a solid by making sure he got home okay. I was wondering if you could do that again."

"Jason?"

"No. Someone else."

"Now?"

"Do you mind? Vince usually does it, but his truck still isn't running."

"I'll be there in a few minutes." He disconnected the call and rubbed Max's head. "Want to go for another ride?"

THE ORANGE HUES of dusk had turned to black and the stars were twinkling brightly by the time Caden got back to the cabin. He'd driven three people home. Three people who made it home without hurting someone or themselves. Driving hadn't got easier, but having Max sitting next to him seemed to ease the fear.

He was used to being in a constant state of exhaustion, with all the physical activity he did on only a few hours' sleep a night. But with the added pressure from driving, he'd reached a whole new level of exhaustion. This time it was more mental. Last night he'd got almost four hours of sleep and was at the beginning of a nightmare when Max had woken him. That was a record for Caden. If he got that much sleep tonight, he'd feel like a new man.

With Max still recovering, Caden had worried about leaving him alone downstairs, so he'd been sleeping on the sofa. He patted Max on the head. "Be right back, boy. I'm going to get our blankets."

At the top of the stairs, he spied a large box on the floor next to his dresser. Stacy had dropped it off, and from the feminine handwriting scrawled across the label, he knew it was from his mother. He lifted the box off the floor and put it on the bed. With shaking hands, he opened the top and gasped. His mother had filled it with his favorite things.

He held up his favorite University of Arizona T-shirt. Next, he pulled out a pair of pajama bottoms and grinned. Kicking his jeans off, he slid them on. The soft flannel greeted him like an old friend.

He spent a few more minutes going through things he'd almost forgotten he owned. At the bottom of the box, he found a small manila envelope. His fingers traced the letters of his name. Sinking on the edge of the bed, he turned the envelope over.

A noise on the stairs startled him. He looked over to see Max sitting at the top of the stairs. Caden grinned. "You made it. Good boy."

The dog limped over to him and waited. Caden set the envelope on the nightstand and scooped Max up to put him next to him on the bed. "Maybe we can sleep in a real bed tonight. What do you think?"

The rustle of the pine trees outside the open window was the only sound. His eyes closed and visions of him and Grayson drifted through his memories. Every image in his head was of Grayson smiling. Just like real life. Everyone liked him and trusted him. Grayson was the rational one, the thinker. Caden was the doer. He would get an idea and run with it. More than once, Grayson had been the voice of reason, talking Caden out of doing something rash.

Except that night.

He picked the envelope up and stared at it for a few moments before opening it. Tears filled his eyes when he recognized Grayson's mother's handwriting.

Dear Caden,

I forgive you. Are you listening? I forgive you. Grayson would forgive you, too. No one loved him more than you did. I know that. He knows that. And he would want you to forgive yourself. Stop punishing yourself by hiding from everyone. It's time you started living again, for Grayson. Make his death count for something. Do something big. Help someone. Fall in love and get married and have a dozen babies. But live.

I know you're still grieving. I am, too. But not just for Grayson. I grieve for you. I feel as though I've lost my second son. You're all I have left of my son. Come home.

I love you,
Miranda

It was as if the truck that had been parked on his chest for the last seven years finally decided to move. With the weight gone, he could breathe. Tears threatened him again as he reread the letter. Max nudged him and licked his face. Caden scratched the dog behind his ears. "I'm okay."

He lay down on the bed to read the letter again. This time, he didn't try to stop the tears.

CADEN BLINKED. Was that sunlight streaming through the window? He blinked again. Yes. He bolted upright. He'd slept through the night? How was that possible?

The letter from Grayson's mother was still in his hand. He carefully folded it and put it back in the envelope. The bed shook as Max shifted next to him.

"Good morning." He patted the dog's head. "Looks like you had a good night's sleep, too."

Max wagged his tail, and they went downstairs together. Caden let the dog outside to do his morning business and crossed the room to turn the coffeepot on. He let Max in and pulled a hot dog from the refrigerator. Max wiggled with excitement. "Hold on, boy. Not until I get your medicine."

With practiced ease, he stuffed the antibiotics into the end of a hot dog and fed the impatient animal. It had been several weeks and Max was finally filling out. His ribs no longer showed and his limp improved daily. The swelling around his eye had gone down and Caden had removed the stitches. Soon, the only remnant of his experience would be the scars running along his hindquarters. "We're a good pair. Our scars match," he said as he gave Max the hot dog.

His phone vibrated and he checked the text message.

We need to talk. Dinner tonight after you're done working in the store.

His heart leaped. She wanted him to come back to the store. It wasn't exactly forgiveness, but it was close.

STACY LOOKED AT the calculator. That couldn't be right. The printout from the cash register stretched across the table and fell into a pile on the floor. She scanned the totals, matching the large amounts with the entries in her books. Hope bubbled up in her chest. Yes! The market had doubled its income for the month of June. She could afford to make a payment on her mother's bill. She couldn't pay it off fully yet, but she would put a good dent in it.

This coming weekend was the Fourth of July celebration and the town's busiest time. Income often tripled for that weekend alone. Between the rising profits on the campground and the store, she was going to be able to pay for the added expenses of her mother's care.

She glanced at the wall clock. If she hurried, she could make it to the nursing home before the office closed. She didn't want to take any chances that something might happen and the money wouldn't be there tomorrow. She ducked into the market to find Millie and let her know she'd be gone for a few minutes.

Millie was making sandwiches for a customer. The young man leaning on the counter had Millie giggling. Stacy fought the pang of jealousy. It'd been a long time since anyone had flirted with her like that. Trouble was, the only person she wanted to flirt with was Caden. And she didn't know what to do about that.

She was still angry with him. He had lied to her, or at the very least, he'd been less than honest. His revelation about Grayson stirred up a lot of emotions. Caden thought he'd destroyed a future she hadn't even known could exist. The truth was, he hadn't.

Even if Grayson had come to Coronado, they wouldn't have got back together. Seven years ago, she was still too bitter over her parents' divorce to trust Grayson or anyone else. She'd been on a mission to prove she could manage on her own.

Caden was allowed to feel guilty for causing the death of his best friend. He wasn't allowed to feel guilty over her. She didn't want his guilt or his pity. What she wanted was for him to trust her enough to tell her the truth.

Where was he? He was supposed to come back to work today. She looked up every time the bells chimed, expecting to see him. Once, she heard a motorcycle go by and looked out the window to see if it was Caden. But she hadn't been quick enough. She wasn't even sure if his motorcycle was running yet.

Her thoughts were still on Caden when she pulled into the parking lot of the nursing home. A Kawasaki stood in the far corner of the lot. It looked a lot like Caden's motorcycle.

Her breath caught in her throat. Maybe he

wanted to tell her he was leaving and couldn't wait until dinner tonight?

Sliding out of her truck, she tossed her purse over her shoulder and headed for the office. As she rounded the corner to her mother's room, she saw Vince leaving. She stepped into a recessed doorway.

Stacy held her position until Vince disappeared and then made a beeline for Mrs. Hernandez's office.

Mrs. Hernandez looked up from the computer. "Stacy. What a surprise. What can I do for you?"

Stacy said, "I'm here to make a payment on my mother's bill."

The director looked confused.

Stacy pulled the monthly statement from her purse. "This one. The one that I have to pay by the end of August or you were sending her to the county facility."

Mrs. Hernandez put on her reading glasses and scanned the letter. "Oh, that account. It's been paid in full."

Stacy's mouth dropped open. Paid in full? Impossible. "When?"

The director punched a few buttons on her computer and stared at the screen. "Today, actually."

"By who?"

"I can't tell you that."

"You can't tell me, or you won't tell me?"

Mrs. Hernandez took her reading glasses off and laid them on her desk. "Does it matter who paid it, as long as it's paid?"

Vince. Had he really followed through on his word? "I guess not."

Stacy left the office and raced for the front of the building. The summer sun blinded her when she burst through the door. She squinted and looked for Vince, but he was gone.

She ran back in and went straight to her mother's room.

"Oh, *sykhaara*, how nice to see you." Nina looked up from a book she was reading to her friend.

"Hi, Nina." Her eyes darted around the room. "How long was Vince here?"

"Only a few minutes today." She closed the book. "He'll be back this evening, as always."

Missy's eyes fluttered open and she smiled. At least, that was what Stacy saw. All thoughts of chasing Vince down fled as she sank into a chair next to her mother.

"How's she been today?"

Nina shrugged. "Not much response, but

every once in a while she twitches, so I know she's trying to talk to me."

Stacy squeezed Missy's hand and pressed it to her chest. The world always seemed to stop spinning when she sat with her mother. How she wished she really could stop time. Except she would've done it ten years ago, when her mother was happy and healthy. When her parents were happy just being together.

"Vince never misses a day, does he?"

On the other side of the bed, Nina hummed a tune and straightened the sheets around Missy's feet.

Stacy stroked her mother's hair. "Mama, Vince did it. He followed through. He did it for you."

Nina sat back in her chair. "He didn't do it just for her. He did it for you, too. He would do anything in the world for you."

"Except quit drinking."

Nina gave her a sharp look. "You have walked in his shoes? You have fought the whole world for the one you love, just to lose it all?"

Stacy lifted her chin. "Don't make excuses for him."

"I don't need to," Nina said. "You already

have it all figured out." With that, Nina got up and left the room.

Stacy took her mother's hand. "Tell me what to do, Mama."

STACY WENT FOR a drive before returning to the market. Between her father's strange behavior and her conflicted feelings for Caden, she felt like a guppy who'd been tossed in the ocean.

When she arrived at the store, Caden was already there. He stayed in the back. She stayed in the front. When she closed the market for the evening, he was still in the attic, so she went to her apartment. Would he remember dinner or would he avoid her?

She almost made chicken enchiladas again but changed her mind. She made shepherd's pie instead. It was her favorite. The rich aroma of gravy was drifting out of the oven when she heard a light knock on the door leading into the store.

Caden looked at her with his stormy gray eyes and she didn't know if she wanted to hit him or hug him. She pushed the door all the way open to allow Max to follow him inside. "Dinner is almost ready."

He came inside, not looking her in the eye.

Finally, while she was putting their meal on the counter, he cleared his throat. "Thank you for letting me finish the work."

She shrugged. "Dinner first. We'll talk later."

They had sat in silence before, but never like this. She pushed the food around the plate with her fork until Caden finally shoved his plate away. He hadn't eaten much, either.

She went to sit on the couch and motioned for him to join her. "I have some questions," she said.

"I'll answer them the best I can."

She bit her lip. "You said Grayson was in love with me and ready to move to Coronado. If that's true, why didn't he call me?"

His brows drew together. "After you moved back to Coronado? I don't know. I was in the military and only got home a week before the accident."

"We only went out for a few months. Honestly, I thought he'd found someone else and moved on. And I was so busy with the market and taking care of Mama that, eventually, I lost touch with everyone in Tucson."

Caden scratched his head. "You don't think Grayson was really in love with you."

"I don't think you're lying. I just don't

think Grayson felt as deeply about me as you think he did."

"You are all he talked about that night."

"And that's the only reason you're here. To apologize? You didn't have to come to Coronado to do that. And why didn't you say anything when we first met? Why stay here the whole month?"

"I wanted to apologize face-to-face. Then, when I got here and saw things falling apart around you, I wanted to help."

"Why? How is anything in my life your responsibility?" Her heart felt like it was being stomped on.

"Because if Grayson was alive, your life would be..." His eyes darted around the room. "Different."

She stared at him for a moment. He had this all wrong. "You're only here because of guilt?"

His brow furrowed. "Is there any other reason?"

She wiped a tear away and stood. "I'm sorry about Grayson. He was a wonderful person. But the truth is, even if he had come here, I wouldn't have taken him back. So, I'm sorry you've spent the last seven years of your life feeling guilty about me. I'm sorry that your overinflated sense of responsibility for my life has brought you here instead of taking you to see a family that loves you and wants you home."

Confusion covered Caden's face and he stood as well. "I couldn't go on with my life until I apologized to you in person."

"Okay. Mission accomplished. You can go back to Tucson with a clear conscience." And she could start repairing her heart.

"I'd like to finish the job first. If you'll let me."

She shook her head. "I don't need charity. And I don't need your pity."

His chest puffed up. "If I was doing it out of pity, I would've handed you a check and walked away. But I couldn't. The truth is, I'm still here because—"

Stacy waited for him to finish, but he just turned away. She put one hand on his arm and stopped him. "Why? What is keeping you here?"

His eyes searched hers. "You are like a ray of sunshine and I have been in the dark for a very long time. I'm drawn to you and I shouldn't be."

Her heart leaped. "Why? What's so bad about being drawn to me?"

He gave her a sad smile and cupped her face with one palm. "If Grayson were here, I'd fight for you. I'd do everything in my power to steal you away from him. But he's not. So I can't."

The touch of his skin sent goose bumps down her spine. She covered his hand with hers. "I don't belong to Grayson. I never did."

Caden dropped his hand and shook his head. "You have for the last seven years, at least in my head. I can't think of you without thinking of him. And every time you look at me now, you'll think about him."

Heat flooded her neck. She cupped his face in both her hands. "You're wrong. Every time I look at you, I see the man who put his own needs aside because he thought mine were greater. I see a man who swallowed his fear to get a dog some help. I see a man who needs to see himself the same way others do."

Caden tilted his head until his forehead rested against hers. "You have no idea how badly I want to be that man."

"You can be," she whispered.

A split second before his lips touched hers, his cell phone rang.

He stepped back and pulled the phone from

his back pocket. He glanced at the number and frowned. "Hello?"

Butterflies danced in her stomach. How could she make him see that Grayson would want them to have some happiness?

He hung up the phone. "I have to go."

"We're not finished talking."

"I'm sorry, Sunshine. It'll have to wait."

Within moments, he and Max were out the door.

CHAPTER EIGHTEEN

"HERE COMES YOUR MAN."

"What?" Stacy balanced on top of the ladder, a long fluorescent tube in one hand and the cover of the light fixture in the other hand. She couldn't look down to see what Millie meant.

"Burned-out bulb?" Caden's deep voice jolted her.

Stacy twisted the four-foot tube into place and snapped the plastic cover back on. She stepped to a lower rung before hopping to the floor, then shot Millie a look. Caden wasn't "her" man.

"Yes." She stooped to pick up the old tubes off the floor, but he beat her to it. "I thought these things were supposed to last a while, but it's the third time I've had to replace them in the last few months."

Caden examined the light in his hand. "This bulb isn't bad. What was it doing?"

"Flickering."

"I've already replaced the wiring for these lights, so the flickering should have stopped. Mind if I take a look at the ballast?"

The what? Before she could say anything, Caden scaled the ladder. With a speed she didn't think possible, he'd removed the cover and both bulbs.

"Hold this for a sec." He handed her the lights, then popped a cylindrical silver piece out of the frame. A few seconds later, he was on the floor, his six-foot frame towering over her.

He smelled like the ocean, fresh and salty. She swallowed and fought the urge to lean closer. *Don't look straight at him.* Instead, she focused on the silver apparatus in his hand. "What's that?"

"The starter. But it's really hard to tell if it's bad. I'll switch it out with one that's working and see if I can tell. It might be the ballast."

"And I'm guessing that's not good."

"It can get expensive, depending on what kind you have. More than likely, it has to do with the faulty wiring." He turned the starter over and over in his hand. "By the way, I'll be done with the wiring by the end of next week."

"That's great." She forced a smile. It didn't feel great. What would happen then? Would he leave like he'd planned?

Caden moved around silently as she went back to work, or tried to. Climbing to the top of the ladder again and again, he carefully checked each light fixture. She snapped her fingers at Millie and mouthed, *Stop staring at him*.

Millie's face turned red and she buried her nose back in her book. That left Stacy with the arduous task of trying not to stare herself. Easier said than done.

Caden folded the ladder. "I checked all the lights. I'll be in the attic if you need me. I'm going to get the wiring in place before it gets too hot up there."

Just like that, he was back to business.

She headed to the front of the market and Millie came to stand next to her. "Do you know that Caden and Jason Peterson have been hanging out together?"

Stacy was surprised. Millie wasn't normally one to listen to gossip. "Where did you hear that?"

"Jason's wife told Cora Lancaster, and she told Kelsey Barton, that Jason went out the other night and didn't get home until after 1:00 a.m."

"So?" She didn't give a whit about what Jason did. The man had a reputation for spending more time at the bar than with his family.

Millie pressed her lips together. "Caden brought him home."

Stacy pushed an invisible strand of hair out of her face and turned back to the cans she was counting. "You don't need to listen to a bunch of idle gossip. It just causes trouble."

Millie shrugged. "Donna saw his motorcycle there three times last week, so it's not just gossip. I know how you feel about things like that, so I just thought you should know."

There had to be a logical explanation. But she couldn't think of a single one. The best way to find out information was to come straight out and ask.

As she walked into the storeroom, Caden had his arm looped through a large role of wire and was about to climb the ladder.

"Hey." She stopped him. "Why did you have to rush off last night? Is everything okay?"

He shifted the wire from one arm to the other. "Yeah. Everything is fine. A friend needed to talk."

"Where did you go?"

He avoided her gaze. "Home."

Stacy watched him climb back into the attic. If he had nothing to hide, why was he acting so weird? Something was off.

Back at the counter, she called Frank. "When was the last time you did a drug and alcohol test on Caden?"

"A few weeks ago. Why?" Frank was quiet for a moment. "Do you have reason to believe I should do another one?"

"No, not really. Okay, maybe. One of my employees has seen him at the bar a few times and I've heard he's hanging around Jason Peterson."

"His tests have all come back clean, but I'll do another one if you're worried."

"It might be a good idea." She hung up the phone, ashamed that she'd even been thinking that.

Less than an hour later, Caden emerged from the back, hot and sweaty.

"Done for the day?"

"No." He wiped the back of his neck with a rag. "Y'all are fixing to get busy for lunch, and Frank needs me to come into the office. My parole officer wants a surprise test. I'll be back in a little while. I wanted to wait until the market closed to finish up some work anyway."

Her throat tightened. She knew his parole officer had nothing to do with it.

Caden didn't seem worried.

"Okay. See you later."

Her stomach felt like it had rocks in it as she watched him walk out the door. Would Frank tell him that she was the one who'd wanted the test? She felt guilty for doubting him. But what bothered her more was that he'd given her a reason to feel that way. One way or the other, she needed to know.

CADEN LEFT THE market and walked toward the sheriff's office. He could have driven the motorcycle, but he hadn't registered it yet and didn't want to risk getting a ticket.

As he walked, people he knew waved at him. A few even stopped and offered him and Max a ride. He wondered how they would feel about him if they knew he'd just got out of prison. He was glad they didn't. He enjoyed feeling part of the small community, even if it was only for a little while.

He had plenty of time to get to the sheriff's department, so he took his time and looked around. He couldn't remember the last time he'd wandered aimlessly. Even before prison, he'd never been one to go window-shopping or enjoy the sights. His mother, on the other hand, could spend hours in antiques stores. She would love this town.

The streets were busy now that it was almost noon. The candy store beside the market drew a large crowd, as did the restaurant across the street. The Coronado Market had its own steady stream of customers, but the people milling about town were different. It wasn't hard to figure out why. Fishermen, hunters and outdoorsmen flocked to the market for bait and camping supplies, while the more urban clientele entered Paisley's Tea Garden on the far end of the street.

Almost everyone he passed on the sidewalk said hello. Caden stepped off the sidewalk to allow two women, barely out of their teens, to stroll past. One of them slid her sunglasses down her nose to give him a once-over. He averted his gaze. There would've been a time when he'd have been flattered. Maybe even flirted back.

She elbowed her friend and smiled brightly. Too brightly. "Hello."

He nodded politely but didn't speak.

The women exchanged glances. "Maybe you can help us. Are you from around here?"

"No, ma'am, I'm not."

"Well, can you tell us which restaurant is better? The Bear's Den or the Tea Garden?"

"Sorry. I haven't eaten at either of those places."

The second woman gave him a coy smile. "Where do you usually eat?"

"The deli at the Coronado Market."

Another exchange of glances. "Is it good? Maybe we'll join you."

The woman didn't give up easily. Time to change tactics. He shrugged. "Better than the prison food I'm used to."

Her face paled. In seconds, the pair disappeared into the closest store. Caden tried not to laugh, but he couldn't help it. Maybe being an ex-con had its advantages after all.

He stopped in front of the forest service ranger station and looked at the brochures showcasing all the activities in the area. Trailheads and fishing spots in the summer, snowshoeing and snowmobiling in the winter.

Back in Tucson, Caden and his brother Patrick had spent many weekends hiking the trails of Sabino Canyon. Maybe they could explore some of the area together someday.

The knowledge that he could come back to Coronado filled him with a peace he hadn't known existed. Stacy knew who he was. She knew what he had done. And she accepted him.

How he wished he could be the person she deserved! It didn't matter that she was willing to take a chance on him. Sooner or later, the truth would come out for the rest of the town, and most people would react just like the two women on the sidewalk had. That was why he had to leave. He'd developed an attachment to the town and many of the people in it. He couldn't bear to see their faces turn away, too.

And whether Stacy wanted to admit it or not, his past would affect the future of her store. No one would want to give their business to someone associated with an ex-con.

He entered the large building that housed the sheriff's department. The receptionist greeted him with her usual terseness. Frank emerged from his office. He was friendly, but not as friendly as usual.

Caden could tell Frank was preoccupied, so he waited in the reception area after the test until Frank got the results and sent a report to his parole officer.

While he waited, he got information about registering the motorcycle and getting a driver's license for it.

"You got that old clunker running, huh?" Frank entered the lobby.

"Yes, sir," Caden said. "She runs like a top."

The sheriff nodded. "Come to my office. There's something I want to talk to you about."

Frank's tone was serious, so Caden wasted no time following him, taking his usual seat across from the desk.

Frank sat in his chair and leaned back. "Want to know why I really called you in today?"

He frowned. "I assumed Lieutenant Erikson asked you to."

"There's a rumor going around town that you've been hanging out with some of Coronado's rougher crowd."

Caden straightened. "I'm not sure what you heard, but I'm not hanging out with anyone. Not socially, anyway."

"Were you at the Watering Hole last night?"

He swallowed. It was against his parole to be inside a bar. But what about outside? "I was in the parking lot, yes."

Frank shook his head. "Your test came back clean, so I know you weren't drinking. But if you keep hanging out there, with heavy drinkers, eventually you're going to fall back in it."

Caden clenched his jaw and took a cleansing breath. "I wasn't hanging out."

"What in the blazes were you doing there, then?"

"Freddy asked me to give a few people a ride home."

"How do you give them a ride home when you don't have a car?"

"I drive their car," Caden said. "Then I hide the keys so they can't drive after I leave."

Frank crossed his arms. "And how do you leave? Walk?"

He shrugged. "I jog a lot."

Frank's mouth fell open. "You're serious, aren't you?"

Caden looked Frank straight in the eye. "I couldn't stand by and let someone make the same mistake I did."

"Does Stacy know what you're doing?"

"No. It's nobody's business." He couldn't explain why, but he didn't want anyone to know. Drawing attention to what he was doing would take away the significance of it. He did what he did for Grayson, not accolades or attention.

"You're almost done with the store. What's your plan?" Frank's demeanor was more relaxed now.

"My brother Patrick has offered me a job in Prescott. I'll probably go there."

Frank nodded. "You ever think about staying in Coronado? I could use someone at the campground with your handyman skills and knowledge of horses."

There was nothing he'd like more than to stay. "I appreciate the offer, but I've done what I came here to do. The Mitchells arrive tomorrow, so I'll spend the rest of this week with them, and after the weekend, I'll finish up the store. Then I can leave."

"What about that mutt?" Frank nodded at Max. "You can't take him on a motorcycle."

Caden laughed. "Actually, he loves riding on it."

"This, I will have to see." Frank reached out and shook his hand. "This is the busiest week of the summer, so if I don't get a chance to see you before you leave, thanks for everything you've done."

He shook Frank's hand and exited the building with Max at his side. He didn't like the feeling that this was goodbye. Staying wasn't an option, but leaving felt wrong.

He left the main road and walked on a few of the dirt side roads that snaked through the town until he got to the store.

The trail between the market and the cabins was smoother than it had been just a few weeks ago. How many times had he walked back and forth? The crisp air, infused with the scent of the forest, lightened his spirits.

Not once while he was growing up had he ever imagined leaving the desert. He loved the emptiness, and he even loved the heat. Now the thought of going back made his heart beat harder. He stopped walking and tilted his head up to see the tops of the tall pine trees, whispering in the wind. The chatter of squirrels and birds surrounded him. This was the furthest thing from the desert he could find.

He closed his eyes and inhaled the woodsy aroma. This place was making him rethink his plans. Not that he could stay here. But maybe he could find someplace to belong. Would Prescott be that place?

Just like that, his light mood was gone, replaced by weariness. It was too easy to imagine what life would be like here, if things were different. If the accident had never happened. Of course, if it hadn't happened, he wouldn't be here now. The thought bothered him more than it should.

STACY GLANCED OUT the large picture window facing the forest trail for the hundredth time. Where was he? He'd said he'd be back before the market closed. He had thirty minutes.

The Reed sisters sat at the table, eating ice cream cones and chatting. Well, not really chatting. It was more of an interrogation. Stacy ignored their questions the best she could.

Max appeared first. Her eyes searched the tree line, looking for Caden. There. He walked slowly, the phone to his ear. Just before reaching the dirt parking lot of the store, he stopped, presumably to finish his conversation. He tucked the phone in his back pocket and made a beeline for the entrance to the store.

Pretending to be busy cleaning the deli, she waited for the bells on the door to ring before turning around. "Oh. Hi." She smiled. "You're late, aren't you?"

Caden walked around the counter into the deli area. He wrapped his arms around her and held her for a moment. She was so shocked at the display of affection that all she could do was hug him back.

She inhaled the scent of shampoo and evergreen. He spent so much time outside, he even smelled like the forest.

"Thank you." He pressed a kiss to her forehead.

"For what?" She leaned back to stare into his clear gray eyes.

He touched his forehead to hers. "For forcing me to be alive again."

Her heart pounded at his nearness. He held her tight and she had no desire to move. "And to think, all this time I was working with a zombie." She leaned in to sniff his neck. "You smell a lot better than a zombie, though."

Deep laughter shook his chest and he pulled her closer. "I'm going to miss you."

"Then don't leave."

Applause from the table area erupted. Edith and Margaret stood at their table, clapping.

"Well done, young man, well done," Edith whooped.

Margaret elbowed her. "Maybe we should go outside and let them finish."

"And miss the show? No way."

Caden stepped away. "I better get to work."

Stacy watched him stroll to the storeroom, Max at his heels.

"Told you this was going to be an entertaining summer." Edith winked at Stacy.

Her checks burned, but she refused to let the elderly woman bait her. She stepped out from behind the deli counter. "Are you ladies done? I'm going to start getting ready to lock up soon."

"Of course, dear." Margaret dabbed her lips with a napkin. "How's your mother?"

And just like that, her balloon burst. All the giddiness from Caden's hug disappeared. "Not good."

She didn't want to talk about how her mother hadn't eaten in days, or how she'd lost so much weight that she was barely recognizable. Stacy wiped the counters down for the third time when bony fingers wrapped around her arm.

Edith gave her a solemn look. "It'll be all right. You'll be all right. This is the way your mother wanted it. She didn't want you to carry the burden of her disease."

Stacy swallowed. "I need to check on Caden."

She escaped to the back of the store. Dust hung in the air, and sheets of drywall had been pulled away from the wall in between the storage room and the store, exposing the wires that had been run down the wall from the ceiling.

Caden had warned her that it would be a messy project. She was glad he could wait until after the Fourth of July weekend to start in the main part of the store. He was turned away from her, and the muscles in his back rippled as he twisted the screwdriver in his hand.

"What happened to the electric drill?"

"Battery died." He never looked up from his work.

"I forgot to plug it in again." It was her fault. When the delivery truck dropped off the milk, one of the jugs had leaked all over the floor. She'd unplugged his drill to move it while she'd mopped. "I'm sorry."

He dropped his arms and turned around. "Doesn't matter. I'm done now."

"Are you ready for the Mitchells tomorrow?"

"Looking forward to it." Caden started putting the tools back in his toolbox. "By the way, do you have cabins available this weekend?"

She grinned. "I only have two left. Those will probably be gone before the weekend."

It had been a long time since the campground had been so full. She had Caden to thank for it. All month, reviews had praised the campground. That wouldn't be possible without his hard work.

"They are now." He gave her a crooked smile. "My family is coming up for the weekend."

"Really?" This was a big step for him. When he'd first arrived, he wouldn't even talk to them on the phone. "Is that who you were talking to when you walked up?"

He nodded. "I figured it was time I faced them."

"That's great. Family is important."

He arched one eyebrow at her. "Isn't that the pot calling the kettle black?"

"What do you mean?"

"Don't you think it's time you talked to Vince?"

"No." She bit her lip. Ever since she'd found out he'd paid the bill at the nursing home, she'd been thinking about that. "All right, yes. I'm just not sure how to go about it."

"Why don't you invite him to the barbecue at the campground on Friday night?"

She cocked her head. "You know I don't have time to plan a barbecue this late in the week."

He grinned. "My mother is the ultimate party planner, and my father is pretty amazing at cooking meat."

A barbecue at the campground? Just like when her grandfather was alive. "I couldn't let your parents do that. Besides, it's probably too late to order that much meat."

Caden shook his head. "My parents own a ranch. He'll bring his own meat and everything else we need. And you can't say no, because he'll use it as a tax write-off."

"I don't know what to say." Stacy placed one hand to her racing heart. "Why are you doing all this for me?"

He pressed his lips together, his brow furrowed. "You know why." His voice was little more than a whisper.

Her heart dropped. It was always about

Grayson. She admired that about him. But a selfish part of her wanted it to be about her.

"Please." He stepped closer. "Let me do this for you."

For you. She swallowed. "Okay. Thank you."

CHAPTER NINETEEN

CADEN STEPPED OFF the sidewalk to let a crowd of people go by. He'd never expected to see this many people in Coronado. Red, white and blue banners hung from the eaves of each storefront, and American flags flew every twenty feet on both sides of the main street. Stacy hadn't been kidding when she'd said Coronado went all out for Independence Day.

The small paper bag he carried was full of brochures from the forest service station. The forest ranger had allowed him to leave flyers advertising the Whispering Pines Campground and, in exchange, he'd promised to leave a few brochures in all the cabins so the guests could see what the White Mountains had to offer.

Everyone who walked past smiled and said hello. He reciprocated and it felt good. When he'd first arrived in town, he'd been burdened with guilt from Grayson's death. Then when he'd kept the truth from Stacy, he'd felt as if he would break under the weight of his lie. Now that the truth was out, he felt like a new man.

Even Max noticed. He bounced next to Caden as they walked down the street. He stopped at the hardware store to see if Denny needed anything. The elderly man beamed when Caden walked in.

"How are you doing, Denny?" Caden leaned on the counter.

"Never better." Denny reached behind the counter to produce a dog treat for Max. "Looks like this guy is all healed up."

Caden nodded. He suspected Max would always have a slight limp, but it didn't seem to hamper him. "I just wanted to make sure you had my number if you needed anything this weekend."

Denny handed Caden a pen and a piece of paper. "I hear you're planning on leaving us soon."

"Yes, sir." Caden wrote his cell phone number down. "As soon as I'm done with the store. Should be sometime next week."

"We'll miss you around here."

"I'll miss being around here," Caden said. Next, he stopped at the market to pick up the picnic supplies Stacy had packed for the Mitchells' trail ride.

The market was bustling. Both Donna and Millie worked the registers and Stacy was in the deli. Caden caught her eye. She smiled as she wrapped up sandwiches for waiting customers.

When she finished, she carried a large backpack over to him. "Here's sandwiches and chips for the Mitchells' ride today. Remember, don't go down the washed-out trail, even though it's the best."

"I fixed it."

Her eyes widened. "What do you mean you fixed it?"

"Last weekend I went down there and filled in the parts that had been washed out. I checked it yesterday and it's good to go."

She shook her head. "Thanks. I don't know how you have time to do all that."

He started to tell her he'd needed something to do when she'd forbidden him from coming to the store. Instead, he gave her a wide grin. "None of your business."

She laughed. "Okay, cowboy. You got me. Now go take care of the Mitchells. And give Maze an extra scoop of grain when you get back."

Caden took the backpack full of food and Stacy turned to greet a waiting customer. Her smile lit up the room.

It was too bad her uncle was the one who now owned the campground. It seemed to be where her heart really was. As he topped the ridge and looked down on the cabins, he thought of Stacy's vision. He pictured a rep-lica Western town at the main entrance. The field behind the barn could hold dozens of horses. There was plenty of space to build some smaller pens for riding lessons.

There was even enough room to build a main house. A house big enough to raise chil-dren in. A house built for a woman who'd lost one family and gained another one, only to lose most of it, too. A house for a family that would never leave her.

His chest ached. He wanted to be the one to give her that family. But that wasn't part of the deal. Caden shook his head. He needed to stop dwelling on what he wished could happen and concentrate on the here and now.

He stopped at every cabin and left bro-chures with the tenants. By the time he'd made his way across the entire campground, the sun was climbing and the heat was rising.

At the barn, the Mitchell family and their

friends were already busy. The horses were saddled and they were ready to go. One palomino caught his eye. He stroked the mare's nose. "This must be Maze."

Mr. Mitchell nodded. "Yes, although we almost didn't bring her."

"Why not?"

"Every time we bring her, she is depressed for weeks when we leave." Mr. Mitchell gave Caden a sad smile. "She still thinks of this as her home."

Caden frowned. "It could be again. Would you sell her to me?"

The man laughed. "Are you serious?"

"Yes, sir."

He clapped Caden on the back. "Let's talk about it while we take these kids on a ride they won't forget."

"Sure thing."

Caden saddled the same horse he'd ridden on his trail ride with Stacy. As he did, he wondered if Stacy would approve of his offer to buy Maze back. She wanted to do things herself. He could understand that but, sometimes, everyone could use some help.

Once the group was mounted and ready to head out, he gave quick instructions. "Parts of the trail are a little narrow and windy, but trust your horse. We'll stop at the bottom of the trail to have lunch and the horses can get water from the stream. Now, does everyone have their water?"

They nodded and Caden led a group of fifteen riders toward the trail. The group chatted and asked him questions about the area. He kept a close eye on one of the teenage girls. She didn't seem very comfortable on the horse, and the horse knew it.

Caden maneuvered his horse close to her. "Take a deep breath. Relax."

The girl nodded. "But he's so big. What if he takes off?"

"First, he is a she. Second, she's not going to just take off. Horses are herd animals. They prefer to stay with their buddies. And if she does take off, most likely she'll head straight to the barn to get some food, so all you have to do is hold on until you get there."

He gave her a few tips on how to relax in the saddle and she seemed to do better. Still, he wanted to stay close to her when the trail got steeper. To distract her, he kept chatting with her. As they got close to the part of the trail that had to be repaired, he asked her questions about school, friends, her plans for the future.

By the time they reached the meadow, he felt like he knew about everyone in her family. He pointed out the grove of trees where he'd set up the picnic, and the groups dispersed to explore the meadow on their own. He dismounted and was unpacking the backpack.

"You did a good job with Amber." Mr. Mitchell had also dismounted, and he came over to Caden. "She fell off a horse when she was a kid and has been scared ever since. I was actually surprised when my daughter was able to convince her to come with us today."

"Sometimes the key is keeping them from being focused on the problem by distracting them with something else." The same way Stacy had distracted him when they'd driven Max to Springerville.

"I have some soldiers that could benefit from your techniques. Maybe I'll send them up here for a weekend."

"Soldiers?"

"I'm a psychologist at the veterans administration. I work with a lot of young men suffering from various forms of post-traumatic stress disorder."

Caden nodded. He had seen his share of

therapists while in prison. The PTSD he suffered from the accident had trumped any PTSD symptoms he may have had from Afghanistan. "I've heard horses can be very calming for that."

"Now that you're running the campground, maybe we can talk about the possibility of sending a few soldiers up here once a month or so."

Caden just nodded. Maybe the next person she hired could do it.

His phone dinged and he checked the text message.

Gonna be a busy night. Hope you're available.

He'd text Freddy back later.

STACY WAS WRAPPING green chili burros and placing them under the heating lamp. The first set she'd made had disappeared in less than an hour. She couldn't remember the last time the little market had been so busy.

Millie walked around the deli counter, tying an apron around her waist. "You're needed up front for cabin rentals."

"Did you tell them we were full?"

"Yeah, but she wanted to speak to you."

Great. She hated starting off the day with an argument. Hopefully they would accept her word for it.

A lady stood at the main counter. Stacy almost groaned. She exuded sophistication from her freshly styled hair to the manicured nails that were emphasized by the sizable diamond on her left hand.

Stacy adjusted her ponytail, tucking loose strands of hair back into the rubber band. "Can I help you?"

"Yes." The woman flashed her a bright smile. "I'm here for two cabin rentals."

"I'm sorry, ma'am." Stacy shook her head. "Like Millie told you, we are full up this weekend."

The door opened and a tall, stocky man entered. Wisps of red hair poked out from under his cowboy hat. "Did you get us checked in yet?"

Stacy glanced at the man, then back at the woman. The woman's eyes were gray. An unusual steel gray. "Are you Caden's parents?"

"Yes." The woman held out her hand. "I'm Jackie Murphy. You must be Stacy."

"I am." Stacy shook her hand. Caden had mentioned her? What else had he told them?

"Caden is probably at the campground, if you want to head over there."

"We called him to tell him we were here, but he's not back from his trail ride yet. He told us to come here."

She glanced at all the customers in the store. "I can't really leave right now."

"I can help." Vince stood between two aisles with an armload of groceries.

Stacy's heart did a flip. Where had he come from?

Vince set his stuff on the end of the counter. "I can run the cash register until you get back."

"I don't think that's a very good idea."

He nodded toward Donna. "Donna won't let me get away with anything, will you?"

Donna grinned at Stacy. "I'll watch him like a hawk."

Vince spoke softly enough that the Murphys couldn't hear him. "Please, Anastacia. Let me do this for you."

Conflict raged within her. If she let him do this, she would be letting him back in her life. Did she dare give him a second chance? She glanced at Donna.

"It'll be fine. I'll put him to work. Besides, you won't be gone that long. Go get these people settled in the cabins."

"I'll be back as soon as I can." She opened the cabinet holding the cabin keys. "Follow me."

She walked outside to find a large group of people waiting.

"Is this Stacy?" A tall strawberry blonde stepped forward.

"That's me."

The woman grinned and wrapped her in a large bear hug. "I'm Sarah, Caden's oldest sister."

Suddenly, she was surrounded by Murphys. They all talked at once. Caden's mother rescued her, and a few minutes later, she was driving toward the campground, Jackie sitting in the vehicle with her.

"Forgive my enthusiastic family," she said. "We're just so grateful to you for bringing Caden back to us."

Stacy frowned. "I don't understand."

Jackie reached over and squeezed her hand. "Seven years ago, I thought I'd lost him forever, and it had nothing to do with him going to prison. He shut himself off from us and himself."

"He was dealing with a lot." Stacy wasn't sure what else to say.

"Yes," Jackie agreed. "He was so overcome

with guilt that he didn't think he deserved to have any happiness or any kind of life. The fact that you've been able to forgive him gave him the strength to come out of that place to a better one."

"I don't really think I had anything to do with it. I think he found it out himself."

She turned onto the dirt road that led to the cabins. As she drove by the barns, she noticed a flurry of activity. People and horses were scattered both inside and outside the barn.

"It looks like they're back from the trail ride. Do you want to stop and say hi?"

Jackie stared at the barns. Her gaze scanned the crowd. "No. Don't interrupt him."

Stacy swallowed. The pain in Jackie's voice was obvious. Stacy was sure there was nothing Jackie wanted more than to storm into that barn and hug her son.

She stopped at the cabins she'd reserved for Caden's family. She unlocked the doors and waited for them to get their luggage and enter. As she went in one of the cabins, her eyes fell on the counter. She walked over and picked up the brochure. Had Caden done this?

"I'm going to need room to store this beef overnight," Caden's father called from the door. "I'll start smoking it first thing in the morning and it'll be ready tomorrow night."

Stacy didn't know anything about smoking meat. "We can make room for the beef in the coolers in the store, but how are you going to cook it? We only have a few small grills in the common areas."

"Don't you worry about that," a familiar voice behind her said. "He cooks it in a pit in the ground and it turns out perfect every time."

"Caden!"

"Hi, Dad."

Moments later, Caden was lost in a swarm of people. Stacy's heart warmed at seeing how excited his family was to see him. What would it be like to be part of such a large family?

Speaking of family, she needed to get back to the market so Vince could leave. She slipped out the door and around the crowd of Murphys. She got into the truck, but before she could leave, someone knocked on her window.

"Hey," Caden said when she rolled her window down. "My mom wants you to come over for dinner after you close the store."

"I think you need some time with your family."

"Please," Caden said. "It would mean a lot to me. I need you."

Stacy's heart raced when he reached in and touched her cheek with one finger. "Okay. I'll try."

She went back to the market and Vince was still behind the register.

"I'm back. You can go now." She stepped behind the counter.

Vince nodded. "Do you need me to do anything? I can stock, clean up, whatever."

Stacy lifted her chin. What she needed was someone she could count on all the time. Before she could open her mouth to answer, Donna spoke up.

"Vince, you could restock the soda shelf."

He gave a half salute and headed for the storeroom.

Stacy turned to Donna. "What are you doing? We don't need his help."

Donna shook her head. "Yes, we do. You should have seen him. We got slammed right after you left and Vince never missed a beat. He really saved us this afternoon."

Stacy bit her lip. Could Vince have changed?

She had initially judged Caden too harshly. Had she done the same thing with her father?

STACY CLOSED THE market later than normal. People came in all day. If she'd stayed open until nine o'clock that night, the market still would have had customers. If she hadn't wanted to go see how Caden was doing with his family, she may have stayed.

She didn't like showing up at the cabin with nothing to offer. She should've baked a pie or something. Like she'd had time for that.

Loud country music blared from the cabin that the elder Murphys were in. She knocked on the door and waited. A few minutes later, Sarah opened the door.

"Stacy, come in." She swung the door wide. "Stacy's here."

She was greeted like an old friend, even though she hadn't officially met most of them. Patrick waved at her from the large table in the dining area. She scanned the room. There was no sign of Caden or Max.

"Hi." A petite and very pregnant woman held out her hand. "I'm Beth, Caden's other sister."

Stacy tried to remember what Caden had

told her about all of his siblings. "Your husband is in the air force, right?"

"Yes." Beth pointed at one of the men at the table with Patrick. "That's Greg. I'd introduce you, but I never interrupt the men when they're playing pitch."

"Pitch?"

Sarah joined them. "It's a card game. We learned to play when we were young but, apparently, it's difficult to learn. But you're not considered a true member of the family until you know how to play."

"I see."

"I'm sure Caden will teach you soon." Beth looked over her shoulder. "Where is he? Didn't he come in with you?"

"I haven't seen him since this afternoon." Her chest tightened. Maybe Caden hadn't been as ready to face his family as he'd thought. Was he hiding out somewhere?

"Huh?" Beth shrugged. "He got a phone call and said he had to go. We all thought he went to get you."

Another mysterious phone call. A bad feeling rolled itself into the pit of her stomach.

"This is the rowdy cabin." Sarah looped her arm through Stacy's. "The other cabin is nice and quiet. Mom is over there putting the kids to bed."

"No, she's not," Beth said, rolling her eyes. "She's letting them sit up late, eat popcorn and tell spooky stories that will take us weeks to get out of their heads."

Stacy smiled. "How many children do you have?"

"I have two," Sarah said. "Sean Junior and his wife, Lynn, have five."

"Lynn is at the quiet cabin," Beth whispered. "She can't handle getting too far away from her children. We all think she's a little overprotective, but we love her for it."

Stacy could hear the affection in her voice. She pointed at Beth's protruding belly. "Is this your first?"

"Oh, no. This one will be number three."

A dark-haired woman stood behind Patrick's chair, one hand on each of his shoulders. "Is that Patrick's wife? How many children do they have?"

The sisters exchanged glances. "None yet. They lost a baby a few months ago."

Sarah whispered, "We think she's pregnant again, but we're afraid to ask."

Stacy's gaze zeroed in on the woman's midsection. There did seem to be a small bump, but it was hard to tell.

A loud roar from the card game got their attention. Caden's father raked in the cards. With his cowboy hat off, the resemblance between him and Caden was much more noticeable. Mr. Murphy looked more like a rancher than a district attorney.

He got up from the table and came to greet Stacy. "Glad you could make it over. Caden showed me around this afternoon. You've got a fine operation going here."

"I can't take much credit. The campground belongs to my uncle."

"Yes, but you do most of the work, don't you?"

Her phone vibrated in her pocket. Maybe it was Caden. She pulled it out and checked the caller ID. It was the nursing home. "Excuse me for a moment."

She stepped outside the cabin before she answered the call.

It was the evening charge nurse. "Miss Tedford, I wanted to let you know that you need to get here right away."

Her heart leaped. "Why? What's going on?"

"Your mother's condition is declining rapidly and, to be honest, we aren't sure if she'll make it through the night."

"I'll be there as soon as I can." She disconnected the call.

She opened the cabin door. Beth and Sarah were both standing by the kitchen counter, dipping potato chips in dip. They glanced at her. "Are you okay?"

She shook her head. "No. I have to go. My mother is ill."

She took off for her apartment as fast as she could go in the dark. As she jogged, she dialed Caden's number. He answered on the third ring. When she heard the sound of his voice, she let out a sob.

"What's wrong, Stacy?"

"My mom," she said between gasps. "I'm going to the nursing home. Can you go with me?"

Silence.

"Caden?"

"I have to take care of something first, but I'll get there as soon as I can."

"Thank you."

She slipped the phone into her back pocket and started running. She was out of breath by the time she got to her apartment and grabbed the keys to her truck from inside.

At the stop sign at the main intersection, she turned left toward the nursing home.

Across the road was the Watering Hole, and something caught her eyes.

Caden was standing outside. His arm was wrapped around another man and they were stumbling toward a car.

Bile rose in her throat. Millie had been right. Caden was hanging around with the party crowd. How could he? His family had come all this way to see him and he was at the bar.

She sped on to the nursing home without him.

CHAPTER TWENTY

IT HAD TAKEN almost two hours for Caden to get Stephen Jackson home. First, the man had fought getting in the car. Then Caden had had to stop several times and wait for him to throw up. Finally, it had taken the man forever to find the keys to his house. Caden had deposited him safely on the couch, then hid the keys to his vehicle in the mailbox.

Stephen's house was three miles out of town. Although Caden jogged the entire way back, it felt like forever. He arrived at the bar and Max jumped up on the seat of the bike. Caden pulled the shirt over his head and tucked the dog close to him.

"Hold on, Max," he told the dog. "Stacy needs us, so we'll go faster than usual."

At the nursing home, he parked the bike, ran inside and stopped outside the door to her mother's room. He peeked inside. Vince was standing next to Stacy. Vince's arm was wrapped protectively around his daughter and they both had tears streaming down their faces. In the background, a nurse pulled the sheet up to cover Melissa's body.

Caden's heart broke for her, but he was happy to see that Vince was with her. He stepped into the room and waited for her to notice him. He didn't want to interrupt them.

Vince kissed her on top of the head. "I'm going to get us both some coffee. I'll be right back." She nodded and stepped back. That was when her tear-rimmed eyes saw him.

Vince patted his shoulder. "Thanks for being here. I'll give you a moment."

Caden held his arms out to hold her. "Sorry I'm late."

Her face was hard and cold. "Get out."

"What?"

She glanced at the bed where her mother lay before she opened the door and stepped into the hallway.

He had no choice but to follow her. "What can I do?"

She lifted her chin. "Nothing. Go back to the bar with your friends."

He'd never heard her voice so full of venom. She'd either seen him or his motorcycle at the bar. "It's not what you think."

"I don't care." She blew her nose with a tissue. "I'm not going to say anything to Frank this time, but only because your family is here and I don't want to see them hurt again. But as soon as this weekend is over, I never want to see you again."

He swallowed. "What do you mean 'say anything this time'?"

"I don't know how you managed to pass the drug and alcohol test last time, but it doesn't matter anymore. You're done."

Anger built in his chest. "You're the reason I got called in for a test? Why didn't you just ask me?"

"Because I knew you'd lie to me," she said. "Just like you lied about who you really were and why you were here. What else did you lie about? Who else have you lied to?"

He knew she was lashing out because she was in pain and grieving her mother, but now he was mad, too. "I've never lied to you."

"You skate around the truth, just like my dad always did. He didn't think what he did was lying, either." She turned away and ran her hands through her hair. "I can't deal with this right now. Just leave."

Caden gritted his teeth. "You're getting good at pushing people away, aren't you? If you push them away, you don't have to deal with the truth."

"You're one to talk, aren't you? You pushed your family away for seven years."

"At least I pushed them away because of my own mistake, not one I thought they made."

She shook her head. "Just go, please."

The coldness in her voice hurt. The fact that she'd jumped to conclusions and didn't give him a chance to explain hurt more. He turned and walked away.

"WHERE'S CADEN?" VINCE came into the room. "I got him coffee, too."

Stacy wiped the tears from her eyes. "I think he wanted something a little stronger than coffee."

Two nurses and a couple of orderlies came into the room. The charge nurse looked at them sadly. "I'm sorry, but we need to take Mrs. Tedford now. Who should we call when the morgue releases her body?"

"Montgomery's funeral home," Vince answered. "Phillip has all of her information."

"Very good," the nurse said. "Feel free to stay as long as you like."

Stacy felt numb. She looked at Vince. "I need to get out of here."

He nodded. "I'll walk you out."

"What did you mean by Phillip has all Mom's information?"

"Missy met with him years ago and arranged everything. He even came to visit her every so often to check and see if anything had changed."

Stacy pressed her fingers to her mouth to stop a sob. "It makes sense, I guess. She knew what was happening. But why didn't she just tell me? I would have taken care of it. I *wanted* to take care of it."

"But she didn't want you to," Vince said. "She knew it would be hard enough for you to accept losing one more mother, and she was afraid of how it would affect you. Everything is arranged and paid for."

How many times had her mother said she didn't want to be a burden to her? Yet going into a nursing home had been more of a financial burden than anything else. Stacy let out a bitter laugh. "She arranged for her death, but not for her care."

Vince squeezed her hand. "She arranged for that, too. But I messed it up."

"You mean by drinking away all the profits from the market and stealing the money from Mom's savings account?"

He looked at her. "You can accuse me of a lot of things, but you need to get your facts straight. I'm a recovering alcoholic—I admit that. But I never took your mother's money."

Stacy opened her mouth to argue, but she stopped. She was too emotionally drained to argue. At the front door, she told him goodnight and got back in her vehicle to drive home.

The apartment felt emptier than normal. Her mother's presence seemed to be everywhere. Her gaze fell on her mother's rolltop desk. She had refused to snoop through it before. Was there a receipt for what had been paid to the funeral home? With shaking fingers, she opened the desk and looked through the documents inside.

An envelope held paper checks from the bank. Stacy opened it up. She found checks written by either her mother or her father, stamped Paid. They must have been written before debit cards became more common.

She flipped through the checks, mostly out of curiosity.

Dozens of checks had been written by Vince, all with names of medical facilities. The notation on the checks all read *Melissa Tedford*. She opened her laptop and searched the names of the medical facilities. They were located all over the country and specialized in experimental treatments for everything from Huntington's to Alzheimer's. So this was where all the money had gone. Vince had been looking for a cure for her mother.

She kept digging and found the receipts for both the funeral home and the nursing home. Her mother had indeed planned far ahead. Not far enough, though. The last check in the envelope was for a drug and alcohol rehabilitation center in Phoenix. The check was dated shortly before Vince had disappeared from Coronado. Stacy recognized her mother's scrawled handwriting. Her mother had sent Vince to a rehab center. Vince hadn't taken the money and run away.

The hole in her chest grew bigger. Nothing she'd found changed the fact that Vince was an alcoholic, but it completely changed what she thought of him. Just like nothing would change the fact that Caden had been to prison for drinking and driving.

She had seen him at the bar. So how come he'd seemed sober when he was at the nursing home?

CHAPTER TWENTY-ONE

STACY WOKE UP on the couch. The envelope of canceled checks lay on the floor and her eyes were swollen from all the tears. She stood and stretched. The clock on the microwave said it was eight thirty. She gasped and ran through the entrance to the market.

Millie and Donna were already working. Millie was in the deli section and Donna was behind the cash register. Millie came out of the deli when she saw her.

"Thanks for being here. I didn't mean to sleep in. I hope we didn't lose a lot of customers when I didn't open this morning."

"Donna opened at the regular time this morning, so you didn't lose any customers."

Stacy always opened the store. "How did Donna know to do that?"

"Caden suggested it. He called us both to let us know. I'm so sorry about your mom. We're both going to be here all day so you can take care of things."

Stacy looked around the store. Everything seemed to be running smoothly.

Millie added, "And Vince called and said he would pick you up at noon to go to the funeral home."

"I'm going to shower. Please call me if you need anything."

On her way back to the apartment, she noticed that all the beef Caden's father had stored in the refrigerated cooler was gone. He'd said he would put the meat on to cook this morning. Had he? Or had everyone packed up and left?

After she showered, she headed to the campground. There was no way to save the barbecue if the Murphys were gone. But why would they stay after she'd ordered Caden to leave?

Mr. Mitchell's SUV was at the barn, so she pulled off the road. She walked into the barn and saw him brushing down one of his horses. Maze stuck her head over the gate and nickered at her. She stopped and stroked Maze's nose.

"That girl is glad to be home." Mr. Mitchell came out of the stall he was in.

She leaned her forehead against Maze's neck. How she longed to climb on the horse and ride until all her problems went away.

"I'm glad to have her home too, even if it's just for a few more days."

"Few more days?" He frowned. "What are you planning on doing with her?"

"I mean when you take her back to your house."

"I'm not. Caden convinced me that you needed her more than I did. He bought her."

Stacy's head jerked up. "When?"

"We talked about it on the trail ride, and he paid me this morning. He said it was for you." Mr. Mitchell's eyes grew wide. "Oh, no. I bet it was going to be a surprise. Don't tell him I ruined it."

Her mind raced. Caden had bought Maze back for her. Was he trying to buy her off to keep her from telling Frank about the bar? But the trail ride had happened before that…

"I stopped by to see if the barbecue was canceled."

"Canceled? I don't think so. They've got enough meat in the ground to feed an army. My wife and daughter are helping with all the sides."

"What about Caden?"

"Who do you think dug the pits for the meat?"

Stacy got back in her truck and drove into

the campground. Outside the Murphys' cabins, smoke drifted in the air. It seemed everyone in the camp was outside. She didn't want to risk another scene with Caden, so she turned around and went home.

CADEN SAW STACY turn around. His pulse thundered in his ears. Was she here to make him leave? She'd told him to leave after the weekend. Why hadn't she demanded he leave right then? Had she wanted to give him more time with his family? No, most likely she'd wanted to keep things pleasant for the Mitchells.

"Isn't that Stacy?" Patrick poked Caden's shoulder.

"Yes."

Patrick quirked one eyebrow. "Aren't you going to see what she needs?"

"If she wants to talk to me, she can come to me." Caden shrugged.

He wasn't going to go after her. Not this time. He'd done everything he could to redeem himself in her eyes. But it wasn't enough. It wasn't even enough to make her ask him. She'd just made assumptions. That was something he couldn't get over.

"Caden," one of the teenage boys called, "can we go on a trail ride?"

Patrick grinned. "Sounds like fun. I'm coming, too."

The rest of the morning was spent at the meadow. The teenagers would've stayed all day, but Patrick had promised them there would be a dance after the barbecue.

"A dance?" Caden asked his brother as they headed back up the trail.

"What's a barbecue without a dance? Wait until you hear my playlist. It'll have them dancing for hours."

Patrick tipped his cowboy hat back. "Is Stacy coming to the barbecue?"

"I don't know. She's not exactly speaking to me right now."

"Uh-oh. What did you do?" Patrick pulled his horse to a stop. "Whatever it is, just apologize so we can move on."

"I didn't do anything to apologize for." Caden was a little irritated that Patrick blamed him so quickly.

Patrick must have picked up on it, because he changed the subject. "How's the job going?"

The rest of the ride back to the barn centered on the job at the store. Originally, Stacy had agreed to close the market for one day the following week so Caden would have full access to the store. He needed to run the new wires down the walls and connect them to the outlets, and that required the electricity to be shut off.

Stacy would be too busy with her mother's funeral to be worried about what he was doing. The market would probably be closed for a few days. He wasn't going to walk away and leave the job half done. What was the old saying? It was better to ask for forgiveness rather than permission? Too bad Stacy wasn't good at giving either one.

BY DARK, THE barbecue was in full swing. A makeshift dance floor had been set up in the middle of the common area. Tables had been arranged all along the edges. One table held meat, one held drinks, one held side dishes, and the last held desserts. Caden had to hand it to his mother. She was a genius at getting everyone in the camp to pitch in and work together.

Mr. Mitchell found him sitting alone at a picnic table. "Nice shindig," he said at Caden's approach.

Caden nodded. "Yes. It turned out well."

"I hope you'll stick around here for a while. I have to be honest—this was probably going to be our last year here."

"Why?" Caden wasn't going to volunteer any information yet.

"Every year, the place was getting more and more run-down. Coy showed up long enough for a trail ride or two, but he didn't go out of his way to make sure we had a good time. We stopped bringing clients with us several years ago."

"Will you be back next year?" Caden held his breath, waiting for the answer.

"Absolutely!" Mr. Mitchell nodded. "This is the best time we've had in a while. You've worked absolute wonders with the teenagers. Even Amber looks forward to getting on a horse."

"I'm glad."

"And don't worry about Stacy. You'll both get through this little lovers' spat and be back together in no time."

Caden rubbed his hands on the denim of his jeans. It was more than a spat. In a way, he was almost glad it had happened. At least now he could leave with a clear conscience.

He couldn't pursue any type of relationship with her. Not without betraying Grayson.

And that was one thing he wouldn't do.

CHAPTER TWENTY-TWO

STACY COULDN'T BRING herself to open the market on Monday morning. Donna and Millie had insisted on keeping the market open through the weekend. It was the busiest one of the year and Stacy was grateful that they'd helped out so much. But she couldn't ask them to work all week. She put a sign up in the window that said she would reopen on Thursday, the day after her mother's funeral.

She hadn't heard from Caden. By all accounts, the barbecue had been a huge success. Mr. and Mrs. Mitchell had stopped by her apartment on their way home. They'd offered their condolences and thanked her for the best time they'd had in years, and promised to be back the following summer.

Her mother's funeral was simple and exactly how Melissa had wanted it. It all seemed to pass in a blur. Stacy had known for years that Huntington's disease would kill her mother, but it didn't make it hurt any less.

After leaving the cemetery, Stacy drove over to the barn and took Maze on a long ride. She chose a different path than the one used for the trail rides. This trail led to a meadow as well.

She lay down under a tall pine and watched the squirrels play in the trees. For the last several years, her life had been consumed with taking care of her mother, at least financially. Every decision she'd made had been based on being able to cover her mother's care.

Without that expense, life would be easier now. Easier, but empty. What was she supposed to do now?

Her thoughts drifted to Caden. He was in the same boat. Now that he'd told her about Grayson, would he go work for his brother in Prescott? Would he go back to Tucson? She missed him, but the fact that he hadn't tried to defend himself spoke volumes. She needed to get him out of her head.

She took her time riding back to the barn and putting the tack away. She fed Maze and brushed her until her arms hurt. Finally, she couldn't put off going home any longer. When she got back to her apartment, Vince was waiting outside.

"I thought we could talk."

Stacy unlocked her door and let him in. "What do you want to talk about?"

Vince glanced around the apartment. "You always did like lots of color."

She sat on the sofa and hugged a bright yellow cushion to her stomach. "What do you want?"

He sat on the far end of the sofa, rubbing his hands up and down his thighs. "I'm sorry, Anastacia. I'm so sorry I wasn't there for you when you needed me. I'm sorry I let you down. Can you ever forgive me?"

Vince expected her to say no. She could see it in his eyes. He expected her to say no, but he'd asked anyway. Maybe he'd needed to say it as much as she'd needed to hear it. A lump formed in her throat and she licked her lips. He was all she had left.

"Yes, Dad." She moved over to sit next to him. "I forgive you."

He pulled her into his arms like he had when she was a little girl and hugged her. "Thank you, *chemi mze*."

Her heart skipped. *My sunshine*. Caden called her Sunshine, too.

Stacy pulled away from him and stood up. "I'm glad you're here." She walked over to the dining room table and found the bill marked Paid In Full. "Thank you. I don't know how you did it, but thank you."

Vince looked at the paper. "I didn't do it."

"What do you mean? Of course you did. Who else could have done it?"

"Caden loaned me the money," Vince said.

She let out a whistle. "He really goes all out to earn his redemption."

"If that's what you think, you're a bigger fool than I am." Vince stood. "He didn't even want you to know."

He walked over to the door. "It's been a long day. I'll work the market in the morning so you can sleep in."

"You don't have to do that."

"I find myself with a lot of free time on my hands," he said sadly. "I need something to do."

After he left, she sank down into the sofa cushions. It had been a long day. Her body felt as if she'd run a marathon. Every part of her was drained, physically and emotionally.

Maybe some warm milk would help.

She opened her refrigerator but there was none. That was the advantage of living in a store. She went into the market to grab a gallon of milk.

All the overhead lights were off, but a glow at the back of the market made it as bright as day. Stacy walked to the rear corner of the market where all of the refrigerated coolers were on. The lights inside the units were proof that they were indeed up and running. She opened the door to one and checked the temperature. She opened all of them and checked. They were all running at the same time.

She walked to the front of the market, where a set of refrigerated coolers holding sodas and drinks was running as well. Her heart skipped a beat. He had finished the job, despite her being angry with him.

She got her milk and went to bed. In the morning, she would go see Caden.

STACY KNOCKED ON Caden's cabin door. There was no answer. She checked the doorknob. It wasn't locked and the door swung open easily.

"Caden?"

The cabin was clean. Too clean. She went into the loft. Plastic covered the mattress. She opened the dresser drawers. Empty.

She hurried downstairs. On the kitchen counter was a notebook. On the front of it, he'd written *Jobs for the Groundskeeper*. Inside was a maintenance schedule for all the cabins, as well as a detailed list of things to be done on a regular basis at the campground.

There was a separate notebook for the care and upkeep of the barns, stalls and horses. He'd gone to a lot of trouble to make sure the next person knew what to do.

He had gone above and beyond anything he'd needed to do. Her chest squeezed. She was going to pay him for the store, whether he wanted her to or not. If he wouldn't take the money, she'd send it to his brother's company. She didn't want to feel like she owed him anything. She needed to get back to life. A life without her mother and a life without Caden.

Things at the market were running smoothly without her. Vince had shown up to open the store, just like he'd promised. After the lunch rush, Stacy told him he could go home, but he refused. She wasn't sure if he was staying for her or because he wanted something to do. Either way, she was grateful for his presence.

Early in the afternoon, Denny Morgan stopped by the store.

"Sorry about your mom," he said. "She was a fine woman."

"Thank you," she said. "Is there anything I can do for you?"

"No," the elderly man said. "Caden took care of everything. Where is he, by the way?"

"Gone," she said. "He went to work for his brother in Prescott."

She had no idea if that were true, but it was the only answer she could think to give.

All day, people stopped in to offer their condolences. Almost all of them also asked about Caden. It seemed he'd worked for more than one person around town.

Vince was still there when Frank stopped in just before she closed the store. "I need you to sign off on this so I can send it to Caden's parole officer."

Stacy read the paper. "I can't sign this."

"Why not?"

She pointed to a line on the paper. "It says that the parolee fulfilled all his obligations and requirements."

Frank crossed his arms. "What did he not do?"

"Stay out of the bar, for one," Stacy said. She didn't feel guilty for saying anything now that Caden was gone. "I saw him stumbling out the night Mom died."

Frank shook his head. "You don't believe that."

"I do. I saw him."

He pulled his cell phone out of his pocket. He dialed a contact and put the phone on speaker.

"The Watering Hole. Freddy speaking."

Stacy crossed her arms and glared at Frank. What was he trying to pull?

"Freddy, this is Sheriff Tedford."

"What can I do for you, Sheriff?"

Frank said, "Can you tell me what Caden Murphy was doing at your bar last Thursday night?"

"Same thing he did for me almost every night. Drive people home."

"Did he ever come inside the bar?"

"No."

"Did he ever have anything to drink?" Frank looked at Stacy.

"Never. I call when I have a customer too drunk to drive and too stupid to listen to reason. Caden always talks them into letting him drive them home."

"Thanks," Frank said and disconnected the call. "Thanks to you, the Watering Hole's guardian angel is now in Prescott."

Her heart pounded in her chest. Caden hadn't

been drinking. "Why didn't he tell me himself?"

"Did you ask him?"

Her hands shook. "No, but he could have told me. He didn't even try."

Frank shrugged. "It was the one thing he was doing for himself. He wanted others to avoid his mistake. Telling you about it would make it seem like he had an ulterior motive."

"I've been so stubborn." Her voice was little more than a whisper. "First with my dad, then with Caden. What am I going to do?"

"I suggest you go get him." Vince leaned on the counter.

Stacy went over to him. "I'm sorry. I didn't give either of you the benefit of the doubt."

"It's not me you should apologize to. It's Caden. Don't you think it's time you told him you loved him?"

Did she love him? Yes. Her heart sang with the knowledge of it. He wasn't just a puzzle she wanted to solve. He wasn't just someone she enjoyed teasing. She loved him. She loved everything about him.

"What about the store?"

Vince rolled his eyes. "I'll run the store."

"I don't even know where he is."

Frank laughed. "Lucky for you, I happen

to have some inside information." He handed her a piece of paper with an address written on it. "He's staying at his brother's for now."

"I'll leave first thing in the morning."

CADEN HUNG OUT IN the kitchen, not wanting to intrude on the happiness going on in the living room. His parents and two of his siblings had driven up for Kimberly and Patrick's big announcement. Kimberly was now past her first trimester and they finally felt confident enough to let everyone know they were expecting a baby.

It wasn't that he wasn't happy for them. He was. But it was just another reminder of something he'd never have. He'd put his heart on the line with Stacy. If she couldn't believe him, no one would. He missed her. He missed Coronado.

He handed Max a piece of his hamburger. "You miss being there too, don't you?"

The doorbell rang. Probably one of Kimberly's friends coming over to help celebrate. Another reason to avoid the living room. Kimberly had made it her mission to find Caden a date. Her friends had been dropping in all day and seemed more interested in flirting with him than in congratulating Kimberly and Patrick.

"Caden, someone is here for you," Patrick called from the living room.

"I'm busy."

Caden's father poked his head in the kitchen. "Stop hiding in this kitchen and get out here right now. You've got a visitor."

"If it's another one of Kimberly's friends, I'm not interested."

"How about a woman who didn't realize how stubborn she was until it was too late?" Stacy stood at the kitchen door.

"Stacy." He couldn't believe his eyes. "What are you doing here?"

She shrugged. "I wrote you a hundred letters, but I couldn't get the words right. I decided the only way to apologize was in person."

His heart raced. "I can understand that."

She stepped closer. "I'm sorry. I should have had more faith in you. Can you ever forgive me?"

"Yes. But that doesn't change anything."

"Why? Because I dated your best friend eight years ago? Because you're an ex-con? I love you. And I know you love me. Stop making excuses to hide from life."

Hiding from life. That was what Grayson's mom had accused him of, too. Did he dare let himself be happy?

"Grayson brought us together. He would understand." She took his hand. "You don't belong here. You belong in Coronado. Come home."

Home. The words sang to him. "I'm an excon. What happens when people find out?"

She laughed. "People have stopped by the market looking for you all week. I'm pretty sure you could grow three horns and they'd still want you around. They love you almost as much as I do."

She was close enough now that he could smell her shampoo. He reached up and brushed her hair back. "I've lived under a cloud for so long, I'm not sure if I know how to live without it anymore."

"It's easy," she whispered. "Just let the sunshine in."

Wrapping his arms around her, he pulled her close and kissed her. This time, he didn't let go. Not even when his family invaded the kitchen.

Kimberly glanced at her husband. "Does this mean I can call my girlfriends and tell them the plan worked?"

Caden kept Stacy locked in his embrace but looked at Patrick. "What plan?"

Patrick shrugged. "We figured if we had enough women stop by, it would scare you enough to go back home."

"Tucson?"

His entire family roared with laughter.

Sarah came up behind him and wrapped her arms around Caden and Stacy. "Coronado. Everyone can see that's where you belong."

His heart swelled with love for his family and love for the woman in his arms. "You heard them. Take me home."

* * * * *

Get 4 FREE REWARDS!

We'll send you 2 FREE Books <u>plus</u> 2 FREE Mystery Gifts.

FREE
Value Over
$20

Both the **Love Inspired**® and **Love Inspired**® Suspense series feature compelling novels filled with inspirational romance, faith, forgiveness, and hope.

YES! Please send me 2 FREE novels from the Love Inspired or Love Inspired Suspense series and my 2 FREE gifts (gifts are worth about $10 retail). After receiving them, if I don't wish to receive any more books, I can return the shipping statement marked "cancel." If I don't cancel, I will receive 6 brand-new Love Inspired Larger-Print books or Love Inspired Suspense Larger-Print books every month and be billed just $5.99 each in the U.S. or $6.24 each in Canada. That is a savings of at least 17% off the cover price. It's quite a bargain! Shipping and handling is just 50¢ per book in the U.S. and $1.25 per book in Canada.* I understand that accepting the 2 free books and gifts places me under no obligation to buy anything. I can always return a shipment and cancel at any time. The free books and gifts are mine to keep no matter what I decide.

Choose one: ☐ **Love Inspired**   ☐ **Love Inspired Suspense**
　　　　　　　　Larger-Print　　　　　**Larger-Print**
　　　　　　　　(122/322 IDN GNWC)　　(107/307 IDN GNWN)

Name (please print)

Address　　　　　　　　　　　　　　　　　　　　　　　　　　Apt. #

City　　　　　　　　　　　State/Province　　　　　　　　　Zip/Postal Code

Email: Please check this box ☐ if you would like to receive newsletters and promotional emails from Harlequin Enterprises ULC and its affiliates. You can unsubscribe anytime.

Mail to the **Harlequin Reader Service:**
IN U.S.A.: P.O. Box 1341, Buffalo, NY 14240-8531
IN CANADA: P.O. Box 603, Fort Erie, Ontario L2A 5X3

Want to try 2 free books from another series! Call 1-800-873-8635 or visit www.ReaderService.com.

Get 4 FREE REWARDS!

We'll send you 2 FREE Books plus 2 FREE Mystery Gifts.

FREE
Value Over
$20

Both the **Harlequin® Special Edition** and **Harlequin® Heartwarming™** series feature compelling novels filled with stories of love and strength where the bonds of friendship, family and community unite.

YES! Please send me 2 FREE novels from the Harlequin Special Edition or Harlequin Heartwarming series and my 2 FREE gifts (gifts are worth about $10 retail). After receiving them, if I don't wish to receive any more books, I can return the shipping statement marked "cancel." If I don't cancel, I will receive 6 brand-new Harlequin Special Edition books every month and be billed just $4.99 each in the U.S or $5.74 each in Canada, a savings of at least 17% off the cover price or 4 brand-new Harlequin Heartwarming Larger-Print books every month and be billed just $5.74 each in the U.S. or $6.24 each in Canada, a savings of at least 21% off the cover price. It's quite a bargain! Shipping and handling is just 50¢ per book in the U.S. and $1.25 per book in Canada.* I understand that accepting the 2 free books and gifts places me under no obligation to buy anything. I can always return a shipment and cancel at any time. The free books and gifts are mine to keep no matter what I decide.

Choose one: ☐ **Harlequin Special Edition** ☐ **Harlequin Heartwarming**
  (235/335 HDN GNMP)   **Larger-Print**
      (161/361 HDN GNPZ)

Name (please print)

Address   Apt. #

City   State/Province   Zip/Postal Code

Email: Please check this box ☐ if you would like to receive newsletters and promotional emails from Harlequin Enterprises ULC and its affiliates. You can unsubscribe anytime.

Mail to the **Harlequin Reader Service:**
IN U.S.A.: P.O. Box 1341, Buffalo, NY 14240-8531
IN CANADA: P.O. Box 603, Fort Erie, Ontario L2A 5X3

Want to try 2 free books from another series! Call 1-800-873-8635 or visit www.ReaderService.com.

---

*Terms and prices subject to change without notice. Prices do not include sales taxes, which will be charged (if applicable) based on your state or country of residence. Canadian residents will be charged applicable taxes. Offer not valid in Quebec. This offer is limited to one order per household. Books received may not be as shown. Not valid for current subscribers to the Harlequin Special Edition or Harlequin Heartwarming series. All orders subject to approval. Credit or debit balances in a customer's account(s) may be offset by any other outstanding balance owed by or to the customer. Please allow 4 to 6 weeks for delivery. Offer available while quantities last.

Your Privacy—Your information is being collected by Harlequin Enterprises ULC, operating as Harlequin Reader Service. For a complete summary of the information we collect, how we use this information and to whom it is disclosed, please visit our privacy notice located at corporate.harlequin.com/privacy-notice. From time to time we may also exchange your personal information with reputable third parties. If you wish to opt out of this sharing of your personal information, please visit readerservice.com/consumerschoice or call 1-800-873-8635. **Notice to California Residents**—Under California law, you have specific rights to control and access your data. For more information on these rights and how to exercise them, visit corporate.harlequin.com/california-privacy.

HSEHW22

COUNTRY LEGACY COLLECTION

19 FREE BOOKS IN ALL!

Cowboys, adventure and romance await you in this new collection! Enjoy superb reading all year long with books by bestselling authors like Diana Palmer, Sasha Summers and Marie Ferrarella!

Get 4 FREE REWARDS!

We'll send you 2 FREE Books plus 2 FREE Mystery Gifts.

Both the **Romance** and **Suspense** collections feature compelling novels written by many of today's bestselling authors.

YES! Please send me 2 FREE novels from the Essential Romance or Essential Suspense Collection and my 2 FREE gifts (gifts are worth about $10 retail). After receiving them, if I don't wish to receive any more books, I can return the shipping statement marked "cancel." If I don't cancel, I will receive 4 brand-new novels every month and be billed just $7.24 each in the U.S. or $7.49 each in Canada. That's a savings of up to 28% off the cover price. It's quite a bargain! Shipping and handling is just 50¢ per book in the U.S. and $1.25 per book in Canada.* I understand that accepting the 2 free books and gifts places me under no obligation to buy anything. I can always return a shipment and cancel at any time. The free books and gifts are mine to keep no matter what I decide.

Choose one: ☐ **Essential Romance**   ☐ **Essential Suspense**
　　　　　　　　(194/394 MDN GQ6M)　　　　(191/391 MDN GQ6M)

Name (please print)

Address   Apt. #

City   State/Province   Zip/Postal Code

Email: Please check this box ☐ if you would like to receive newsletters and promotional emails from Harlequin Enterprises ULC and its affiliates. You can unsubscribe anytime.

Mail to the **Harlequin Reader Service:**
IN U.S.A.: P.O. Box 1341, Buffalo, NY 14240-8531
IN CANADA: P.O. Box 603, Fort Erie, Ontario L2A 5X3

Want to try 2 free books from another series! Call 1-800-873-8635 or visit www.ReaderService.com.

---

*Terms and prices subject to change without notice. Prices do not include sales taxes, which will be charged (if applicable) based on your state or country of residence. Canadian residents will be charged applicable taxes. Offer not valid in Quebec. This offer is limited to one order per household. Books received may not be as shown. Not valid for current subscribers to the Essential Romance or Essential Suspense Collection. All orders subject to approval. Credit or debit balances in a customer's account(s) may be offset by any other outstanding balance owed by or to the customer. Please allow 4 to 6 weeks for delivery. Offer available while quantities last.

Your Privacy—Your information is being collected by Harlequin Enterprises ULC, operating as Harlequin Reader Service. For a complete summary of the information we collect, how we use this information and to whom it is disclosed, please visit our privacy notice located at corporate.harlequin.com/privacy-notice. From time to time we may also exchange your personal information with reputable third parties. If you wish to opt out of this sharing of your personal information, please visit readerservice.com/consumerchoice or call 1-800-873-8635. **Notice to California Residents**—Under California law, you have specific rights to control and access your data. For more information on these rights and how to exercise them, visit corporate.harlequin.com/california-privacy.

STRS22

COMING NEXT MONTH FROM

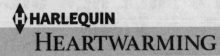

HARLEQUIN
HEARTWARMING

#427 THE BRONC RIDER'S TWIN SURPRISE
Bachelor Cowboys • by Lisa Childs

After weeks of searching for his runaway wife, rodeo rider Dusty Haven gets a double shock when he finally finds her. Not only is Melanie Shepard living at his family's ranch—she's pregnant with their twins!

#428 HER COWBOY WEDDING DATE
Three Springs, Texas • by Cari Lynn Webb

Widow Tess Palmer believes a perfect wedding beckons a perfect life. Roping cowboy Carter Sloan in to plan her cousin's big day might be a mistake—unless she realizes this best man might be the best man for her.

#429 AN ALASKAN FAMILY FOUND
A Northern Lights Novel • by Beth Carpenter

Single dad Caleb DeBoer hires Gen Rockwell to work on his peony farm for the summer. When she moves her daughters to the farm, the two families become close—but a startling secret threatens everything.

#430 THE RUNAWAY RANCHER
Kansas Cowboys • by Leigh Riker

Gabe Morgan found sanctuary as a cowboy in Barren, Kansas. But he can't reveal his true identity—even as he falls for local librarian Sophie Crane. How can he be honest with Sophie when he's lying about everything else?

YOU CAN FIND MORE INFORMATION ON UPCOMING HARLEQUIN TITLES, FREE EXCERPTS AND MORE AT HARLEQUIN.COM.

HWCNM0522

Visit ReaderService.com Today!

As a valued member of the Harlequin Reader Service, you'll find these benefits and more at ReaderService.com:

- Try 2 free books from any series
- Access risk-free special offers
- View your account history & manage payments
- Browse the latest Bonus Bucks catalog

Don't miss out!

If you want to stay up-to-date on the latest at the Harlequin Reader Service and enjoy more content, make sure you've signed up for our monthly News & Notes email newsletter. Sign up online at ReaderService.com or by calling Customer Service at 1-800-873-8635.